Howling to Restore Honor

A Sharp Investigations Novel

Book Seven

BY: E. N. CRANE

EDITED BY: A. O. NEAL &
SUE SCOTT

Dedication

For my dad, Jeff Neal, who served in the military and law enforcement for most of his adult life. As a retiree, he still supports his new community as a volunteer fire fighter and member of the county's search and rescue team.

Thank you for sharing your knowledge of both and of the VA Medical system. I still remember seeing you in full uniform on 9/11 before I walked to junior high and having no idea what happened.

Thank you for always being willing to protect and serve.

Chapter One: Code Blue

T he shrill alarm of life-saving equipment cut through the once peaceful hospital like a hurricane in Southern Florida. Every hair on my neck stood up at the sound, a slow building weight of dread settling in my chest that something traumatic had happened in the once calm trauma ward of the Veterans Affairs Hospital of Ohio.

A terrible something that was somehow my fault.

Except hospitals were rarely quiet and anyone out during a hurricane in Florida was an idiot because they gave plenty of advance warnings to get out of Florida. The entire state was a red flag of inhospitable conditions and yet no one fled the gator, humidity, and hurricane plagued state shaped like an anatomically correct display of male genitalia.

People who lived in Florida made poor choices daily... the most obvious being they lived in Florida.

There was no advance warning for sudden attacks on patients.

Especially not by volunteers court ordered to improve their mental wellbeing.

Every surface reflected the strobing blue lights. Each sterilized metal instrument reverberated with the sound of incoming tragedy even as I struggled to do something, anything, to help the unassuming victim laid out before me. One by one, each machine had an ominous tone joining the original alert until it was an unholy assault on the senses that reminded me of a war zone.

A war zone that could have been avoided if I hadn't been running through a hospital in socks while my shoes dried.

"Winnie! Off!" I shouted again, even as the not-quite-in-jeopardy patient laughed. My body fought to move forward and forcibly remove the dog, but no amount of tugging and pulling could get me any closer to the rogue canine. In the hallway, I could hear the tell-tale squeak of a crash cart barreling toward the room and a herd of hospital worker shoes following behind.

Any second they'd reach the glue, and their cushioned shoes would be toast.

As would the hospital's willingness to let me do community service here.

We were either going to prison or cleaning garbage on the side of a highway.

I couldn't see any other option for us.

"Winnie!" I shouted again at my former military partner, but she would not be dissuaded from her objective by alarms, orders, or even her once beloved handler who was certainly on the fast track to a women's penitentiary for homicide charges. Winnie's front two paws were planted on the patient's chest, her pink tongue offering him a sponge bath even as her feet kneaded his chest like an aggressive baker with anger issues. The bath focused solely on the removal of the crumbs and peanut butter coating his face and shirt, the massage focused on making sure the residual bruising from the land mine never managed to fade. The German Shepherd Malinois mix continued to ignore me, reminding me why we had been "contractually terminated" from the Army.

As in they "forgot" to mention my contract was ending and I was conveniently not an employee when I tried to burn down Florida. Winnie's retirement wasn't exactly planned, but I heard rumors it was celebrated with a keg of meat.

None of that was particularly helpful at the moment, surrounded by the sights and sounds of a hospital gone mad.

A battalion of pea green scrubs arrived, my face getting redder and redder as they took in the sight in front of them. No amount of positive energy or witchcraft would turn me invisible fast enough to avoid the glares and disapproving head shakes that accompanied my ill-fated ability to serve the military community.

Court ordered or not, it was unlikely the scene before me wouldn't cost me my volunteer badge.

We're going to end up picking up trash on the side of the road and Winnie is going to eat a used diaper and barf baby poop on the police escort and that will be an assault on an officer and we'll be incarcerated forever.

I glared heavily at the canine as though it would do more than give me a headache.

In her bid to rid the world of consumption detritus, Winnie had ripped off the adhesive pads connected to the patient's heart monitor. His chest hair had been mercifully shaved for the treatment of burns, but the removal launched phase one of the auditory warfare.

She'd also dislodged the tubing that was clipped to his nasal passages to supply oxygen, phase two that brought on a lower pitched tone and a flashing red light.

Phase three was anyone's guess, but it was loud, flashing rapidly, and covered in slobber.

To get to the man's face, which was naturally at the *head* of the bed, she'd also activated the bed's adjustable head and foot functions. A non-issue if her paw wasn't resting on the remote for the fifteen seconds it took for the glue to dry. Every shift in her weight raised the head of the bed, and then lowered it, caused it to vibrate, and then stop.

If this were a ride at an amusement park, I'd call it Dolphin Discomboulate.

If I were a judge, I'd call it assault with a deadly dog.

"Ms. Sharp!" I turned to the sound of my name being spoken like a curse and stood at attention. Or the closest to attention I could manage in an exaggerated pigeon-toed ballet fourth position.

Definitely crossing ballet off the list of ways I can amuse and entertain soldiers, I noted in my head.

If fourth position hurt, fifth would pop my knee out of its socket.

In front of me were several doctors and nurses. A light sheen of sweat graced a large number of their faces, but it was unclear if it was from the mad dash to the room or the laughter sending them folded over at the middle. It was as though a switch had been flipped and professional helpers were now snapping pictures and joking about how Winnie neutralized the threat of ants by ensuring no crumb had been left behind...

Kind of.

"Would you care to explain *this* catastrophe?" Dr. Burt Ernesto spoke in a tone that reminded me of my time in Afghanistan. You accidentally get mashed potatoes on the pants of one Army Ranger battalion and suddenly you're "incompetent" and a "disgrace to the uniform".

I wonder what they would have said if I'd let her eat the arm of the man who had taunted her and initiated the whole scene in the first place. Yeah, the bench weighing her down gave him a head start, but if I hadn't tied the leash as tight as I did, he'd have been a goner. Then what would they have called me?

A hero?

The modern-day embodiment of natural selection?

Probably, it still would have been incompetent and disgraceful but with "attempted murderer" thrown in for fun.

Then I could have been featured on a True Crime podcast, so... missed opportunities.

My internal speculation lasted a second before I broke down and answered him.

"Private Luna had a peanut butter sandwich and Winnie was helping him clean up," I offered, wondering if that would be the end of it. The thought turned into a fervent wish as I watched about half of the medical staff who'd rushed in begin to discover they couldn't leave.

"Why didn't you stop her?" Dr. Ernesto's voice boomed throughout the room and I looked down at my feet. My toe-nail polish was a glitter-based silver, and both the nails and toes looked paler than usual beside the heavily trod upon industrial grade laminate. "And where are your shoes?"

"Sir," I began, going silent when one of the nurses let out a small scream and stepped out of her immobile shoes. "Can I explain after you get some acetone?"

"What do I need acetone..." his question was cut off as he started to turn and discovered much like the rest of us, he'd been glued to the floor.

"I'm on it," a male nurse who must have come from the un-contaminated end of the hallway started toward the door. His red hair and hobbit height made him look like a resident of the shire setting out on a quest.

"Just don't go left!" I called out and he offered a thumbs up as he went right, passing the textured glass window. The thumbs up turned into a hand jive as he tried to redirect a gurney being pushed by a quartet of EMTs.

It resulted in a larger audience to entertain when both the EMTs and the patient whipped out their phones to take videos.

A real feat for the man in the gurney considering half the fingers from his hand were in an ice bucket on his lap. If I were losing blood and risking the nickname "Stubby" or maybe "Fingerlicker", I might insist they reattach those instead of documenting another patient's misery.

Private Luna cackled under Winnie's tongue, and I sighed.

No one was miserable but me.

The reality is, I am far too good at my job of providing levity and entertainment for the injured soldiers at the VA Hospital. A job that was court ordered after I "misappropriated" some military explosives to take out a genetically motivated weapon in an underground tunnel where it couldn't harm others. While the security council thought it would be "beneficial" for me to spend 8 hours a week here, the medical staff with sticks in places that are traditionally 'Exit Only' thought it was the military's way of saying "don't you wish you were in a war zone?"

A dangerous place to be with the aforementioned sticks.

The perforation potential in the rectum was extremely high.

"Cynthia Sharp, answer me!" Dr. Ernesto repeated himself and I snickered into my hand before masking it as a cough. The number of people who have demanded answers and been further thrown into confusion when provided them could fill... well, a war zone.

Or a room full of hospital workers glued to the floor.

Hello, captive audience, I thought and wondered if in the end they'd be spell bound or threatening to bind and gag me for torture.

Anyone's guess at this stage.

"Remember earlier when someone activated the emergency shower by the eyewash station and partially flooded the hallway?" I started, noting that more than just the people who were glued to the floor were staying to hear this story.

It was getting to the point I should start charging admission to my humiliation to pay establishments back for the damage associated with it.

At the very least they should cut me in on the kickbacks from YouTube

"That was the teenage son of Sgt. Ryan over in room 408. He has a thing about textures and perceptions of cleanliness. Winnie gave him kisses and he reacted like Lucy from Charlie Brown, all 'get some hot water, get some iodine' so a floor orderly pulled him into the chem-shower and activated it. The man thought it was a biological or chemical exposure and not an overreaction, sir. But once the freezing water hit the teenaged Ryan, his scream turned into something from the shower scene in *Psycho*."

You could hear a pin drop in the room. The nurse seeking acetone returned with an industrial sized bottle and a handful of rags. He wielded the semi-transparent jug like Arthur in the animated movie with Excalibur... confused and in a hurry.

When no one looked away from my storytelling he tried again to get their attention, but with words.

"Where should I start?" he asked, noting the empty Crocs frozen in place beside lounging stocking clad nurses. Apparently, the comfort of rubber shoes was greatly diminished when they were forced to remain stationary.

"Winnie's paws, please. I'm fairly certain Private Luna would like to stop being folded in half," I said, gesturing toward the bed where Winnie had flopped over. The patient was stroking her fur, eyes at half-mast. On the end of one of her paws was the bed remote and part of his sheet adhered to the second one. Her rear paws were on either side of his hips, but he had the forethought to hold that portion of the sheet in place.

Hospital gowns were not lower-body privacy friendly.

Winnie's soft snoring indicated she was mostly done causing chaos and mayhem for at least the next fifteen minutes. An hour if no one unwrapped anything that smelled good.

"Sharp!" Dr. Ernesto hollered and I narrowly resisted rolling my eyes at him.

"Right, so my shoes were soaked by the shower when I saved Oscar the Grouchy Orderly from getting an elbow to the nose. I put the shoes near the autoclave in the instrument storage to dry and was continuing on in my socks. There was a Marine who came in, he was the human half of an explosives detection team and he was missing his partner. So, Winnie was going to go offer him a temporary companion to alleviate some of the stress and to improve healing. On our way there, a kitchen worker slipped in the water and the food tray crashed to the ground. Winnie took off after a rolling hamburger patty and barreled into a worker holding tubes of blueish purple gunk. I let her chase the patty while I helped the kitchen worker to her feet, then the person who had the tubes..." I swallowed hard as recognition sent snickers through the audience.

A small yelp escaped my lips as the cold acetone touched my feet.

"Cold!" I squeaked and the nurse in front of me laughed.

"Well, we can't warm it up. Not that we've ever needed to put it directly on a patient, but if we warm it, it goes boom," he used a coarse rag to rub the edges of my feet to loosen the adhesive. "Also, the socks you left in the hallway are toast."

Chewing my bottom lip, I tried not to sigh in despair.

"Yeah, I figured. If you get them removed, just toss them."

My eyes found their way back to the doctor. His thick salt and pepper hair contrasted heavily with the unlined features of his face. Genetics were strange, deciding arbitrarily which part of you aged gracefully and which part like Winnie glued you to the floor of a hospital.

"So, it took awhile for me to get the worker back upright and the purple goo had started to become clear at the thinner parts. I was half stuck to the ground in socks when I saw the word 'Dermabond' on the tubes. Before I could register the implications of the word 'bond' and its relationship to my feet, Private Luna had let out a..." I looked at the patient and considered how sweet he looked with an arm around Winnie. He'd been through enough without the notoriously emasculating humor of soldiers regarding his... undignified scream. "Very manly shout for assistance. My feet came out of the socks and I ran through the goo into this room. I stumbled on the cords, caught myself on the bed, and the Dermabond cured. It was also then that I noticed she was glued to the patient and any attempt to physically remove her could harm him."

"So, your plan to get assistance was to make us think a patient was dying?" his nostrils flared and I could see some more of his hairs turning gray as he stared at me. At six feet and a size sixteen, I was mostly used to being stared at. My lavender eyes and dishwater blonde hair made me look like Godzilla in a wig, sending normal citizens into "escape the freak" mode faster than a toddler with feces on its hands.

This was the first time I'd received the look from a medical professional while not actively bleeding.

Or covered in someone else's blood.

Usually both.

"I actually hadn't gotten to the plan making portion of the incident yet. Winnie took it upon herself to call for help. " I glossed over the fact it had been an accident. "Now that you're here and we've come unglued..."

I paused watching Nurse Hobbit apply more solvent to the many pairs of footwear trapped in the room.

"What? What do you plan on doing, Ms. Sharp?" he shouted, as I saw my Cuban American canine training sergeant standing in the hallway with a half smirk on his face. It may have been several years since he paired me with my best friend, but it had only been a few hours since I'd seen that smirk on his face for *other* reasons.

"Leaving. I have to be at work in an hour and my ride is here." I shrugged and let out a single long whistle, summoning Winnie to my side. We strolled out, barefoot and making slight squelching sounds until I made my way nose to nose with Sgt. Ian Cruz. We were nearly the same height, and he lowered his nose a quarter inch to rub it against mine while maintaining the minimum possible distance from me to avoid cross contamination from my clothing.

"Your ride, chica?" he asked with a suggestive brow wiggle.

"Just shut up and start walking before someone sees what Winnie did to the X-ray lab," I hissed and hurried barefoot toward the exit.

Chapter Two:
Indecent Exposure

"Do you want to run that by me again?" I asked, not quite able to take Joseph seriously as he stood before me in the remnants of a pink princess's pinafore gown. Behind him, a half-dozen children posed with his "noble steed", not in the least missing my boss in drag from their fun and photography session. Staring at the "steed", his sanity was definitely slipping into white coat and butterfly net territory.

Though we worked on a dairy farm and had actual horses, his noble steed was Winnie in a jousting match costume sporting a plush knight right behind her shoulder blades.

Her height, ears, coloring and wagging tail were far from the least believable parts of the outfit. It was completely unrealistic that the knight was still on her back, in the custody of his head, and no one had dripped ice cream on it yet.

It was a low-priority miracle delivered to Joseph, giving him a false sense of optimism that everything would go smoothly today.

The glue residue on my feet said we were ten seconds from disaster and his naked butt was the least of our concerns.

In terms of costumes he'd put on Winnie for the "Photo Spot with Winnie" booth, it was the only one thus far to acknowledge she was an animal of some sort. In terms of accuracy, the velociraptor costume I'd seen on the internet would have been more fitting, but "Jurassic Mint Julep was a summer flavor and we were headed into fall".

Another statement that called into question the legitimacy of the man having a wife.

The Photo Spot with Winnie was his concession to the dog needing a job to keep her occupied while on the farm. She'd objected loudly to herding, pulling, and not sampling all of the dairy products. Sitting outside the ice cream parlor posing for pictures in exchange for treats was her new job for the safety of livestock, guests, and dairy sanitation standard requirements.

Why Joseph insisted on dressing up right beside her was probably something he'd be working on in therapy after they tackled his alcoholism and refusal to wear clothing that wasn't two sizes too small. Maybe after they got to the root of his love of drag, the doctor could get him to admit his wife was as fake as the terrifying voicemails we'd hear her leave him.

If they weren't fake, maybe the drag was prep work for witness protection.

The alleged Mrs. Joseph sounded like turning humans into mince meat pies was child's play.

"It was the only outfit left at the store and I need you to wear it!" He insisted, and I blinked back my horror at his suggestion. Though I'd spent the morning glued barefoot to a hospital floor and nearly completed the work of a land mine in permanently disabling a soldier, it was the most insulting job someone suggested I perform today.

And that included the not-so-subtle invitation to take advantage of Cruz's joystick while he drove.

The VA hospital was in Dayton, about forty-five minutes from my storefront apartment on Main Street in the small town of Sweet Pea, Ohio. The Sharp Investigations office was on a quarter of the library's building lot and consisted of a single cube of space on street level and a back staircase to a studio apartment above. There was no oven or stove, but I had two coffee makers, a fridge, a microwave and a George Foreman, so I was pretty much set unless I wanted to bake something.

If I wanted to bake something, I had to visit my mother.

My mom was an adventurous spirit who had me at least a decade after her three previous children. Heidi and Molly, the two eldest sisters, were fully in favor of my parents' adventurous lifestyle. Seth tolerated it from the safety of being the only male and a newly married man in his 40s with two kids.

I, on the other hand, was regularly accused of being uptight and having toys foisted on me.

Not cute ones like plush unicorns and fidget spinners.

Nope, my mom gave me inappropriate ones that twitched, vibrated and went in the freezer.

As a result, I baked only in emergencies.

We'd stopped at the apartment so I could get socks and trade my waterlogged shoes for work boots, stuff water and snacks in my pockets, and drive to my "real" job as an Animal Technician at The Dairy. It may have had a proper name at some point, but like every freeway and highway in California, that name had been replaced with "The" and "the simplest description that could be applied to it without confusing strangers".

The 5.

The 14.

The Road That Dead-ends at Apollo Park.

The Apartment Above Sharp Investigations was fifteen minutes from where I was standing right now, but somehow felt like another planet. I was surrounded by the suction machines of dairy retrieval on a line of cows, excrement, and the very judgy gaze of Berry the Goat, my archenemy. I'd moved him and a few chatty male farmhands outside of the barn until the ladies were done fulfilling supply requests. While the cows didn't seem to mind their publicly exposed nipples being milked, I felt a sisterly solidarity to make the men keep their eyes above udder level.

It usually granted me peace and quiet to measure the output temperatures and sanitation protocols. That I made all of them blush and squirm uncomfortably was just an added bonus. It was a reminder that in Health class, the males had all said "ew" and "yuck" to female reproductive health even as they made passes to play with it. There should be some kind of How Lady Parts Work test men have to pass before they are allowed to have sex.

Or work at a dairy.

The Dairy sat a half-dozen miles outside Sweet Pea, Ohio and consisted of a dozen paddocks, at least two barns, and an ice cream parlor that served as the backdrop for Winnie's photo spot. Tourists thought she was adorable, but I knew the spot existed only to keep her busy and away from the livestock. I'd been born and raised in the area, but I was still at a loss to explain the appeal presented by our town to tourists and people looking for a "simpler life".

Maybe I wasn't a city slicker, but shoveling cow poop was far from simple or relaxing.

Now that I'm an adult, I encourage them to leave so I'm not criminally liable when they inevitably find themselves exposed to something visually, auditorily, or olfactorily horrifying.

Like Joseph in a torn pink princess dress.

Or Mr. Meden's Skunk Stash.

Or my mother and her seniors' swinger club on Slingshot Dildo Night.

An event that left me with an unfortunately shaped red mark on my face that had been photographed and posted online like gangbusters at the VA hospital. If the gaggle of cell phone mommies behind Joseph were any indication, he was also enroute to Insta-fame. Though the images would probably be posted in mommy blogs to condemn the loss of Christian values in America, the only explanation for a half-naked man in drag.

Capitalism had nothing on the self-righteous condemnation of the Lululemon crowd.

"That can't be true! You could switch to being the knight and make Winnie a dragon. I've seen the outfits, I know you have them! I even helped you repair the chain mail when you needed someone to show you how to use needle-nose pliers without being mocked by the farmhands! Hell, I even sewed the wing back on the dragon costume when an unsupervised toddler ripped it off while being saved from having its ice cream hand removed!" I countered, not daring to look at the deep green crushed velvet outfit with the ogre horn headband tucked under his arm.

"But today's flavor is Passion Fruit Princess! Someone has to be the princess, and you're the only person who fits the back-up costume! It's not my fault that you're my most ogre-sized employee on-duty today." His normally gruff demeanor had dissolved into a plea for mercy as his not-so-tighty-whiteys caught a stiff breeze on his exposed backside.

"Winnie can be the princess," I countered, more concerned about being forced to pose in a dress with children than his unflattering comparison of me to an ogre.

Fiona was a badass.

"Winnie was the princess last week. We can't repeat costumes that frequently! It's business, Cyn!"

"It's humiliating, Joseph! I don't want to be a princess, find a different sucker!"

"You're the only sucker with the right build! And she's your dog!"

Scanning the barn, I started praying to dog for a beanstalk to drop a giant and solve my problems. Around me, the farm hands were all looking strangely busy for a group that normally had a few too many extra minutes to chew the fat. All of them were wearing denim pants and some sort of top that showcased tan skin, calloused hands, and moderate levels of muscle.

They were also all a minimum of four inches shorter than me.

And completely incapable of standing near Winnie without upsetting her.

"Look, I know you are an animal technician and I have regularly added to your job duties in ways that do not align with your education and training, but I will give you a half gallon of any ice cream flavor you want if you put on this costume and distract those monsters!" he shouted, but a little too loudly.

An army of little girls turned to him as a single unit and narrowed their eyes.

Jurassic Park music sounded in my head and I nearly whispered 'clever girl' as their sharp gazes lasered onto their target.

"I would recommend running," I whispered, but he looked frozen in place, clutching the Princess Fiona costume he'd been so desperate for me to wear. His prominently displayed underwear didn't take on any new colors, but his trembling fingers were proof enough he knew where he'd gone wrong. Monsters or not, you don't mess with females and he'd poked the bear. "You don't have enough costume left for them to remove. They'll go for the skin."

Winnie stepped to the front of the mob of little girls, her gallant knight seated lopsided on her back. She'd been called a

19

monster by a lot of men, and none of them were disproven... or dumb enough to say it a second time. The dog hadn't been the best personal protection canine, her skills leaning heavily toward scent work and chaos, but at that moment, I had vivid memories of her teeth wrapped around Cruz's arm and the bruise that had been there for at least a week after. He may have been wearing a bite sleeve, but her jaw had pressure to rival a drill press, and he started farming out her decoy work to soldiers who annoyed him.

As soon as Winnie raised her tan tail, twitching just the tip, Joseph should have cowered and begged for mercy. He should have pulled out beef jerky, bribed her allegiance, and tried to harness her herding skills on the skinned-knee and ponytail collective. Offered all of them free ice cream, knowing I'd survive Winnie's lactose intolerant gas far better than he'd survive the wrath of pre-teen girls.

Instead, he tried to reason with a mob.

Like every stupid man before him, he said the three words that guaranteed his demise.

"Just calm down! I didn't mean..." but he raised his hand, Winnie's signal to advance. Winnie accepted the invitation, charging forward with the screaming horde behind her. None of the girls listened to their scolding mothers as they raised their tiny fists.

When they got closer, their screaming turned into a bone chilling chant.

"Into the Unknown! Into the Unknown!"

The battle cry forced Joseph backwards, where his too-clean cowboy boots collided with each other and he landed on his exposed butt in the straw and sand floor of the barn. Sensing his weakness, the group Winnie led picked up speed, closing the distance as he crab-walked backward and barely made it six inches before Winnie launched herself onto his chest and started giving him a facial.

"Cynthia, do something!"

I shook my head and cleaned the thermometer, the little girls pulling out make-up and markers from their pockets. Winnie kept her paws on his shoulders, but stopped licking him so the girls could exact their artistic retribution.

"I told you months ago the photo spot was a bad idea. You're on your own," I answered, moving to the next pasteurization drum. "Next time I tell you your idea is dumb, I recommend listening to me."

Everything hurt and I still had to drive my car.

I'd allowed the attack on Joseph to go on for about seven minutes before intervening. My solution, while inelegant, had involved free pony rides and discounted ice cream. The mommy brigade was satisfied by the proposition of getting more social media worthy photos of their crotch fruit and readily signed onto my plan. Joseph was rescued, most of the marker was water-based, and he only kind of looked like a clown for the rest of the day.

Unfortunately, the dairy didn't have a pony.

A few of the girls rode Heather, a temperamental mare who only got worse with age but was often too lazy to take any real action. She was actually the safest option as long as Winnie stayed ten yards away, but most of the parents felt that a full-sized horse was too dangerous for their precious offspring to perch upon. Carrying around tagging markers and weaponizing nail polish was perfectly suitable, but potentially falling six feet into straw was "far too dangerous".

My assertion that I fell from six feet onto the ground daily did nothing to convince them of its safety.

Apparently if I fell less, ate less, and was generally more pleasant I could have amounted to more.

No one was particularly clear on what their definition of *more* was, but it seemed to involve wedding rings and children.

Apparently, some life goals were non-negotiable.

Like promising pony rides when the dairy didn't have a pony and everyone wanted you to fix it.

A particularly put together woman pointed to Esther and suggested that mules took hikers into the Grand Canyon all the time. The suggestion quickly got majority support and before I could inform them that Esther was a donkey and not a mule, they descended onto her enclosure and started lifting their offspring onto her back.

Though I was fairly certain if any of them had been men, they'd be dead, Esther allowed the little girls to pose on her. So long as Winnie remained behind me and our female farmhand, Ezzie, did most of the negotiating, the sudden need for donkey rides on the second most temperamental female at the dairy went better than expected.

Until after about six pictures, then Esther wanted to walk away.

I may not have amounted to much by their standards, but I knew better than to fight with an ass.

The trim, posh, and heavily perfumed "Viv" as the others called her, would not hear of it. Her pointy manicure ripped the reins from Ezzie's hand and tried to drag the donkey back into the "perfect backdrop". Then, much like the chicken flying seminar she hosted a few months back, Esther proved once again that kicking things was the only way to solve a problem.

Unless you had hands, then I usually opted for punching my problems in the face.

To each their own.

"Viv" got stomped on before screeching and hurrying away on designer heels that had no business on a farm. Within minutes, the rest of the Lululemon crowd had scattered to the far corners of the farm. The bucking donkey cleared the area faster than a Winnie fart and I considered applauding her but thought it might get me a hoof to the ass, no pun intended.

Then Ezzie and I got to spend the next forty minutes trying to calm the donkey.

Esther was livid, bucking backward and forward, contained only by easily dented aluminum pipes. In a perfect world, we'd have been able to let her work through her rage on her own

23

time. Sadly, reality had seen fit to return the mommy brigade to spectating positions, cameras at the ready to document the unsafe nature of farms.

Ezzie and I both took a few hooves to the shins, but we got her calm before any Mad Ass videos could hit the internet. Since we didn't break any bones, I high-fived Ezzie and went back to work while the shrill voice of "Viv" carried across two paddocks.

The Kardashian wannabe was threatening Joseph with lawsuits and criminal child-endangerment. No amount of customer service voice calmed the woman, and we considered our bruises well worth it to not have to participate in the conversation. After another hour, the woman stormed from Joseph's shack of an office with an insistence that he'd hear from her lawyer tossed over one shoulder.

I watched her limp toward her car, not putting weight on the foot Esther *hadn't* stomped on. Fake as her nails and puffed lips, the woman was just another gold digging overly litigious monster of American Capitalism.

A wannabe Kardashian with a smaller backside.

The woman tossed a huge leather bag onto her passenger seat and I looked around, but all the children had left. It was possible she was someone's aunt, but something told me no one would claim relation to her unless they had to.

Either way, Joseph dived face first into a six pack of beer and disappeared for the remainder of the day. Winnie returned to her photo spot and the whole farm carried on as normal.

An oddly accurate truth that started when he hired me.

"Ugh," I stared at my Jeep, tugging open the door. Winnie leapt in, slipped into the back and promptly fell asleep on the bench seat. My leg barely bent enough to get my foot on the running board and then I had to stay still while I breathed through the pain. My dog let out a snore and mocked me. "You know you suck, right?"

A small *pooft* of gas rustled her tail and I choked, my eyes watering from the smell.

"I swear, if the military really wanted to throw peace conventions to the wind, they'd be unstoppable if they weaponized your ass," I grumbled, hauling myself into the front seat with an audible pop from my hip joint. "Since you're a *German* shepherd and Hitler was German, I'm guessing you gave him the idea for Mustard gas too. Or tear gas... whatever debilitating gas they threw into trenches."

My brain registered that trench warfare was more of a World War I thing and II had a lot more plane dogfighting, but I was in too much pain to care. Most of my impressions regarding the Second World War came from watching comic book movies, so it hardly seemed worth my energy to look into fiction.

And I'd never had any energy to look into real history in the first place. It mostly showed that humans sucked and treated each other like crap. Then, when things started getting a little better, someone else came along and did something more awful to remind humanity it was the virus destroying the planet.

Mistletoe on the tree of life.

Tapeworm in the bowels of the ecosystem.

Decaf coffee.

I shuddered at the last. Any species that broke coffee for their own sick purposes was definitely headed to an apocalyptic event.

Despite my brain's vacation, we pulled up to the alley behind my office and cruised to the street parking at the far end.

"We need to move," I groaned, looking at the twenty-yard walk between me and my darkened building. It was never intended to be residential, so there was no overnight parking near the building. Just a long scary walk in a dark alley to a dark building...

Why is my building dark?

My dash clock said it was ten, late enough that Cruz should be there waiting to nurse me back to health. He had his own place that looked like a dog-training facility he wasn't allowed to open until his Army contract ended, but he rarely slept there, and it was starting to look like the backdrop of a horror film. Ian Cruz, fearless member of the Army Criminal Intelligence Unit, hated being alone in the quiet countryside.

Since I liked using him as a personal space heater, it worked out for both of us.

Main Street was a bustling metropolis of hourly cars cruising down it, Thursday morning dumpster retrieval, and semi hourly yowling cats. It also housed the building of my unpaid labor and residence, but that was the least interesting place on the street. There were banned books in the library window, naked mannequins in the appliance repair shop, and personal lubricant samples at Phil's sex shop. On the weekends, the bar remained open until two in the morning and nearly ten whole people knew how to turn on the Karaoke machine.

We were practically a nighttime hotspot and if more than one person knew where the song book was for karaoke, I'd have to move.

To the moon, because "yowling cat" described the singing skills of half the drinking age population in Sweet Pea. Combine that with my parent's affinity for public nudity and we were on the fast track to getting put into one of those bubbles like The Simpsons.

Except the street was eerily silent and when Winnie jumped from the car, her claws tapping on the asphalt were the only sound on the usually busy street. I felt my stomach tighten as we walked closer to the back door, my ears joining Winnie's as we listened for sounds of danger. At my back door, I tested the handle and was relieved to find it locked.

Sure, I had no idea how many people possessed keys to the door, but at least it was locked.

What criminal took the time to re-lock the door behind themselves?

Unless they were still inside and locked it to trick me.

Someone could be lurking up there waiting to murder me.

Or force me to take a pill that gave me a coffee allergy.

Inserting my key, Winnie nudged the door open. She scented the air, her tail picking up speed as she charged up the staircase with a clattering of claws and jingle of her collar. I picked up the faint scent of man and got excited, darting up after her only to find my dark apartment empty.

On the counter beside my coffee pots was a note and the cell phone I must not have brought with me to work. Just as I picked it up, the wall of windows facing Main St erupted in an explosion of color and light, the loud boom of fireworks tugging me closer until I could just make out the well-lit high school football stadium, the game clearly representing the town's only source of entertainment on a Monday night.

Main Street wasn't deserted due to serial killers, just over-involvement with local high school sports.

With a sigh, I relaxed slightly and plopped on my couch. My eyes started to drift shut even as my lower body begged for anti-inflammatories. The day had been too long and now I needed to shower, brush my teeth, and take my old lady vitamins.

Being a hygienic adult was the worst.

Winnie leapt up next to me and draped her head across my chest with a soft whimper and I stroked her ears. She whimpered again and I peeled open an eyelid to look at her, finding a piece of paper in my hand that I'd forgotten about.

One that had my name on it.

CYN,

I'M SORRY. MY SUSPENSION ENDED, THEY'RE MAKING ME COME IN.

I'LL COME BACK WHEN I CAN. THEY OWN ME FOR TWO MORE YEARS AND THEY INTEND TO KEEP ME.

–IAN

I blinked at the note and felt a knowing weight settle in my chest. It had been fun having him here, but the thing about Ian Cruz was, he always left us.

As the saying went, he was here for a good time not for a long time.

It didn't really hurt anymore.

Not that I'd notice any additional pain at the moment.

"Guess it's just us again, girl," I whispered, rubbing small circles on the tips of her ears. "We knew we couldn't keep him."

With a whimper of my own, I hauled myself off the couch and got ready for bed.

Chapter Three:
Family Affair

D ropping my forehead against the glass, I fought the urge to beat my fists against the glass and weep uncontrollably. The day had gone off the rails faster than any before and if I were a fictional princess, I'd have flung myself on the nearest cushioned surface and had a minor melt down.

Instead, I lifted my face and dropped it on the glass a second time, and then a third, before someone put their hand between me and the vending machine.

A cold hand covered in a rubber glove that smelled suspiciously like menthol rub.

"Look, I'm not sure you can afford to get any less coordinated or pass out while in a hospital. Normally, it would be a safe place but with your track record..." I grabbed the wrist beneath the glove and felt the cool sting on my forehead of mentho-lated jelly reacting with air. Having already been vomited on by two patients with concussions and chased Winnie down after she stole the removed incontinence shorts of an amputee soldier, the last thing I wanted was something else on my body to give me nightmares.

"What were you putting VapoRub on before you touched my face?" I asked, turning to the short nurse. The gener-ic scrubs hung on an androgynous form, a paper mask concealing the lower portion of the pea green wrapped mocha-skinned nurse.

"Tongue depressor sticks," the shrug accompanied a voice that gave no additional indicators of age or gender. I labeled the nurse Gumby and moved on. The Claymation character had been way ahead of its time and should have been rightly permitted gender neutrality.

Also pants.

Being clay without pants seemed like a bad way to lose parts of you when they just... fell off.

"Sticks?" I blinked at Gumby.

"For distribution to the patients on the next set of rounds."

"Just the sticks?" I questioned them warily, checking the latex gloves for tell-tale signs of mucus or fecal matter. Why the latter would be associated with menthol rub was not as relevant as my need to check that it wasn't there.

"Just the sticks, Sharp Attack. Though if I'm going to get the third degree, I'll just let you knock yourself out next time. Don't be surprised when you wake up with penises drawn on your face and a 400 lb dog in need of emergency care for eating all the things only you can stop her from consuming."

Nurse Gumby snickered, and I swiped at the smear on my face. My fingers came away shiny but otherwise untainted with bodily fluids. Just residual sharpie from a poorly exccuted attempt to entertain children so their parents could have a private moment to discuss the doctor's prognosis.

That assignment had been worse than the one that got me vomited on and I'm fairly certain their father just wanted to make out with his injured wife.

"Sharp Attack?" I puzzled, wiping my hand on my cargos. I felt a cellophane wrapper crunch and pulled out a small pouch of cheese crackers. Tearing at the perforated edge, my fingers kept slipping off and got me no closer to the crunchy cheese goodness.

Nurse Gumby took the packet, ripped it open, and passed it back. I offered a muttered thanks, but I wasn't sure the nurse heard before continuing.

"Oh, yeah, after the Private Luna incident last weekend, you're practically Jaws around here. Whenever you're around, things are getting chomped, cracked, or obliterated. Might get you a theme song." Nurse Gumby's smirk transformed into a cackle. Wincing, I dumped the whole bag of crackers into my mouth at once and stuck the wrapper in my pocket. "Winnie has been code-named PacMan."

I looked down at my partner, crunching a mouth full of dry crackers. It had been an unwise choice without water on-hand, but the vending machine refused to accept my dollar in exchange for crappy hospital coffee and I was not going to skip coffee *and* my snack.

That's how you ended up on trial for robbery... maybe murder.

Depends on if whoever I came across had coffee they were unwilling to trade for their life.

Robbery with a side of murder?

That sounded right.

"Good luck getting her to answer, many men have failed before," I said after a giant swallow. Part of me considered sharing the story of how hard the military tried to rename the wayward canine from the Hocus Pocus inspired name given to Sgt. Pupperson by the breeder's daughter. Another part of me thought that sharing the story would lead to questions and comments regarding my sanity when I'd agreed to work with the dog anyway.

I thought it was more insane that I couldn't verify Cruz was telling the truth about a mysterious breeder's daughter.

Or was it the trainer's daughter?

I was never sure if the puppy makers were also the puppy teachers.

I'd tried to track down her sire, or the man who had hooked up her parents to ask that question as well as countless others. I was extremely curious whether any of her litter mates had fared better, and a strong desire to meet the girl who named her. From the name alone, I couldn't determine if Winnie and the child had actually bonded or if the girl was an angry anti-magic villager commenting on the dog's possessed behaviors.

I remember Cruz saying she *liked* Hocus Pocus, I was hoping it was the former.

Hoping, like happy thoughts without Pixie Dust, got me no closer to answers.

So I kept looking.

But the breeder went into Witness Protection sometime after we foiled an arms heist that resulted in munitions discharge injuries but before we blew up a marketplace in Afghanistan. Last I had heard, the little girl had named at least three more strong willed canines after she'd named Winnie, but none of them had handlers willing to accept my calls.

Apparently, their research indicated my dog and I would be a "bad influence".

My research indicated they were giant man babies.

A fact that was confirmed when I posted it online and they got snippy.

"We can call her whatever we want, she doesn't listen to anyone but you anyway." Just then an overhead page summoned Nurse Pluto and Gumby gave an exaggerated bow. "I'm off, Sharp Attack. Stay out of the water."

Like Neil DeGrasse Tyson booting the planet of the same name out of the solar system, Nurse Pluto departed rudely and without reason. The relationship to the Roman God of War also seemed a little too on the nose and I sent out a silent request for a peace treaty between Pluto and the Hospital Galaxy.

As though Pluto would even be on the radar as long as Winnie and I continued to come in.

"I need a break," I grumbled, spotting the lit-up neon green exit sign. Following the arrows, I made my way to the industrial gray metal barrier between sanitary and unsanitary existence.

Not that anywhere near Winnie could be considered sanitary.

Normally the crash doors were alarmed, but I learned during my second week of service that most ground floor doors were disarmed by hospital workers so they could sneak out for a nicotine fix. We'd discovered this by chance when no alarm sounded as I burst outside choking on noxious fumes. A brief investigation and I learned these doors were always disarmed.

Useful information if your partner has a nasty habit of eating anything that looks or smells like food.

Like petroleum jelly.

Or laxatives.

The outcome of both was similar, and the color and texture of them would haunt my nightmares for years to come. While a putrid stench still lingered in the back parking area of the hospital that custodial blamed on an unreported sewage leak, the original smell had burned my olfactory sense into a lingering state of fear.

We arrived at the door, my fingers searching for the electrical tape used to keep the flap down until you were ready to come back in. When I couldn't find it, I pushed lightly, and the door swung outward. Though my nose resisted, I gave a cautious sniff for cigarette smoke.

"I can't risk your lungs, kid," I whispered to Winnie. "Your stomach is tortured enough without adding lungs into the equation."

"Not smoking, but am I gonna need to run from your partner?"

We peeked around the corner and saw a middle-aged man in a white coat leaning against the building.

"Not today," I conceded, stepping outside and around the door. The doctor was one I wasn't familiar with personally, but he looked well-versed in hospital politics and sleep deprivation. "I don't think we've met yet, I'm Cyn and this is Winnie."

He shook my extended hand, but I noticed his eyes remained trained across the street.

"Dr. Denicourt, audiology."

"Audiology? Like... hearing loss?" I queried, following his gaze to see a homeless man pushing a metal shopping cart between trash bins.

"Yup."

The man with the cart paused at the next city owned trash can and flipped the top back. He started going through the contents meticulously. Every dip into the bin led to an observation and then careful placement in one of the cart's sections. Despite the distance, it was clear he was sorting out the recyclables and had a system that bordered on obsessiveness. Dr. Denicourt's eyes trailed from the trash man to the far corner where another man stood wearing jeans, a plain black T-Shirt, sunglasses and... crocs.

"Friends of yours?"

I watched the doctor giving a subtle nod to the man on the corner, before tacking my question.

"In a manner of speaking," Denicourt answered, and Sunglasses started toward The Recycler. About two strides from him, Sunglasses slid his hand in his pocket and pulled out something small.

"Oh my dog, are you going to hurt..." my words cut off as I saw the man in sunglasses stop at The Recycler and ask him a question. After a short exchange, he slipped something into his hand and walked away. The Recycler called after Sunglasses, but the man didn't turn. Confused, I watched him study the paper in his hand before his eyes locked on Dr. Denicourt. With a slight head shake , he dropped it on the ground and walked away pushing his carefully curated metal basket of garbage.

"Damn it," Dr. Denicourt said and he pulled out his phone, typing a quick message. Sunglasses reappeared and scooped up the paper, darting across a couple of lanes of traffic to stop in front of the doctor. He looked more familiar than the doctor, but without a name badge for reference his name was a blank.

"Sorry, doc," Sunglasses spoke and held out a hundred-dollar bill. "Want me to try again?"

"Nah, don't worry about it, Clyde. Head on home. Thanks for trying."

Clyde clapped the doctor on the shoulder and squeezed slightly.

"We'll keep trying, man."

They both nodded silently at one another before Sunglasses, aka Clyde, slipped back through the fire door. Dr. Denicourt scrubbed his face, shifting his glasses to rub his eyes while his palms scraped against barely visible stubble. When he shoved too hard, the nose pieces caught in his hair.

"Do you... want to talk about it?" I had tried curbing my curiosity with a healthy reminder that when I ask questions, people usually give me answers. Instead, the question came out and I braced for the usual outcome.

People asking for my help.

I'd been asked for my help getting a dead lover back from the realm of spirits that trapped him in a single mirror... which faced a painting... of the man.

I'd been asked to search a house for an escaped "pet" that turned out to be a spider.

Once, I'd gotten scratched to pieces trying to rescue a happily sunbathing cat from a windowsill it did not want to leave.

"Homeless man is a former soldier," Dr. Denicourt spoke through his palms and I looked again at The Recycler. "His name is Arturo, joined up toward the very end of Vietnam... Maybe after it entirely, dates aren't really my specialty. After that he was part of a specialized unit working prep for Desert Storm. Though as far as I know, he was never actually *in* Desert Storm."

"Do you mean in Kuwait or in the Persian Gulf War?"

"Both," he answered me. Pulling his hands from his face, he started working his glasses back out of his hair.

Nodding, I watched the way Arturo moved. He had a slight limp, his hand had a slight tremor, and I watched him pull a cigarette from a pack in his pocket and light it. The little plastic lighter flickered out and missed twice before he finally got the tip to glow orange. In the cart behind him, I looked more closely at the recyclables, noticing they were perfectly ordered not only by material, but size and color as well.

"What happened to him? If he wasn't at the Persian Gulf War... In the Persian Gulf War?" I studied his clothing and waited for an answer I wasn't sure would make sense based on the clothing. It was worn but clean, miscellaneous pieces of combat fatigues filling out an otherwise benign outfit. The uniform pieces were not the uniform style of Vietnam but the late 80s and 90s military dress.

None of which explained the clear and present injuries impeding his movement.

"Do you try to give money to all homeless former soldiers?"

Dr. Denicourt pulled a pack of cigarettes from his lab coat pocket and placed them on the bench beside the trash can. Beside it was a plastic bag with what looked like clean undergarments that had to have been sitting there the whole time.

It was an odd mix of gifts for a homeless stranger. Larry, the commercial vet in Sweet Pea, and I had dated for months, and I'd never bought him underwear. Sure, I saw and removed them... but I didn't buy them for him.

Buying someone underwear was a much bigger commitment than just telling someone you love them. Yet, the doctor stood there with socks and underwear for a man he was also giving cigarettes. An oddly mixed message, like 'I don't want you to get genital warts or a UTI' while at the same time saying 'But it's cool if you die of lung cancer as long as you do it in clean underwear'.

"Money, underwear, and lung cancer?" He scowled at me, but he was still putting cigarettes with the socks.

"Not exactly. He's dying."

The doctor continued to watch Arturo as he reached the corner and pressed the button to cross.

"When they let him out of military prison, his medical chart went to the VA, even though he never followed it. His skull has a minor fracture, but there was an untreated lung infection that's been getting worse for the last decade. I used to try and get him medicine and inhalers, but he won't take them. Says he deserves to die for what he's done," Dr. Denicourt's voice was a robotic monotone, but the pain he felt was etched on his face.

"Desert Storm? That was... thirty years ago. How does someone have an untreated illness for thirty years? Who thinks they deserve to slowly suffocate to death? Were you even alive then? And if he wasn't there, how did he get... Did you say military prison?" I asked and Winnie leaned against my leg, a clear indication that I was getting anxious.

To be fair, watching a doctor give a man lung cancer has that effect on people.

Dr. Denicourt let out a long breath as he watched Arturo start the meticulous process of separation on our side of the street. He didn't hesitate or pause with his cigarette in his mouth, the tip slowly turning to ash as he inhaled through and around it. The paper wrapped tobacco remained ramrod straight between his lips, a mirror of his posture, even as his whole body skewed to one side.

But he never coughed or struggled to get air... or cigarette smoke.

"Are you sure he's sick?" I questioned, hope building that maybe he was mistaken. Maybe that man was homeless by choice and not because he was punishing himself for a past decided by someone else. Most soldiers went where they were told, followed the rules of engagement, and shot at whoever the government thought "bad" enough to kill.

"Yeah, I'm sure. And yeah, I was alive. I was ten when Desert Storm started, and ten when the military sentenced him to thirty years for war crimes. He got out and... fell off the face of the Earth. Took a year to track him down. Never thought I'd have to leave the dry heat of Arizona to live in Ohio... Who wants to be homeless in Ohio?" Dr. Denicourt gave Arturo one last look before heading back to the fire door. I couldn't help wondering why he thought being homeless in Arizona would be better. Even being housed in Arizona still meant going outside in triple-digit heat. "I can't give up on him, but it's getting harder to stay here, so close and no closer than I was on the other side of the country. They can claim his actions and decisions got a whole team of men killed, but true or not... He can't... I can't... I just wanted... I don't know what I wanted. I never looked up the reports, but my gut says he's smart and careful. There has to be a mistake. If there wasn't a mistake, he still didn't kill anyone."

"Why did you spend a year tracking down a man who's been in military jail for three decades?" I asked, even as I looked between the two men. His knowledge of the man's personality and patterns was slowly becoming clearer as I matched eye color and ears.

"He's my dad, Cyn. Whatever he did, he still deserves to come home."

Chapter Four:
Sleepless Nights

F our pots of coffee and the characters on my computer screen still wouldn't focus.

I'd checked the display port, the router, and the power outlet only to discover the worst had happened. All of those were completely operational, as was the laptop I'd abandoned upstairs an hour ago to sit at the main desktop CPU in the Sharp Investigations Office.

The problem was me.

I'd become the punchline of a Taylor Swift song.

And not an empowering one.

One that meant I needed therapy.

Though the monster on the hill part sounded oddly enjoyable barring any human interaction to disturb my new feral life.

I sighed when my brain shook itself free and I still couldn't turn the hieroglyphs in front of my eyes into English words.

Apparently, I'd crossed the threshold of maximum coffee to minimum sleep ratio that broke my eyes. The useless flesh flaps refused to stay open and I knew little more now than I had ten hours ago standing outside the VA Hospital.

His name was Arturo Denicourt.

He'd been born in the 1960s. Parents were deceased, graduated high school in Nowhere, Nebraska in the seventies and then... nothing.

There was nothing about Arturo Denicourt joining the military. Despite the microscopic habitat of his hometown, there wasn't a wedding announcement or a birth announcement mentioning him as the father of Dr. Roberto Denicourt. A baffling realization when the news story on Roberto's birthday was about a bale of hay rolling into a major intersection and obstructing the roadway for fifteen whole minutes until someone could find a tractor to move it.

It was like after he graduated high school, he died.

Which didn't make any sense, because I'd seen with my own two eyes he was alive.

Not to mention proof that he had lived long enough to procreate.

"Who has the power to erase someone who's still here?" I asked Winnie, who'd come downstairs with me. She was on her dog bed against the wall beside my desk. Her paws were twitching as the soft purrs of her doggy snores broke the silence.

Without an answer from her, I pressed refresh on my browser window. When the screen still refused to show something else, I refreshed it again.

Then again.

My body finally gave out and the world tilted sideways. There was a brief sensation of freefall, followed by a soft thud and then something cold and wet on my face.

"So you could hear me," I muttered, shoving the large dog head away from my face. Now that I was somewhat flat and my eyes half closed, it no longer seemed necessary to make sense of the world. Every cup of coffee that added up to every pot of coffee I'd consumed gurgled uncomfortably in my stomach. There was a war brewing between needing sleep and chugging bean water. A war that had turned my life into Voldemort drinking unicorn blood.

It was a half-life, a cursed life, and I was paying the price.

"Need more coffee," I rasped, dragging my lower body across the floor of my office to the coffee cart. "Must defeat sleep."

Bitchcraft by Jax erupted from my desk and I jumped out of my suddenly itchy skin. The vibrations bounced it along the surface, dropping it not-so-gently on my head.

"Ow," I muttered.

"Cyn?" I looked over at the device. When it landed on my head, it answered the phone call and I recognized the voice from The Before Times.

Before humans were disappeared and coffee stopped keeping me awake for days on end. Perhaps he'd dialed 888 to go back in time and we were enroute to hover boards and DeLoreans.

We'd already lived the version where the bullies win and treat the country as their personal chess board.

"Ungh," I grunted and a soft chuckle trickled through the line, sending a jolt of heat through my body. It felt good, but also infuriatingly like someone insisting I do something while knocking on death's door.

All I wanted was a peaceful death.

The nerve of some people.

Making me feel alive.

"Chica, are you dead?" Cruz's question drifted to my ears, and I followed up with another half-dead groan. We were no longer half-alive, only halfway to dying but growing no closer. Like a cassette tape from the nineties, I could neither be re-wound to start over or played through to the end because my technological time had passed and kids no longer used number two pencils. "Did I wake you up?"

"No. No sleep."

Winnie thumped her tail against my head. I peeled back an eyelid that had fallen closed. She'd somehow laid down with her butt pressed against my face, nose steadily nudging the phone closer to my face. It was both impressive and disconcerting that she seemed hell bent on making me talk to the man.

"Sorry, I didn't mean to wake you up so early. It's just been a week and I wanted to talk to you," his voice made my nerve endings hum in excitement even as my brain registered his words.

"What do you mean early?" I asked, trying to look through the tail draped on my face to see the clock on the wall. As far as I could tell, the ancient battery powered circle had succumbed to the suggestions of the Salvador Dali painting and had melted.

Time itself had dripped and dropped into a giant nothing coffee pot. A coffee pot shaped like the earth with a handle and a spout. Little coffee beans were dripping into the opening, making the world sharper and brighter, while another part faded.

"Chica!" The voice startled me, and my eyes snapped back open.

No melting clocks, no globe in a coffee pot pouring coffee beans into a dying lifeform.

"Yeah?" I answered the disembodied voice. My small rectangle of glass, plastic and magic... science? What were computer chips made out of?

"I asked why you were awake," he was practically shouting now.

I reached over to poke the speaker phone button before he damaged something in his throat.

"Dead man, walking around. Went to military prison for many years, doesn't exist after high school. Definitely not dead but also not that real..." I muttered, shifting my head to rest it on Winnie's haunch. A sharp pain pierced my left eye, so I closed it. When that helped, I closed both of them and wondered how I managed to stay awake for days on end in my early twenties.

Probably hormones.

Or cocaine... did I take cocaine? Did I know where to buy cocaine? The only drugs I'd seen in Sweet Pea were little blue pills on my dad's dresser... pills that had not been the anti-inflammatories I'd been looking for.

Then I started searching for a metal rod to damage my brain. I'd found one in my parents' "playroom", but I didn't know if I wanted to aim for my frontal cortex's working memory or one of the other two regions. Probably procedural and semantic wouldn't have been helpful, but by the time I'd decided to go for the frontal cortex, my mom had shown up in a leather bustier and kicked me out for noontime nookie.

I'd decided I needed to chug vodka until I blacked out, but it was disgusting so I quit after a few sips and started researching lobotomies.

"Cyn!" I scrunched my nose, focusing back on the box even as I refused to open my eyes again. "Cyn, are you there?"

Right, on the phone in my office. Not reliving last week's trauma in my parents' house.

"Not dead," I answered him and I could nearly hear his eyes roll.

"I know you're not dead. What's the man's name?"

"What man? My dad or the one who sold him the pills?" I swiped at a pool of drool that slipped out of the side of my mouth. "Because there's a waitlist for lobotomies and I didn't ask for anything else I'd want to use to forget."

"What the hell... no, not... The man from the military prison who isn't dead! What is *his* name?"

Oh, right, that, I nodded to myself.

"Arturo Denicourt? His son... Roberto Denicourt, is a doctor at the VA hospital. The God of War got VapoRub on my face and I went outside. He's pushing a cart and smoking with lung damage, won't go home and he's from Knowhere."

47

"Everyone is from somewhere, chica," he chuckled, but I could tell I'd piqued his interest.

"Not nowhere, Knowhere. It's somewhere in Nebraska. Then he must have moved to Arizona at some point... maybe?"

I'd have to check with the good doctor to find out when exactly he'd moved to the land of sunshine and cacti. It was possible Arizona had happened after his dad's incarceration and there was somewhere between Knowhere and Phoenix... it would be great if it was called Somewhere.

I would laugh.

"Interesting..." he muttered, and I practically shot up, my eyes snapping open. The unbearable pain shut them again and I cried out.

"What's interesting?"

"Can you get me a photo?" His question was in a more clinical tone and a gentle clicking on his end told me he'd pulled out his computer.

"Yeah... Wait! You're Criminal Intelligence! You can make him reappear! Pull him out of whatever black sack the government stuffed his life into! Restore him to the last previously saved version, like that time my computer fried. Do a reverse grid-offing!" I fluffed my pillow and tried to settle back against it, but a gentle nibble followed by a *pooft* that released a stench so foul I could market it as smelling salts, reminded me the pillow was Winnie and her butt was not even remotely ideal to have next to your face.

"You can't reboot humans like a computer, chica."

He was speaking with only half his attention, and I'd have been offended if I wasn't gasping for air.

"And I'm guessing no one was able to rescue your computer. When you fry something, you *fry* something."

"Yeah, yeah, whatever. So... can you re-introduce him to the digital land of the living?" I asked hopefully.

"Maybe? I'm not really sure... that's why I need the picture. This is weird, Cyn," he'd grown quiet, and I lifted my head off of my partner's backside, grabbing for the edge of my desk. When I felt something solid under my fingers, I gripped it tightly and pulled, trying to get myself back into a seated position. The desk slipped through my fingers and when I pulled harder, something crashed to the ground with a metal clang.

Winnie bolted to her feet, barked at the fallen CPU while letting out another fart and then took off up the stairs to our apartment. Her toenails clicked on the hard surface flooring, a scramble as she lost traction and a final thump as she landed on the bed and sent it slamming into the wall.

"Chicken!" I shouted after her and then studied the computer tower. One of the metal sides had popped off, but it still illuminated with power. "Please don't be broken."

"What's happening, Cyn?" Cruz demanded from the floor and I picked up the phone, propping it on my desk while I tried to right the desktop computer.

"Nothing. Gravity and a chicken dog. Please don't be broken," I begged the computer again, wiggling the mouse. "Please don't be broken. It took so long to get the porn off of you and I can't afford one that isn't second-hand..."

"What?" Cruz was distracted on his end, but I could almost see his interest at the mention of porn.

"Nothing. My desktop came from a client who had his web server hacked and I figured out it was his mom trying to stop him from distributing porn. It was super weird, but he had this old desktop and I needed one, but getting all of the pictures and videos off was a challenge," I lied. Some of those pictures of naked beefy men holding puppies were too good to delete and my folder of images a man might call a spank-bank was the closest I was getting to action for a while.

"Cyn, I know about the folder," he smirked, and I wished he was here in person so I could throw something at him. Then maybe give him a hug and use him as a pogo stick before ultimately wrapping myself around him like a baby koala and depriving him of his personal space.

"Well, then you know I don't want to lose... damn."

The tower had started to click maniacally.

Then the display wavered back and forth.

So I smacked the side of the box and everything cleared up. My life motto had been "try fixing it the way you broke it" for years and this was the first time it worked.

The name Arturo Denicourt at the top of my browser window brought me back to the phone call and the reason I was fighting my biological need to collapse into dreamland.

"Why is Arturo Denicourt weird?" I thought his statement was a bit *pot calling the kettle black* considering who he was and who he was talking to.

I listened for an answer as he seemed to strain before a door closed on his end.

"Look, I'm not saying the military disappears people, but if they did... there would be a record of it that can be restored if the person magically reappears," he swallowed something, but I kept quiet to encourage him not to stop. "Arturo Denicourt isn't in that folder. He isn't in any of my folders. But there's a picture and a note from the prison. It's... unusual. The note just says, 'The missing have nothing to lose. Find the answers'."

My teeth worried my lower lip as I tried to sort through his words with their implications. Was Arturo Denicourt missing or lost?

"What's in the picture?" I asked, hoping it was a man in military fatigues with a name on his chest clearly in focus and a copy of his release papers, also in focus, telling us what he'd done.

"A man is standing beside a hospital bed, holding a baby all bundled up while the woman in the bed is looking at them. The back of the picture says 'R.D. 10/15/1980', is that when your doctor was born?"

I looked at the scattered pieces of paper around me, unsure if I'd found or read Dr. Denicourt's birthdate. There was very little that made sense after this many hours without sleep.

"Not sure... but let me talk to them and I'll get back to you. If he didn't have a file, where did you get the picture?" He shifted on the other end of the call and lowered his voice.

"I went into the prison's computer system. It was listed in someone's exit property."

"Not Arturo's?" I blinked and tried to pop my neck muscles.

"Can't tell... but I don't think so. Date doesn't match the release timeline," his voice was tired and I remembered it was both early and late.

"Why did you call? I'm guessing you didn't see a homeless recently released military prisoner and stick your nose all up in his business."

His hesitation came through the line with more weight than I'd have thought possible in a conversation about not-really-dead former soldiers. I mean, it was a mystery sure, but it wasn't like anyone was dead... that I knew of.

"Come on, out with it," I encouraged, picking up my coffee cup. I stuck my tongue in it, trying to lick clean any remaining drips. It was well and truly empty.

"Did you get your orders?"

"Yeah..." he hesitated, and I licked the outside rim of the cup. A few dried drips were mummified to the side and the burning in my gut could only mean I needed more coffee. "I have bad news, chica."

"Bad news?" I hesitated, wondering if I wanted an answer and picking up the empty coffee carafe. Since the question was already out, I started licking the pot for any leftovers.

"There was a vote, and they need me... in the Middle East."

"That's not that bad, we've been there before and it's calmer than it used to be. Plus, you blend in way better than I do. What are you investigating? Goat thefts?"

"Cyn, you're not listening. They are sending me to the Middle East for at least six months. I've been informed that it's a dead zone, deep cover mission. No cell phones or internet... and they won't tell me when I'm coming back or what the target is. Or if there's a target. I don't know if I'm looking for someone, something or covering up."

He paused for a beat, then a second as I tried to process his words.

"Can they do that? Don't you need background and time to research before they send you on an investigation?" I was no longer licking empty containers as the burning in my stomach turned into something a lot heavier.

"They can if you piss them off."

"What did you do to piss them off?"

The question wasn't necessary, but I asked anyway, knowing deep down that it was what *I* had done.

"The fallout from the Conri Kade incident sent a wave of investigations into other government practices and past events abroad. A squadron was killed in the early nineties and the news media got word of it. They need a clean-up crew to dig up the skeletons and make everything look rosy. It's still a hot area, with media and unfriendlies, and I'm on the shit list so..."

"They're sending you to look into skeletons?"

"Not that they've said. I've just seen the chatter and it's on their radar to do *something*. I don't know if that will be my problem or someone else's but whatever they need, I have to do it," his voice ended in a whisper of regret. "I think you should call Larry, Cyn. No matter what happens, you deserve to be happy. And as much fun as we have, it's not like what you two have."

"So, what you're saying is... what you mean to say is..." I trailed off, waiting for my brain to process his words. I reached for the

53

empty cup and sent it crashing to the floor. It splintered into a million porcelain pieces on the floor, scattering under the desk and toward the far wall.

"I'm saying goodbye, chica. I'll help you look into this Denicourt stuff, but I leave in a week and it doesn't sound like the Army really cares if I come back."

Chapter Five:
Personal Touch

"It's our fault Winnie," I said into her fur. The burning sensation in my stomach had been quelled by two packages of Oreos, a restaurant sized box of cheese crackers and a pint of ice cream. These additions sent the burning from my stomach to my chest and more coffee spiked with antacids had done nothing to make the pain or exhaustion go away.

"What if he... I mean... He could..." My vision of the ceiling blurred, warm tears pooling in my eyes. "Do you think..."

Winnie licked the tears off my face and the mucus in my nose dripped back into my throat. Choking, I rolled to my side in the bed and looked at my partner. She thumped her tail softly and I nodded at her.

"You're right. We couldn't let them have that weapon. And Cruz is tough, he'll be OK." I wrapped an arm around Winnie and closed my eyes again. It was my day off from The Dairy and all I wanted was a few hours of sleep to clear my head.

Maybe also let my body digest some of the garbage I'd shoveled into it before I barfed it back up.

My eyelids drooped, my breathing leveled off and... nothing.

"Alexa, what's the worst way to die?" I asked my robotic roommate.

"Hmmm... I don't know that," she responded and I decided it was probably for the best. Knowing all the ways he could be murdered was probably not going to help me.

"Alexa, can you travel through time?"

"I can travel anywhere with a power source and wifi. Would you like me to add these items to your recurring monthly order of coffee, cookies and..."

"No," I interrupted her and blinked at the ceiling. That order would probably need editing but I couldn't bring myself to access the spider-free web.

"Now what?" I groaned, knowing without knowing that sleep wasn't happening. "We can't do anything!"

Winnie licked my face again and hopped off the bed. She turned in three quick circles, sat down and extended her paw. The eyebrows on her furry face danced the worm and she put her paw down onto the coffee table. Something plastic and weighted fell to the floor and slid over to her.

"Impressive," I said, enjoying my dog's minor circus performance. It was rare that she did anything other than fart and sleep without a treat for motivation.

The dog lowered her head and started nudging the plastic object toward the bed. As she got closer, I saw that it was my hospital ID on the lanyard they gave me declaring me a volunteer.

"You want to go back to the hospital?"

She wagged her tail in response.

A forty plus minute drive to Dayton seemed like more skills and motivation than I currently possessed, but laying in bed not sleeping was driving me mad.

So I split the difference and called my best friend, Mo.

"Mary's Muffins and More, we close in ten minutes and I'm out of anything that doesn't have raisins," she exhaled the words in a single breath that would have left a normal person gasping. The red headed baker was several inches shorter than me, but we'd been in every grade together since she moved to the area as a kid.

She'd also managed to rocket light years ahead of me in maturity and grown-up responsibilities so I trusted her jugement and driving.

Even if we were regularly passed by people on motorized scooters.

"Wanna go on a road trip where you drive and I have a panic attack in the passenger seat while trying not to throw up?"

My question triggered a sound that usually accompanied either an eye roll or an inquisitive brow raise. I could practically see her perfectly shaped eyebrows arching gracefully over circulating retinas as she considered whether this was a prank call or a cry for help.

Since she'd met me, it was a short deliberation.

"Sure. Ten minutes and we take your Jeep?" she answered.

I smiled at the woman who was the closest to a "ride or die" I'd ever experienced within the human population.

Winnie was my "snack or strike" equivalent.

"Yeah... bring anything that doesn't sell. I need to do some recon and also feed strangers."

The idea popped into my head as I pictured Dr. Denicourt's dad and the other homeless people around the hospital. A Mo baked good was usually heaven *and* sneakily filled with what I heard referenced as "healthy fats" and veggies. I never saw any fats or vegetables but her baked goods usually left me feeling a little better.

That I usually washed them down with a medically unrecommended volume of coffee and Oreos was beside the point.

An effort had been made.

I had eaten the vegetables.

"If you give me half an hour, I can bake you something fresh," Mo said into the line and I smiled.

"It's not for me. We're feeding homeless vets."

"Then I'll be over now with everything I've got. I'll make more tomorrow," she answered and then hung up before I could say thanks.

"Guess we need to get dressed," I said, staggering to my feet. My stomach lurched and I rushed to the bathroom to evacuate cheese, cheese crackers, cheese chips and ice cream.

"When did I eat corn?" I muttered from the floor and heaved again.

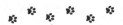

"You're sure about this?" I whined at Mo as we pulled into the hospital parking lot. She had filled my Jeep with bread, cheese, deli meat, muffins and cake. When she'd pulled up to my building with my loaded car, it had taken almost five minutes to find space for me and Winnie.

As it was, that space had to be shared.

And my shoulder was dislocated trying to keep Winnie from eating all of it.

Good thing this adventure was starting at a hospital.

"Ask me that again and I'll start demanding answers for the bags under your eyes and faint smell of vomit coming from your hair," she warned and I clamped my mouth shut. Instead, I pulled a package of Wet Wipes out of my glove box and wiped down my hands and hair. The initial relief I'd felt when my stomach had been reduced to having a reasonable volume of food had quickly faded under the anxiety, guilt and sleep deprivation itchiness threatening to crawl its way out like an alien inhabitant.

To make matters worse, I'd started twitching.

"Ok," I said, inhaling the alcoholic scent of antibacterial cleanser. When life was messy, cleaning supplies were calming.

It might have been related to all those military assigned cleaning details, but cleaning gave me the sense that I'd righted a wrong.

Or in the case of my childhood, washed away a bad memory delivered by school bullies and goats.

My apartment always smelled like dog slobber and coffee, but it was also slightly bleachy.

Especially when everything went to hell.

Sure, my personal life was a wreck and someone I care about could die for helping me, but at least if my dog drank out of the toilet, she wouldn't get any fecal coliforms hitching a ride.

She'd have to get those from licking her own butt like a normal dog.

"So, where do we start?" she asked, eyeing all of the food. We had four arms and a dog who would eat anything she was left in charge of. Not useful in this scenario. My eyes roved the parking structure and spotted Pluto climbing out of a sunshine yellow VW bug.

"Hey! God of War!" I shouted and Pluto gave me a smirk before heading over. "Do you think the hospital would let me borrow a cart?"

The nurse eyed my Jeep, making eye contact with Mo and giving a cursory sniff in my direction. Whatever look Mo had given Pluto must have been pleading for help, because the nurse turned back to me with skepticism and concern. Catching sight of my arm, Pluto stepped to my side, bent the elbow and shoved up, popping the ball joint back in the socket with a loud *pop*.

"Yeah, why the hell not," Pluto waved for me to follow and I left Winnie with Mo for safety reasons. Mostly my safety as I hadn't found Winnie a new vet since I broke up with her old one a few months ago for being a giant mama's boy and dry humping Amber Carter.

I quickly switched to a new line of thought as the visual made the churning in my stomach worse.

No way was I vomiting in a hospital.

Not after I got my arm back where it belonged and could successfully avoid medical treatment.

"You stink, Sharp Attack. Care to share?" Pluto's amusement came through the question loud and clear. I blinked at the green scrubs, wondering which smell needed explaining. "The vomit smell? Alcohol cleanser? Expression of constipated concentration?"

I shrugged but responded with a question of my own.

"Do you know about Dr. Denicourt's dad?"

I wasn't sure if it was common knowledge or a closely guarded secret. If it was the latter, he was screwed because keeping secrets wasn't really my thing. If it was the former, any information would be better than what I currently had.

Which was a name, a DOB, place of birth and weird prison photo that may not have been his.

"Yeah, kind of. The whole hospital helps him care for the man. It's less suspicious the more people who pass him money, food and clothing. Though my solution was a kidnap and rehabilitation plan, it was vetoed and got me on a hospital wide watch list for suspicious behavior. Dr. Denicourt said that if I weren't a damn good nurse, he'd probably have me investigated for unsolved crimes," Pluto shrugged and I wondered whether or not the abduction plan would work.

If Pluto would be a willing accomplice, maybe we could nab Cruz before the Army made him walk the plank.

"Sounds like everyone knows who he is, does anyone know why he feels like he belongs there?" I asked and the nurse scrunched up a freckle flecked nose. We'd arrived at a closet door near a laundry room and Pluto pulled out a canvas lined laundry cart. It wasn't ideal for food distribution, but it was better than dropping the food on the ground.

Probably.

The cart didn't *look* like it had transported bloody and poop stained clothing, but you really couldn't tell with laundry carts unless it was specifically labeled "clean only" and someone enforced it. The Commandant of Cleanliness.

Rather than asking, I accepted the cart. Sleep deprived, Ate Too Much Cyn Who Threw Up Her Snacks was not allowed to question the cleanliness of others.

At least that's what Mo told me on our way to Dayton when I enquired about some white staining on her pants.

"Dr. Denicourt is pretty well liked and most of us served overseas. We've all seen and lived through stuff... hell, a lot of us are one missed dose of medication away from being on the streets right beside Arturo. Whatever happened, it probably wasn't his fault but defecation is subject to gravity," the nurse winked and I wondered at the formal presentation of the adage *shit rolls downhill* while watching Pluto's sneakers disappear around the corner just as a man cleared his throat behind me.

I spun around screaming and caught the man in the jaw.

"What the hell!" I shouted, my heart racing in my chest as the man attempted to get his stethoscope back on his neck. My punch had barely grazed his jaw, the exhaustion too much to aim effectively. "You can't just sneak up on people, I could have killed you!"

The man in the white coat smirked and I regretted not accidentally hitting him harder.

"From what I've heard around the hospital, that's a possibility whether I sneak up on you or not."

His voice had a weird cadence that combined the subtle whistle of a tea kettle with the harsh interruption of an air horn. A sound that was startling, unpleasant, and encouraged anyone in ear shot to flee or their head would explode.

That or I was tired and he was being a jerk.

One or the other.

"Great. I'm taking this laundry basket to feed the birds so in about ten seconds you'll be out of the danger zone. You won't die today," I grumbled, starting to push past him when he held out a hand to my shoulder.

"Please, I just need a minute of your time."

I stared at the hand not quite touching my arm and sighed.

"What is it now?" I grumbled, searching his eyes for any signs of drug abuse or diagonal pupils indicating a mind demon had taken over his brain.

No normal person asked me for a minute of my time.

They just stole it, rudely and with great entitlement.

"My wife…" he shifted uncomfortably and then pulled out his phone to show me a picture. The woman had curly hair, a broad smile and a chin dimple. It was a super close-up of her face that offered no context or identifying characteristics I'd recognize from a distance.

Unless we were making out, the picture was useless for identity purposes.

"That's not a super helpful picture for recognizing her at a distance. What do you need?" I blinked at his face which was a little too asymmetrical to be attractive.

"What do you think?"

My gut response was that she could do better, but that probably wasn't what he was asking.

"I'm really tired and have vomited a lot in the past twelve hours. You need to spell it out or move," I finished on a yawn.

"I think she's cheating on me. She's been secretive, going out more and returning in an upbeat mood. I thought it was drugs, but she didn't have any of the other trademark characteristics," he scanned the area before dropping his voice even lower. "And she used to gag when she gave me…"

"Stop! Stop right there. That is not what I meant by spell it out. I do not want or need you to finish that sentence," my feet carried me away from the man, but he seemed undeterred.

"It's just, I've seen so many wrappers for sausages and I can't help but wonder if… will you look into it?" He pleaded and my head bounced off the concrete wall behind me. Confused, I looked around and saw that instead of backing toward the exit, I'd backed myself into a corner.

Freaking great, I thought as I wondered how many times the man was going to try to elaborate on his wife's throat muscles before I used the pen in his pocket to puncture his voice box.

"You're an investigator. Like a PI and I need one to confirm... I'll pay you!" He looked excited at the thought and I had my first glimpse into what my life would have been like as a prostitute.

Offered money for services I regretted having the capacity to perform.

And I wouldn't even have the chance to get an orgasm... not that prostitutes probably got those either.

There really was no service job that made women feel good.

My eyes drifted back to the man in front of me and I remembered we were in the middle of a conversation.

"I'm not a PI! I mean, I have an office that says Sharp investigations and a business permit because the government is big on taxes, but I don't own a long-range camera or one of those listening things. Cheating spouses isn't on my list of services offered. I find bananas and lost car keys and..."

"I'm not asking you to cheat on my spouse, I'm asking you to find out if she is a cheating spouse. And if she is, if the guy is seriously hung because the softness of her throat..." I slapped my hand over his mouth and prayed for concrete to become sedimentary and erode around me like quicksand.

"Shut up. Shut up now and give me... a..." My mind went blank. I had no interest in following his wife, but I had even less interest in this man talking to me. "A text message. I mean, message me a better photo, full body, name and work address of your wife."

"Wouldn't it be better if I..."

"Nope. No it would not. Nothing that involves being near you would be better than being not near you and now I'm going to take this laundry trolley and leave and you will stay right there. Stay," I warned again when he twitched like he might follow me. "Stay. Good doctor. The hospital has my number. Don't follow me or I'll..."

I didn't have a threat so I spun around, shoving the cart and sprinting toward the door. Shoving the cart toward the opening, I slammed into it at full force. The metal cart bounced back into my ribs and the world went sideways as I flew backward, landing on the linoleum with the laundry cart on my chest.

The Throat Doctor walked up and loomed over me with a shit-eating grin on his face that I'd have slapped off of him if I could breath.

"That doors a 'pull', Sharp," he said before bursting out laughing and snapping a picture of me on the floor.

"I hate you," I wheezed.

Chapter Six:
Veterans Park

"D o you want to talk about your new bruises?" Mo dropped the question while casually pushing the laundry cart. We were walking down a mostly maintained sidewalk. Every crease between concrete squares was slightly higher or lower than its neighbor. I counted thumps and bumps, noting with concern how some of the softer cheese pastries jiggled in a way that was both mesmerizing and nauseating. "Or the vomit? Maybe why I haven't seen Cruz in over a week?"

Mentioning vomit had me looking away from the pastries and taking deep even breaths as inconspicuously as possible while walking. No need to give Mo anything else to grill me about while I hobbled along beside her. The pain in my ribs was only slightly more uncomfortable than the knot on the back of my head from colliding it into the ground and neither pain was enough to put me down for the nap I so richly deserved.

That probably wouldn't come without Tequila, knockout gas or prolonged pressure applied to my windpipe for a few seconds less than it would take to kill me.

The pro-wrestling sweet spot.

Also a super fun game the popular kids had played in junior high.

Sadly, they all survived to procreate.

"Not really," I answered, guiding us around the corner. While waiting for my lungs to work, Nurse Pluto had reappeared with a cold compress and Doctor Clyde No-Last-Name. Doctor Clyde hadn't been in the military, but he'd lost his partner in Iraq. He'd made it his mission to help vets come home, not just physically, but mentally.

Turns out, he's a doctor of psychiatry.

Also turns out you *can* diagnose a person's mental disorders from YouTube videos and military service records.

But he'd only tell me his findings if I made an appointment and who has time for that?

"Want to tell me more about where we're going?" she asked instead and I gestured toward a white cross-hatched arch with vines and shrubbery creeping up both sides. It served as an entryway for a path that went beside multiple black marble walls, engraved with the names of soldiers from the area who'd been recorded as killed in combat going back through World War I.

"Veterans Park," I said, gesturing beyond the memorial to a few scattered people in battered clothing. They weren't all veterans, but the VA hospital had made the case that allowing encampments in the park would keep those who were closer to medical care.

It was months of hearings and "not in my backyard", but the hospital and the city won. The Veteran's Memorial Park was an open space for gathering, and after hours, for encampments. Many people avoided the park, claiming it was a dishonor to those who served to allow "riffraff" in the park.

I personally thought it was a dishonor to those who served that we couldn't manage to take care of those who came back. Maybe my time in the military was shorter than it could have been, but I don't think I'd met a single soldier who'd be ashamed to let a fellow soldier sleep by a memorial honoring his death.

They might be a little upset about the whole dying thing... and the homeless issue of people who fought alongside them... maybe a little bit about how many birds pooped on the stone monument...

"Cyn!" Mo pulled me from my downward spiral of *things that would bother me if my name was on a block in a park.*

"Sorry. We are here to bring them some food... and get information," I said quietly, noticing a group of men with hole-filled green duffels watching us. Their eyes drifted warily from me to Mo before landing on Winnie. Creases formed along the edges of their weather worn skin as they smiled at the crazy canine.

You wouldn't be smiling like that if you had to sleep with her after she ate a block of cheese, I thought and tried to transmit a plea that they not let her get any cheese. Despite my mental transmission, they leaned invitingly toward Winnie and she pranced over with her head up and tail waving merrily in the cool-aired sunshine.

Then they gave her cheese.

No, wait, that was just affection.

"Should you just let her walk over to them like that?" Mo hissed and my eyes darted between what I could now see was a group of men and women, and the German Shepherd enroute. "Don't they deserve some kind of warning?"

Mo's words sunk in just as she got to the group. One stepped forward, rubbing her ears. A second moved closer, running a hand down the dog's spine as I made my way into the circle.

"Don' need your pity, blondie. San'wich lady comes by once a day. Got wha' we need here," a gruff voice spoke from behind the five people who were now petting Winnie. Some were having her sit, lay down, and shake paws, but most seemed to brighten just from being in her company.

It was possibly the first time my dog had helped my fellow soldiers without destroying anything first.

"This isn't sandwiches, it's baked goods. Mo's baked goods. And even though she was a teacher for Teach for America, she didn't date over there so she got really good at making stuff. She's got a male companion now, but that didn't seem to have ruined her talents," I babbled and a few of the people petting Winnie stopped to give me a concerned look.

"I'm sleep deprived, over-caffeinated, and someone I... like a lot, is being sent off to a hostile area without back-up because he pissed off some military bigwig by helping me and I ate my weight in Oreos, cheese crackers, and actual cheese. Then threw it up and started over so... y'know..." I trailed off as a weathered hand touched my shoulder. I looked down into deep brown eyes that shared a lifetime of experience without a single word being spoken.

Her presence was calming and I took a few deep breaths.

"What have you got in the cart?" her question triggering a half-scoff from Gruff Voice. No one walked away and his eyes flashed mutiny. Mo, sensing her true purpose had finally come, started whipping out treats. Despite the amount of sugar and chocolate, I also knew she snuck veggies into her baked goods. I'd had carrot and zucchini cupcakes with a Greek yogurt frosting that was both delicious and managed to stave off hunger.

For everything except more cupcakes.

So, maybe in addition to veggies, she was also filling them with crack.

It would explain why she always has a line, I thought, narrowing my eyes in her direction before remembering she wasn't the reason we were here.

While the red headed baker got down to the business of feeding people, I scanned the crowd for Arturo.

"Looking for someone, blondie?"

I turned, recognizing the gruff voice from the sandwich accusation. My mind started weighing if I should ask him outright or sneak the questions in, when my eyes locked into the amber brown of Arturo Denicourt. Up close, I could see faint scarring along his left cheek, the limp I'd spotted previously more pronounced with a clear view of his left shoulder sitting two inches below his right. Dr. Denicourt had favored his father, but the man before me was too sharp and calculating to be the lost soul his son had described.

"Arturo," I offered with a nod.

"Sharp," he returned, and I nodded again. "Been a long time since that doctor was bold enough to send someone all the way down to the park. He know we don't need his pity anymore 'en we need yours?"

"Doctor? A doctor didn't send me. No one sent me. To be honest, no one ever sends me. I just end up places and sometimes it works out and sometimes it's Florida," I shrugged, breaking eye contact to check on Winnie. With food in the hands of all her admirers, she was in full crumb clean-up detail, threatening to Hoover any food particle that so much as hinted it obeyed the laws of gravity.

"What's that like?" He asked and I turned to see his eyes fixed on me.

"What's what like?" I countered, searching for hidden meaning in eyes that gave nothing away. He lived in a world that didn't seem to intersect this one beyond the physical. He met my gaze, pulled out a cigarette and lit it. A long drag passed as he sized me up.

"Having a partner? Someone who's got your back and is always there?"

He'd switched to watching Mo who had started up a conversation with two of the men. Her laughter, a sound like sleigh bells in a snow-softened night, brightened the world around her. Arturo puffed twice more, the cigarette never leaving his lips, ash raining down onto his graying coat that may have once been black... or a slightly darker gray. Neither of which managed to distract from his faded and graying face, sharp eyes that lost any spark of joy sitting in a face that had to have once been happy. The man had been married, had a son, one who loved him enough to move to Ohio to be near the father who hadn't come home.

"You were married. You had a partner," I said, looking for signs of a reaction. "Why didn't you go home to her? To your family? Did you think they stopped caring about you or did you stop caring about them?"

He remained fixated on Mo, but I saw the tremble in his hand. Arturo started clenching and unclenching his fists, like part of his hand was going numb. I'd either made him angry or upset, but his carefully controlled face wouldn't show me which.

The man had forged a mask of steel over the years that wouldn't be cracked by an amateur detective and her canine.

A real tragedy because Winnie deserved a smile.

She was fluffing adorable.

"How do you know about that?" he barely breathed the words.

I blinked repeatedly, trying to process his words through the haze of exhaustion that settled like a wet blanket on my body. Everything felt heavy and uncomfortable, but there was nothing I could do that would change Cruz's fate.

There was nothing I could do to change what he'd been through.

My only option was to tell the truth and hope for the best.

"From your son," I answered, and his lip lifted slightly... or I blinked a bunch of times and made the optical illusion of his face twitching. I chose to believe it was the first though, and he was silently asking me to tell him more about the child who'd been taken from him. "He's a doctor at the VA Hospital. I assumed you knew that, it's why you wouldn't take anything from him directly. Whatever happened when he was a teenager, whatever shame you carry, he wants you to come home. Don't you want to know the man he's become? Don't you think the Army has taken enough of your life that you should get to enjoy the remainder?"

"Marines," Arturo's eyes had taken on a misty quality, but it might have been my imagination. In a flash, his jaw was set, teeth grinding in his mouth, before he turned on me.

"I was in the Marines, damnit. As far as my family knows, Sharp, I'm dead. Don't deserve a family, or a life, but they just wouldn't let me die. I do what I can out here, because I owe them for those that I let down. But my 'family' is better off leaving me buried. Dead men can't disappoint," he scoffed. I opened my mouth to counter, to point out that he was disappointing his son by *not* coming home, but he was gone. Shuffling toward Mo and the others, dropping the butt of his cigarette on the ground, stomping it once and then picking it up to put in the trash can.

"Man got the short stick," I glanced down to see the brown-eyed woman beside me. Winnie sat beside her, taking gentle ear scrunches while the woman worked through her own demons to share someone else's. Her face had a hair thin scar down her left jawline that went around and under her ear before disappearing into a thick mane of unkempt hair.

"Do you know?" I asked, but she shook her head. "About him? About any of it?"

74

"No one knows, not all of it. Man talks in his sleep though. Shoutin' bout blood, and how was there so much blood..." She twitched a little, head toward me while her fingers seized. Her whole arm jumped and Winnie leaned against her leg, letting the woman ride out whatever neural synapse was misfiring. I tried to study her scar, wondering if there wasn't a piece of shrapnel accidentally left behind. "Asked around, though. He was in the military prison a long time. Rumors come out of there more often than not, and there was an intern... that ain't right. He was doin' file stuff while recoverin' from some'in or other 'round the time Arturo was coming up on his end there."

"Did he see the file?" I wondered aloud, curious how a file existed in the prison that didn't manage to exist in the massive database where Cruz could access it.

Unless they took away his research access because of you, my brain offered bitterly and I tried to shove her back down. There was only enough self-loathing in me to help one person right now, and digging into the past was a lot more my speed than trying to prevent the future.

As cool as it would be to have a Delorean, I could not pull off the Marty McFly look.

"Yeah, but he wouldn't say nothin' bout it. Said we was better off not knowin' and when he got his meds sorted, he went and opened a range. Offered most of us jobs there if we wanted. Can't take the noise though. Most of us can't take the noise, sends us backwards and we ain't made it far enough forward to go back."

I nodded, letting her words settle in. It wasn't definitive, or even enlightening, but it was more than I'd had before and I couldn't bring myself to push her... to push any of them.

This is so not right, my brain offered and I agreed even as I mocked my own statement of the obvious. *We should do something.*

Before an idea could form, two sharp barks cut through the air.

My head jerked to the side just in time to see a skateboarder cruising toward the rail of the memorial wall. Ears on end, Winnie stood at full alert, her tail bristling as the guy continued toward what she had decreed was off limits to him. Before I could re-clip her leash, Winnie took off toward the monument and I ran after her.

"Winnie! No! Bad!" I shouted, but her eyes were laser focused on the wheels of the kid's skateboard. "Come on! Mo has snacks!"

Pumping my arms, I fought harder to keep up, but I was too late. Winnie threw her weight into the guy on the skateboard, knocking him off and sending his board scuffling into the nearby grass. A small black earphone fell out of his ear and I watched him morph from skateboarder into threat.

"What the hell? Get this thing off me!"

Winnie had hold of his left shoe and was tugging as hard as she could until it slid off his foot. He grabbed for her, lunging as she shook his shoe like a captured prey she was about to feast upon. Her head slowed, she scented again and dropped the shoe, turning back toward Skateboarder Man. He looked at me, and I

76

studied his face while my eyes tracked Winnie's laser focus. He was either closing in on mid-30s or had lived a life in ignorance of sunscreen. The bottoms of his black cargo shorts were brushing the tops of his tube socks.

His lumpy tube socks.

"Winnie! Leave it!" I shouted, grabbing for her collar as her teeth settled into the top of his sock. She pulled on the sock, I pulled on the dog and...

The sock slipped off, dropping a small gun on the ground. The man grabbed for it and I kicked it away from his hand, lunging forward to subdue him until the cops could get here. All around the park, strollers stopped and trash can lids popped up to reveal...

"Are you kidding me?"

The exclamation was joined by a man in full police uniform, popping out of the back of a satellite dish van. The man with the skateboard went bug-eyed, dodging my attack and main-lining it for the center of the park where more undercover officers were waiting. One shoved the wheel of a bicycle in his path while another jumped on his back, the whole lot falling on the ground in a tussle that put Hulk Hogan to shame.

I looked down to see the collar I was holding was now empty. I panicked, eyes searching desperately for the dog in case there were any more armed assailants lurking in the area as a dozen more officers breached the park perimeter and tugged cuffs out as more spooked looking deadbeats tried to run from the park.

Where the hell is...

The dog who had occupied the collar had a gun in her mouth. Not only was it a gun, but she'd somehow looped an incisor into the trigger guard and it spun around on her tooth while she was parading around with her prize. On her second pass of armed memorial patrol, an officer approached her and she went still as a statue. He took a step toward her and I saw the tip of her tail twitch.

The officer took another step and I watched Winnie shift her weight to her back legs.

"Crap," I grumbled as the young officer dived to her left, Winnie sprang right, and he crashed into the ground where she'd been standing.

"Your dog is something special," I nearly jumped, seeing the homeless woman standing at my elbow. I'd not only forgotten she was there, I wasn't all that sure this wasn't a prank show. "I think he'd like you."

"Who'd like me?" I yawned at my own question, watching a woman in skin-tight leopard leggings produce a pair of handcuffs from neon pink legwarmers. Winnie had sent another officer into a face slide, then lunged backward with her gun. Backing up, her butt ran into a baby stroller, startling her. The canine stumbled back, bumped it again and darted away as it started to tilt.

The baby carriage shade fell back and a parabolic microphone joined the stroller in crashing to the ground and shattering into pieces of plastic and computer bits. It was like the whole park was the movie set from *Miss Congeniality* and I held my breath for Sandra Bullock to make her grand entrance.

Nothing.

Another movie that would have benefitted from having a dog, I thought, turning my attention back to the woman beside me. She'd said something... something about someone liking me.

"Who'd like me?" I asked again and she laughed.

"Lots of people, but this time I was talking about the intern with the gun range."

"The guy who saw Denicourt's file?" She nodded and I tried to split my attention between her and the four additional units who'd arrived to disarm a rogue military canine.

"Trigger," she answered, slipping me a small piece of paper. I unfolded it to see an address west of the city and a block letter header declaring the address belonged to a business called *Shots Fired*. "Gotta warn you though, he ain't one for sharing. I 'magine if he'd tell anyone, he'd tell you though. Jus' make sure you bring the dog. Man's only got patience for shootin' and dogs."

She meandered back toward the group of spectators. As a collective, they looked like the cast of a post-apocalyptic movie on lunch break. Each of them clutching snacks from Mo's goodie basket while we waited for the director to yell cut... or Winnie to shoot someone.

The way today was going, this was either a movie or a crime scene.

So, I snapped a picture of Arturo and the others, just in case it was both.

Chapter Seven:
Cuffed and
Confused

This wasn't my first time being arrested.

This wasn't even my first time being arrested for my association with Winnie.

It was the first time I'd been arrested, handcuffed to a bench, and left alone for three hours while being actively accused of domestic terrorism.

When Winnie and I had first arrived home, amid tracking a missing fake reverend and not-actually-missing money, Winnie had destroyed a wedding. It was outside, I was forced to attend by Larry Kirby, and it was for my childhood nemesis Amber Carter.

Count Groomula, a psychopath who needed money, had tricked Amber into marrying him with a fake title and grew to regret his decision enough to try to kill her.

Winnie, by getting mud on her dress, demolishing the wedding cake, and rumored to have peed on the Groomsmen, had saved Amber's life. Since Amber was now getting jiggy with Larry after I told him I loved him and almost moved into his house, I partly regretted how many treats I gave the dog for destroying the wedding.

If she'd been better behaved, Amber would probably be a distant memory... like that nightmare where the world runs out of coffee and chocolate. Then I'd still be with Larry, Cruz wouldn't be on his way to a suicide mission, and...

And I'd probably still have ended up arrested somehow, I thought, watching my latest string of drool lower slowly toward the floor. I'd invented a game where I let out a single strand of spit and tried to suck it back into my mouth just before it reached the ground.

The Crater Lake deep puddle on the floor was decent evidence I sucked at this game.

And that I was ill-suited to a life of lock-up.

"There're always homeless people in that park. What difference do they make?" a male voice shouted from somewhere in the bowels of the police station. The strange juxtaposition of a building that both swallowed sound and failed to mute a single one was both alarming and reassuring.

Transparency in policing without a single moment of clarity.

"You don't think that a park full of civilians is something you should have taken into account and protected before approving and executing this operation?" a woman's voice interjected between the sniveling whine of two men accusing me of 'ruining everything'.

"They're just *homeless* people, no one cares if anything-" A sharp crack rang out and died upon echoing off half of the walls.

"Those are people and your lack of regard for their safety is far worse than a dog picking up a gun," the woman seethed, and I nearly cheered but then I'd have to figure out how to sit up. "Your operation was a violation of department and city policy. If I had the power to fire you, you'd be turning in your badge. Who conducts an operation to apprehend domestic terrorists without verifying the safety of all non-operational personnel? You can be certain that a sternly worded letter disparaging you and your..."

Her voice faded out before I could cheer, replaced with a new pair of voices.

"You know that lady is a war hero?" one asked, followed by the metallic click of a soda can opening.

"Half the people out in that park are war heroes. Hell, the only reason I agreed to being on this team was to make sure Skid Marks didn't get any of them hurt," the second man paused, and I assumed he was either eating or drinking.

"Why is he so hell bent on getting rid of them? They're taking care of each other the best that they can and they don't bother anyone," another break in speech, but the echoes were getting clearer. Maybe they were moving closer.

"It's his thing. Says they're leeches on society and too weak to be allowed to live. I heard him once on the phone with someone. There's a dude in that group he really has it in for. I think that the dog stealing the gun ruined his plan to do something bad."

"I think his mom knew what she was doing when she named him Dick," both men snickered.

My eyes closed and I pictured the group I'd photographed. Were any of them the target of uninterrupted attention? The voices outside the door faded as I rewound my own memory but there wasn't much to pick out. Between Winnie and Mo, the whole group had drawn a lot of attention. Picking out who was a police officer before it all went to hell and became obvious would have taken a level of rest and attention I didn't currently possess.

"Did you hear they rounded up the Apple Dumpling Gang?" a woman's voice accompanied the snap of a stapler and I tried to pinpoint the direction. Was it normal to have administrative workers so close to detainees?

"I can't believe how big a task force Dick got to take out a group of deadbeats and washouts based on a social media post," a man with a slight accent answered her. It was either Korean or...

"Did you know, no one found that post? As far as anyone can tell, he's the only one who saw it. Bizarro, right?"

My brow furrowed and I strained for more, but the voices moved, and no more conversations drifted to my bench.

Police people are super gossipy, I thought, even as I made a mental note to get a visual on Skid Marks and see if he was unnecessarily interested in my friends.

Still cuffed to a bench, I swiped my tongue across the top of my mouth to get a solid batch of saliva and pushed it to the corner of my mouth. A grimace to squeeze and felt a new line of spit ooze out and begin its descent .

"What the hell is wrong with you?"

A pair of black boots asked from beside my head. My carefully curated slobber plopped on the floor. Annoyed, I tilted my chin toward my torso and felt an immediate head rush from being upside down for so long.

"Spitcicles," I answered, swiping my right hand across my chin. My left hand was still cuffed to a pole running behind the wooden bench in an unsecured holding area. For a mysterious reason, I was placed on the center of the detainment bench and only my left hand had been cuffed to the wall behind me.

Then everyone disappeared.

Sleep-deprived, I took the opportunity to lay flat on the bench but there was too much noise for a nap. Sitting back upright, my butt went numb, so I slid to the side and put my lower back where my butt had been, sneaker clad feet on the wall caging my cuffed hand. Though the absence of something warm and fluffy in my general vicinity was weird and uncomfortable.

Being arrested without Winnie was the least ideal way to be arrested. She'd been with me in the back of that cop car in Yellow Springs, she'd been with me when I was accused of arson, she'd been with me in Canada when we accidentally flooded a food court with gravy and they needed to bring in a hazmat team.

Not this time, though.

This time, my furry best friend was in the custody of my human best friend, released after a 6 minute car ride when she farted for a minute straight and gassed out the driver of the patrol car. No one wanted her inside, and no one was permitted to let me go until the car had been fumigated.

The dog's toxic colon was somehow also my fault.

Or they were still mad at me and even if she hadn't tried to asphyxiate a police officer, I'd still be cuffed to a wall.

"You thought spitting on my floor was an appropriate activity in my police station?"

The boots were attached to legs and as I rediscovered where my core muscles were, I found the pants were attached to a torso and the torso was topped with some sort of human head.

"*Your* floor in *your* police station?" I asked the kid, swinging my legs around to sit upright with a series of pops and cracks that reminded me I needed to buy breakfast cereal.

"Yes! You got a problem with that?" his rhetorical question coaxed a snort from my throat.

His pimple marked face was going red, the badge patch declaring him a cadet at odds with the air of ownership he had for a facility that probably wouldn't know his name if it weren't on his shirt.

"Kid, my spit is the least offensive bodily fluid that has been on this floor," I rubbed away my tiredness with my free hand while waiting for him to either whine some more or fetch a real adult to scold me for hurting his feelings.

"What the hell did you do this time?"

The faux southern drawl sent a wave of annoyance tinged with delight running through me. It was a voice that meant I was probably going to get to go home soon, but I would suffer immensely for my freedom.

"And why is your face red?" he asked from inches away.

I looked up at the toned and tanned body of Daniel Kirby, Larry's older brother, the hottest guy in high school, and one of Sweet Pea's two deputies. The entire department was Daniel, a second officer named Barney Fife, no relation, and a Chief of Police, Carla Sharp.

AKA my sister-in-law who I would have to grill relentlessly to figure out why she sent a second string law enforcement officer to fetch me.

"Officer Kirby," Daniel introduced himself to the kid, and I nearly burst into laughter when the kid turned up his nose and sniffed.

"Your shirt says deputy."

Our town was as baffled about this weird naming policy as the kid was. It was not unusual to have a sheriff covering an area that also had a local chief of police. The sheriff would have deputies, the chief officers, and away we would go. But Sweet Pea had an identity crisis because none of the town founders paid enough attention during Andy Griffith to figure out if they wanted a police or a sheriff's department, so the county decided for them.

Then they never told us what they decided.

Or came anywhere near the town again because we were, and I quote "crazy".

The town's mothers had not had them tested so the argument died with a rubber and glue comeback that artists had rendered into wall paintings proudly hung in our city hall.

"Daniel," I said, deciding not to answer any of his questions. The Kid, Omar if one believed name tags, was giving Daniel a once over that would have a woman covering her private parts. The Officer was wearing a dark blue polo with his name embroidered into it with jeans in a police casual that didn't look completely legitimate.

"Where's the domestic terrorist?" he joked and I snickered while Little Omar's eyes went wide.

Unfortunately, the snicker got away from me and turned into a full belly laugh. The bench rushed towards my face, tears streaming while I cackled like a madwoman huffing paint in a nitrous oxide factory. Every muscle in my body contracted and spasmed, every laugh more painful than the one before, but I couldn't stop. Everything was hilarious. Daniel. Little Omar. Winnie getting me arrested for "training" her to attack "agents of the government" and "unlawfully removing evidence from a crime scene".

The collective stick up the ass of this establishment was just too much and I snapped.

"Shit, get the key," Daniel said, holding out a hand toward Omar.

"What? You can't..."

Daniel held up his badge to cut off the kid's whining, flashing his gun at the same time.

The kid sniffed at it, dismissing the badge and the gun with equal attitude. Turning his head, Omar jutted his chin in the air and crossed twig arms over his chest.

"You don't work here."

My body shook with renewed laughter until I fell off the bench, strung up by my arm, into the puddle of my own spit.

"You Deputy Kirby?" a new voice interrupted my meltdown. A hand went into each of my armpits and I was dumped back on the bench, slippery spit dripping from my chin onto my shirt with the salty remnants of my tears.

"Yeah. You the judge?" Daniel asked, extending a hand from under my arm to shake hers. My gaze stayed fixed on the floor, it was too much work to see who was wearing the sensible kitten heels with a black robe.

"That would be me, Judge Anita Pestolli. I apologize for calling you, but Miss Sharp and her canine caused quite the disturbance in a sting operation. One of the Captains running the operation split his pants open chasing the gun wielding dog and has been nicknamed Skid Marks, though I understand the name existed long before Miss Sharp stumbled into our town. Naturally, he is attempting to nail charges onto Miss Sharp like Jell-O on a telephone pole. Rather than argue with him, I'm releasing her into the custody of another agency until her court hearing."

"Where is the dog? Who the hell gave Winnie a gun?" Daniel shouted from beside me and I "accidentally" wiped my slobber onto his navy blue T-shirt to avenge my now ringing ears. The man needed to learn volume control.

"It is my understanding that no one armed the dog. It retrieved the weapon from a person of interest and then refused to give it back," the judge spoke with an evident smile in her voice. "I'm reminded of a story involving a trained attack chicken with some sort of laser guidance system and razor blades on its ankles."

"Don't you dare arm any chickens!" I jumped to my feet, head whipping around in horror. "You don't understand the horror you'll unleash! Chickens are the spawn of satanic forces summoned from the depths of manure!"

Seeing a green exit sign, I made a sprint for it.

In two steps, I was face up in Daniel Kirby's lap.

"Thwarted by my own arm," I grumbled, Daniel taking a key from the cadet and releasing the cuff. My eyes finally looked at the short, curly haired woman dressed to preside over the criminal justice system. Her skin was smooth, a milk chocolate color with deep brown eyes and a friendly smile lined just enough to prove she did it often.

"Thanks," I muttered, still staring at her face. She was familiar, but I couldn't place her. "Do I know you?"

Asking was easier than guessing.

Also safer if the memory of a man trying to hit me for confusing him with his best friend was any indication. Apparently calling out the wrong name in bed and then stating you got confused with who you hooked up with the night before was as effective as telling someone to calm down.

Which I also tried.

He did not.

But I did learn how many different words men had for slutty.

89

"Not that I'm aware of, though I'd be surprised if we hadn't seen each other previously," she hinted at a life of crime with a wicked glint in her eyes and I didn't have the energy to argue.

"Yeah, well, thanks for making the kid give Daniel the key. When's my... did you say hearing?" I asked and tilted my head toward her.

"Yes, Miss Sharp. Though I haven't a clue what to discuss, since you didn't actually commit a crime. Scheduling a hearing was the only way to get Captain Preznall to stop stammering and looking like a Big Mouth Bass, so I caved. A man who is that sensitive about skid marks should either do laundry better or buy new underpants," she shook her head, but I nodded in understanding.

You don't end up doing field work solo in a hostile war zone without knowing a thing or two about the fragility of the male ego. It was remarkable that the more volatile of their species was diminished as feminine when nothing is more emotionally unstable than an arrogant man who's embarrassed.

Just look at The Great Orange One.

Or that Falcons player who blamed Pink because he didn't have the stamina to finish a game.

Like pop a little blue pill, sport ball game loser.

"Miss Sharp?" I blinked at the judge who looked like she was waiting for some sort of a response.

"Yeah?"

"Do you want your phone back?"

She gestured toward a man in khaki holding a plastic bag with my wallet, keys, cell phone and pocket cookies.

"I'd rather know why they had to take my cookies," I shot back, taking the bag and emptying it into my cargo pants. "You wouldn't have spit on your floor if you let me have cookies."

"Somehow I doubt that," she shook her head and I shrugged while powering my phone back on. It took a solid thirty seconds to boot up, but it eventually blinked to life and displayed two unread messages. Cruz's name sat above one, and I opened it to see confirmation he'd received the picture and he'd try to have the information to me before he left.

For his doom, my brain finished. I was too tired at the moment to feel the usual guilt. Instead I felt angry and began plotting a Rambo style infiltration into the hostile zone to kill everyone and wear their teeth on a necklace of intestines.

"Making that face will keep them from letting you out, Sharp," Daniel said, pulling me up short before I ran face first into a glass door at the exit. "Can you try to focus until we are outside again?"

His teeth would be the first on my sash of death. I eyed his incisors with an evil glint.

"Just... close your face until we're back in Sweet Pea."

He switched to walking behind me, leading me toward his truck in the parking lot by the shoulders. The second message had a 927 area code but was unknown to my phone.

"What's this?" I questioned my phone as it slowly attempted to load the message and attachments. When it didn't answer, I leaned against Daniel's truck and waited, enjoying the show as he tried to get keys out of his too tight pants. If inappropriate hand gestures were family friendly, the man could start a circus act pulling things out of his pants.

The phone dinged again and I reluctantly looked away. As amusing as it was to watch the man feel himself up trying to get his keys back, there were more important things in life. My eyes drifted to the picture in the message that had finally loaded.

"Why is there a picture of the judge on your phone?" Daniel asked and I squinted at the blurring letters underneath. Dr. Pestolli, whose wife works at the courthouse, told him she'd be late getting home... Friday.

"Oh no," I groaned, half falling into Daniels truck. "No freaking way am I following around a judge."

Chapter Eight: Just Kidding

"Where are we going?"

My question came while pressing my face against the window of Daniel's truck. It came out like the Swedish Chef from the muppets, but I was too tired to move my head.

We'd missed the turn that would take us into the center of Sweet Pea and were heading out to the boonies. Something an outsider might consider a gross exaggeration of the town center's merits, while those who lived here knew that once you were outside Main Street, it was like traveling to Amish country.

Backwards, offensive to women, and smelling strongly of horses.

"I got a call while you were snoring and I need to go check it out," he said, turning off onto an unmaintained dirt road. It rumbled and bumped, large crevices carved out by past rain dried into minor ditches that could masquerade as Ohio's version of the Grand Canyon.

"If the call was that someone lost half the bolts in their car driving down this road, I will testify in agreement with them. This road sucks, case closed," I let out a wide yawn and caught sight of aluminum siding being used as reinforcement on a slowly rotting wooden fence. "Where are we?"

The aluminum siding changed into chain link with green plastic slats obscuring what's on the other side. Small square blocks of wood poked out of the ground and the peaked roof of a playhouse disturbed the skyline, but there was no other evidence of children. Floating particles hung in the air just above the fence, something dusty and off-white. Curious, I rolled down the window to be assaulted by an auditory sound that sent fear piercing my heart.

"No," I whispered, grabbing for the door handle of the car. "No!"

I yanked harder, but the door handle wouldn't budge. Fumbling with the plastic lock, I kept pushing until the red sticker disappeared and then tried again, nothing.

"Child safety locks, Cyn. Keep your pants on, we aren't going to Roger's homestead," he chuckled but it was drowned out by the clucking of a million bird demons. They must have been scratching the ground or dueling to the death, because dust and feathers floated up. Everyday bird squawking was occasionally punctuated by the screech of attempted murder that had my thumb turning the door lock back to red.

"It's like Thunderdome in there. Those chickens are not normal," my hushed voice choked on dust and spit. Hacking and gasping for air, Daniel rolled my window back up and pulled up in front of a yellow colonial-style house with a wide porch, perfectly weeded and curated flower beds in autumn pastels... and a six-foot metal rooster parked in the driveway.

"What's with the cock?" I mused, mentally patting myself on the back when Daniel choked and turned red.

"It's... call it a rooster!" he scolded and I snickered until it transformed into a yawn.

"Where are we?" I repeated, searching the area behind me. Roger's bombed out trailer and attack chicken dystopia were completely gone from view. It reminded me how terrified Dorothy must have been getting sucked from the safety and familiarity of a tornado into the too-bright land of Oz. "Is this where you're going to murder me? Because seriously, I'm bitter and petty enough to kill all of these flowers with my decaying corpse, Daniel."

"Geez you're dramatic. We are here to look into a missing kid," he said, climbing out of his truck and slamming the door. Daniel had reached my side of the truck before my brain could process his statement. "Let's go."

"Go where?" I demanded, holding my breath as he leaned over my lap and unbuckled the safety belt. I may have swapped spit with his brother, but no way was I swapping air with him.

"Weren't you listening? We need to go find a kid!"

His exasperation with me would have been amusing if he wasn't using the 'w' word.

"What do you mean 'we'? Is that like... the royal we? You're the only one here," I declared, trying to take my safety belt back and re-attach it to the car. "Because I don't work for you. Don't work with you. In my current state, the only thing I'm working at is not passing out while vomiting so I eventually suffocate and die before dictating my will, leaving it all to Winnie."

"Don't make me call Chief Sharp," he warned, and I pulled out my phone.

"I won't make you. Like women everywhere forced to canoodle with you, it's more efficient when I do it myself!" I stabbed the button to summon my sister-in-law via telecommunications. Her phone rang six times before switching to a voicemail recording.

You've reached Chief Carla Sharp. I am currently out of town on a family matter. For any requests related to police matters, please contact Daniel Kirby or Barney Fife. Daniel, if this is another voicemail about your need for a more casual uniform to prevent jock itch, I will cure your jock itch with castration. If this is Cyn, you agreed before I left to help Daniel and Barney with cases while I was gone. Backing out will result in blackmail circulation and being handcuffed to Sylvia for a week.

The message ended and I sighed.

Sylvia, my eight year old niece, was the cutest satanic spawn to ever walk the earth. She liked to feed Winnie cheese, torture her brother with loud noises, and steal his noise cancelling headphones, all while throwing knives and swallowing fire.

OK, that last part hadn't happened yet, but it was only a matter of time.

Especially since she started hanging out with Daniel's criminal offspring.

"Damn," I grumbled, snapping a picture of Daniel with my phone and sending it off to Carla. He'd apparently decided he didn't need her permission to dress casual and I intended to see him hang for it. "I guess I do have to help you."

"What the hell is with the picture?" his voice broke. Lunging toward me and the cell phone, his face went white when a low growl rumbled behind him. Daniel froze, sweat beading at his thinning hairline. "How did she get here? I told her to keep that beast inside when we came over."

I smiled wide and unbuckled my seatbelt, jumped out of the truck and ran to... not Winnie.

"Hi girl," I cooed, crouching beside a large Rottweiler with drool tusks on the corners of her mouth and droopy eyes. "Not a Daniel fan?"

We turned to stare at him, satisfied to see he was moving jerkily and with great care. If this were Oz, he'd be a combo of the Scarecrow, the Tin Man, and the Lion. The man had no brain, no courage and belonged in a rusted metal outfit.

Like Hannibal Lecter.

"Don't touch her. I've been called out here before. Athena will rip off your fingers," he hissed, but I held out an arm. Athena sniffed and then bumped my palm with the top of her head. Assuming her ears were itchy, I went to town scrunching and scratching her head affectionately. The dried drool on my shirt was joined by her fresh deposits and we were soon rolling around in the perfectly manicured lawn.

"Athena!"

We both sat up and stared at the porch.

"Is your name Athena?" her question clipped and condescending.

The woman stared at me with a raised brow and I tilted my head, looking toward the dog for a situationally appropriate answer. Athena gave me a blank look in response, then sneezed twice. Her drool rocketed off her face to coat the surrounding area before being quickly replaced.

"No?" I asked, going back to the old woman. She was ramrod straight in a faded floral nightgown that she probably bought off a mannequin advertising the Little House on the Prairie. She clicked her tongue against the top of her mouth and I checked with Athena again.

"You must be Cynthia," she declared, eyeing me up and down. Since I was half laying on the ground, the head gesture seemed a little unnecessarily exaggerated. I'm not ashamed to admit that her sizing me up gave me a tiny thrill of terror, but I was laying down. Laying down meant that I could be murdered without all that unnecessary running and sweating.

New meaning to lie down and take it, I snickered at my own dark humor and realized the woman was still staring at me.

"Yeah, I'm Cynthia. You can call me Cyn."

"I'm Angela. Do not call me Angie."

The lady could have been less dramatic.

"Do you intend to spend all day lying about or will you be getting to work, Cynthia?"

"Can I change my answer? I don't want to be Cynthia. Just once I'd like to be Winnie. Someone else gives me snacks and drives me places. Plus, she gets away with everything and I usually end up..." *Getting asked for help*, I finished in my head.

Athena's human scoffed at me.

Not a normal scoff but a 'pfffth' that was so pointed, I checked to see if I'd been impaled.

No such luck, I thought when I found no fresh bloodstains.

"Get up. My daughter's kid is missing and we all know that Daniel is useless."

Turning on her heel, she let out a piercing whistle, summoning Athena forward. Deciding that I trusted the Rottweiler's judgment, I followed behind her without checking that Daniel was coming too. If we were all openly admitting he was useless, it was hardly worth the effort to pretend.

He was an accessory to an already inconvenient situation.

I choked on a laugh as I pictured Daniel as an accessory.

"What are you laughing at?" he snapped and I turned, mentally adding straps and rhinestones.

"How ridiculous you'd look as a purse." I pictured his wife's face at the sight of a gaudy Daniel handbag and started cackling. "No way would your wife carry you. You'd be too small to hold anything useful and a choking hazard to your children."

"Enough."

Angela, not Angie, had led us into her house. Immediately to the left sat a sitting room with an old-fashioned davenport and a

99

wood pellet stove in the corner. Complimenting the pioneer motif was a stuffed deer head with enormous antlers, a phonograph and a TV that was far too old to have color. Everything was worn but clean in a way that reminded me of beating laundry against a rock. She'd forsaken convenience for the superiority that comes with doing things "the hard way".

She probably locked little girls in closets and threw them over walls by their pigtails.

"Sit down," Angela said, pointing me to an empty armchair. On the faded couch was a small woman holding a red squirming alien creature that appeared to be feasting on her flesh. The sound of wet suckling sent my stomach churning.

"What is that?" My voice broke, and I put the armchair between me and the parasitic life form. "It's eating you. Why is it eating you?"

A dry heave wracked my body. Moisture beaded under my eyes, and I swallowed hard trying to clear the sensation without breaking eye contact with the imminent threat. It turned its head toward me and I braced myself for nostril slits covered in the blood of a unicorn. Instead of a face smeared with red and chunks of human tissue, it was a squish-face baby with half-closed eyes.

"I thought your kid was missing," I looked to Athena, trusting her to tell me the truth.

"Not this kid. Do you think anyone would be this calm if their child was missing?" Athena's human was the one to respond and I shrugged even as my brain said humans were supposed to be freakishly attached to their offspring. *Humans, bears, wolves...*

was I the only member of the species disinterested in ensuring the population had a future?

The thought would have been depressing but I was reassured by the idea that global warming and political fervor would have ensured my offspring's future would have sucked anyway. By not procreating, I was doing my genetic line a favor.

Then I realized Angela, not Angie, wasn't even in the room.

"Where did you go?" I stammered, keeping an eye on the squishy monster that ate flesh. It was by far the biggest threat in the room, but disappearing old ladies were a close second.

"Kitchen. Be back in a second."

"OK, so if it's not your child...?"

My question trailed off, watching Angela back into the room through a swinging door I'd missed upon entry. As it closed, I caught sight of an old oven and a fridge that may have required the delivery of ice to function. Angela-not-Angie turned, holding a wooden tray in her hands and daring me to comment. Instead, I considered the contents of the tray. It held a pitcher of what appeared to be iced tea, little cubes of sugar, a miniature milk jug and five cups. "Who is missing?"

"My kid," Angela's daughter, spoke while watching the baby. It started clenching its hands and making a duck face, so she turned him back toward her breast. "She was born a few months ago and has the perfect temperament for athletic relaxation and joy."

"Is that code for a sex shop?" My wide eyes stared at the women, and I considered running away. Who would train a few month-old kid for that? Or worse, call a robotic pleasure device their "kid".

"No, it's code for goat yoga," Athena's human scoffed and my jaw fell open.

"You lost yoga?"

"No, she lost a goat," Angela, not Angie, corrected me and that somehow seemed worse.

"You called the police about a goat?"

"Not just any goat, I assure you. Cecill, stop crying. It's been forty-five minutes, you've been crying for forty of them. Explain to the woman about Birdy before she calls the looney bin to scoop you up and I help them haul you through the door," the older woman snapped at her daughter and my eyes went back to Cecill.

Sure enough, crying.

Her and the baby.

My own personal hell.

"I already told you! She had the perfect temperament for goat yoga! Do you know how hard it is to get a goat willing to pose on the lower back of a..."

A breeze blew in through an open window and carried the sounds of nature. Mixed in was a soft bleating and I got to my feet. Even if the sound was only a hallucination, I needed to check it out. Any opportunity to escape was one I would seize with both hands.

Especially if there was crying.

Ignoring the bickering women and Daniel's pouting face, I cut through the house and exited a back door that led into a manicured yard housing gnomes and plants that may have been an old-timey poison garden. The fence was a post style with two cross-beams and it looked useless at keeping anything in or out, neat rows tempting critters to come in and sample the produce.

Definitely a poison garden, I thought when I saw no insects or vermin scurrying by.

Another bleat and I snapped my head toward a small meadow. The grass was knee height and fairly dense, perfect spot for goats and assassins to hide. Assassins would be as problematic as goats, but I couldn't think of anything out there an assassin would want, so I declared it safe to search for goats.

Ears straining, I waited for a confirmation bleat, but only the wind rustling grass came on the afternoon breeze.

A loud wail came from the house, confirming I would not be going back that direction.

"What do you think?" I queried, looking down beside me to see that I was alone. "Right... no Winnie."

A soft whimper pulled my attention to the left and I saw Athena with a leather leash in her mouth.

"Close enough," I yawned, as I clipped her leash on and led us into the grassy field. Every few feet, we'd pause to listen over the breeze and cries until we couldn't hear anything at all. The house was now far enough away that none of the interior noises carried, but we could still see it clearly.

"Goat?" I called out.

Nothing.

"Baaaaa!" I tried calling for Birdy in her native tongue.

More nothing.

Maybe the sound hadn't been real after all.

"Do you smell anything?" Athena looked at me confused and lifted her head to the sky. One sniff, two... she shook her head, sneezing all over the left side of my pants.

"Allergies?" I sneezed in sympathy. "Definitely allergies. What about goats?"

She sneezed twice more, her head shaking her ears with a subtle *flap flap*.

We stood there longer, trying to come up with a new plan to get the goat involved in our game of Marco Polo. I went through my mental list of things people find annoying and started trying out their effectiveness on goats.

Whistling, humming, using cookware as percussive instruments... singing?

The last was easiest, so I broke out in a Broadway routine that was an insult to the art.

A bleating goat sounded on my second chorus of *Circle of Life*, and we went right, picking up our pace before it moved again, and we needed to sing *It's a Small World*. The meadow took on a slight incline, leading us upward to the crest. At the top was another rainwater cut, sounds of a struggle getting louder as we followed the crack toward a small dust cloud.

Parting the tall grass, Athena whimpered while I stared.

A black and white goat, one hind leg trapped between two rocks was attempting to ward off a small horde of chickens who were circling like a biker gang.

"Get out of here!" I shouted, charging toward the chickens. They turned as a unit, and I could practically hear them snapping their fingers as they advanced. In perfect lines, heads high, they marched to a perfect 4/4-time signature that had me questioning the phrase *goose-stepping*.

Geese had never been this coordinated.

"Woof!" Athena said, lowering her head and barreling toward the lines. Feathers ballooned out from the scuffle, and I moved to the goat while Athena took up her mantle as sidekick in a manner Winnie never would have managed. Birdie's wedged leg had a few small scrapes, more appearing every time she flailed and fought for freedom.

"Baaaaa!" She shouted. It was accompanied by a wide-eyed goat stare that promised not to kick me if I got her out. "Baa!"

Now she was begging me.

"OK, I'm trusting you," I whispered, moving closer and closer until I could wrap my hand around her leg. It immediately twitched, but she didn't move while I examined the situation. Her hoof had gotten hooked on a protruding rock edge and it couldn't be slid or tugged free and then wedged between two larger rocks that leaned on either side of her leg. The primary rock was half-buried, and the ground was too dry for me to dig it out. Kicking seemed the best option, but it set a bad precedent for the goat. Checking that no skin was in contact, I used her secured leg as a fulcrum and levered part of the rock upward. In seconds, her foot was out and she bleated happily. Prancing like a lovestruck skunk, she circled the hilltop twice before she bounded away.

"You're welcome!" I shouted, just as Athena yelped. She had been circled by the chickens. Tail coiled under her body and ears flat, she begged for help with fear filled puppy eyes. "Crap."

The chickens should have been wearing spiked collars and leather jackets. I picked the biggest one, ran toward it and when it took a single step back, grabbed Athena's leash and pulled her down the hill.

"Run!" I screamed, tugging the dog forward to the soundtrack of menacing clucks and wing flaps that also sounded like a rumble scene from Westside Story. "Faster!"

We got to the meadow and hopped the wooden fence back into the yard.

"What is happening?" Cecill's mom stuck her head out and Athena shoved her out of the way to get in the house.

"Get back inside! They're coming!"

Her face contorted and I chanced a glimpse behind me to see the chickens swarming in a perfect jet fighter formation. It reminded me of the geese terrorizing the Air Force at their airport hangar my third week in the Army.

I turned back toward the house, looking down too late to see the gopher hole before my foot lodged in it. Gravity took over and I careened toward the ground as the chicken sounds reached a crescendo that was blasted into silence with a rifle shot that exploded blood and white feathers exactly where my head had just been.

Chapter Nine: Happens all the Time

"Why is your kitchen covered in broken glass?"

Instead of answering Mo, I pulled the pillow tighter around my head. There were four blankets piled on my bed and Winnie did her part to comfort me by adding her weight to the blanket pile. Normally, I'd be a holly jolly giant, but it was not a good time to come in and demand I answer questions. The only appropriate thing for an intruder into my fortress to do was either kill me or be killed.

Survival of the... something.

Motivated, maybe?

"Go away!" I shouted. Or at least it would have been yelling but my raw throat and blanket fort muted everything to a near whisper. If anyone besides Mo had randomly appeared in my house, I may have shot them.

There was a gun in my blanket fort and everything.

Whether or not there were bullets in the gun, or the fort, was anyone's guess.

"Cyn!" Mo ripped my blankets off and let in the sunlight.

"Hssskkkk!" I hissed at her and the too bright light that was attacking my flesh. Winnie, now having access to my face, began licking every part of me she could reach. It was as though the dog were warning me not to murder or get murdered by anybody.

"You need to get out of bed and explain to me why there is glass all over your kitchen floor!" Mo threw my blanket on the couch and Winnie leapt on top of it. If the bed weren't two feet from the couch, the jump would have been impressive. As it was, when she nearly fell off, I made a mental note to get her glucosamine... just in case.

"You also need to explain to me why I had to hear about someone shooting at you from Daniel! Freaking Daniel, Cyn!"

I opened my mouth in a wide yawn and tried to threaten her with my teeth.

Mo continued glaring and Winnie's eyes were closed... no one considered me a threat.

I need vampire fangs implanted in my mouth...

"The glass is coffee mugs. After several hours in Daniel's company, a fitful nap and two packages of Oreos, I needed coffee. But the shelf came loose and they all crashed to the floor," I sighed, giving up on sleep and hauling myself out of bed. "Then I drank coffee from a bowl, told Winnie to stay out of the kitchen and went back to bed. What time is it?"

"All that... is coffee mugs?"

She stared wide eyed at the floor, and I looked over the top of her head. It reminded me of a pottery place I'd visited in school. They'd smash glazed pieces and attach them to vases or planters in mosaics. Some of the pieces were strategically cut into exact pieces to form perfect pictures, but I'd marveled at the sight of something being destroyed and still beautiful.

Then Amber smashed my cookie snack pack, and the broken cookies were not beautiful.

Neither was the suspension I got for trying to break her face in retribution.

Or her face when I failed to break it.

"Yup." I tried to find a clock in my kitchen to answer the question she'd ignored but it was impossible to look away from the smashed crockery on the floor.

"Just coffee mugs?"

Her astonished tone of voice was baffling. She had to know I had a lot of coffee cups, even if I only used a few of them. Usually, the ones with the snarkiest sayings or that were gifted to me by people I cared about as a show of appreciation and mutual care.

Also, the woman made coffee in my house almost as much as I did.

She'd seen the cups.

Instead of confirming, I walked to the corner where I kept my silicone clogs. Slipping them on my feet, I went back toward the kitchen and picked my way carefully over the mess to the far side of the fridge. Between it and the cabinet was a four-inch gap where I kept my broom and one of those plastic mops that I never seemed to have pads for.

Not that I mopped much, anyway. Winnie tracked in enough dirt and grime to negate any and all floor cleaning efforts.

Dog mom problems.

But I owned the broom and used it at least once a week to keep mice at bay and reduce the number of Winnie fur floof gremlins in the corners. Every time I swept, they reappeared in a matter of hours, it was likely if I *didn't* sweep them, we would probably suffocate in fur.

I also really hated the feeling of dirt sticking to the bottom of my feet.

The two of us were unsurprisingly *very* efficient at making crumbs and dirt.

Only one of us had the thumbs to use a broom, so I volunteered as tribute.

"As far as someone shooting at me..." I said, dropping to a crouch as I guided chunks of sparkly, neon and character festooned ceramic into my dustpan. It was full in three swipes of the broom, so I dumped it into the kitchen trash beside me. "We don't know for sure anyone was shooting at me."

"That's not what Daniel said," Mo stuffed her hands on her hips, and I let out a strangled breath. It was bad enough that I had to clean without coffee, but now I had to deal with Daniel inspired fear and panic by information oversharing.

"What exactly did Daniel say then, oh Great Knower of Things?"

She threw a dish towel at my head, and I gave her my best death glare.

"I'm without coffee, sleep or orgasms. Do you really want to fight me?" I rose to my full almost six feet, towering over the smaller woman like Godzilla at the Eiffel Tower. I took a step forward, bearing down on her.

She rolled her eyes and handed me a paper cup of coffee from her bakery and a doughnut.

"Shut up. You don't scare me."

"Why didn't you hand these to me immediately?" I demanded, and she gave me a look that threatened to take both back.

Instead of pursuing this line of questioning, I stuffed the doughnut in my mouth and guzzled what was most likely just a bunch of espresso shots in a cup. Four swallows later, the cup was empty, and the doughnut was gone.

Ha! Now she can't take it back, my brain shouted and I tried to look smug.

My face declined to participate.

It still wanted to either cry or hit something. Since I'd never hit anything with my face and crying was usually plan Q, I was either still tired, under the influence of hormones, or concerned because someone tried to shoot me. If any of those were out of the ordinary, it would be easier to find the source, but inadequate sleep, cyclic hormones courtesy of mother nature and people trying to kill me came around with a surprising regularity.

One might even consider tracking such things, but no one had invented an attempted murder tracking app yet.

It made tracking the other two frivolous.

"Whatever," I said, and went back to cleaning up the shattered remnants of my only collection. Small pictures of German Shepherds and references to Winnie's velociraptor nature from Larry were mingled with mugs I'd collected from around the world and ones sent to me by friends who were still out there fighting the fight... or who had lost it and were now sipping coffee in the great beyond.

It was like staring at a film reel of my life in splintered images and I found myself eyeing the bottle of Fireball I kept for emergencies.

Sure, alcohol was never the *answer* but it could dull the *questions*.

And I had a lot of questions.

Head aching, heart hurting questions.

"Don't look at the alcohol," Mo warned. Now that I'd swept up a decent chunk of the glass, the baker slipped past me and started making coffee in my drip machine. "I need to know why someone is shooting at you!"

"What did Daniel tell you?" I conceded, dumping my fourth dustpan full of glass, porcelain and ceramic into the trash bin. Winnie and I had been up until four in the morning after a six-hour nap when we got home, so she was fed and empty. The digital display said it was eight in the morning, so she was good for at least two more hours.

I, on the other hand, wouldn't be good until I had a gallon of coffee and some cheesy bacon on something.

Cheese and bacon were as effective as alcohol, if not healthier, then at least more socially acceptable mid-day.

Unless you were eating it near vegans then... well... bottoms up.

"He said you were searching for a kid and on your way back to the house, someone shot at you. This was after he'd told me 'everything was fine' when he collected Winnie from me. If I weren't proofing dough, I'd have figured out something was wrong sooner because no way would you trust that idiot with Winnie. This morning I confronted him, he told me you and Winnie found evidence of a person lying in wait in the woods, an empty shell and a trail back to the main highway."

Her story had taken less time than the coffee pot needed to brew, and I just stood there, processing. It was easy to identify where I'd gone wrong in this scenario. Mo and I had been friends for decades, I trusted her with Winnie's life and I'd sent an idiot to collect her from said best friend.

Not my smartest move if the goal was to keep my attempted murder a secret.

Though with Daniel present at the incident, the concept of a secret was a moot point.

Daniel, The Idiot, had shared every bit of information about an assault with a deadly weapon case with a virtual stranger and it was a wonder criminals didn't just walk free hourly.

Between him and Jenny the gossiping dispatcher, there was nothing you couldn't learn about crime in this town if you stood next to the right person. Criminal defense, thy name is small town loose lips.

We were too far inland for them to sink ships, so I suppose they had to do something.

"What? What do you have to say for yourself?" She demanded.

I blinked at her, wondering if she thought I should bring in a frigate from the Atlantic.

"Huh?"

"Why am I talking to you? You're useless until that's done," she jerked a thumb toward the coffee maker. "Four shots of espresso is not enough in your condition."

Espresso? I looked around the room, *When did I have espresso?*

My eyes landed on the paper bakery cup.

Oh, right.

I returned to watching Mo search my kitchen like an archaeologist in a temple of doom.

Opening cabinets, she kept shifting and muttering until she located another small cache of coffee mugs. It was a surprise for both of us, since I'd forgotten I hid my special ones there and added a few others when I ran out of room by the sink. She'd reached the door above the fridge on tiptoes and was climbing on the counter to get the door the rest of the way open.

"Why don't you own a step stool?" She whined, but the answer was obvious so we both let it fall to the ground. In the meantime, I studied the cups I'd stashed up there. They weren't all special, but I'd definitely hidden them away with reason.

Reasons that flooded back to me as she reached out a hand and nearly toppled one. It was shaped like an exaggerated combat boot, and I'd hidden it up there when the plant that came inside of it died harder than the planet Earth in Wall-E.

"Please be careful with those," I said, eyeing one from a soldier I knew had passed. While a few of the shattered ones had come from people on the other side, the ones above my fridge came from those I couldn't save.

People I'd tried very hard to save.

Mo studied me as she looked up at the mugs from her perch on my kitchen counter. In the silence, I watched her mind work through questions she could answer herself and those that might be better asked later. The wind-up monkey in my brain crashed his cymbals and it was terribly inconvenient with the ringing in my ears as her hand inched closer to a sparkling black color changing mug.

"Which one?" she asked gently but the air I needed to live was stuck in my throat. My mouth moved in time to the ringing in my ears, the pressure growing with every second I struggled to breath around the panic in my chest.

She climbed off the counter and gestured towards the cabinet.

"On second thought, you pull down the cups you don't mind using."

Air flooded my lungs and I took a deep breath.

Nodding, I went to the cabinet and studied the mugs, picking out two Larry had given me when we were still together. They were a little crude and I placed them up there so my mother wouldn't demand he get her a set as well. Though not the best artistically speaking, the protruding handle of one nested perfectly in a crevice created in the other.

It was like a hot dog in geode cake... which he'd also given me.

Both literally and figuratively.

"I understand how it looks, but Mo, there's no reason for anyone to shoot at me. I haven't done anything! Whoever was out there waiting wouldn't have had any idea I would be there, so even if the shot was aimed at me, it was probably because they thought I was someone else," I speculated while doctoring coffee in the "hot dog" mug. "Or something else. Maybe it was a hunter who had a few too many and thought I was a sasquatch."

"A hunter who only missed your head because you tripped and he was drunk? What next? You think aliens landed in Nevada and didn't probe anyone?"

She took a long drink from her "geode cake" and I made a face. Aside from the borderline pornography that our morning coffee was turning into, her reasoning was flawless and a small twinge in my stomach confirmed what I already knew but refused to believe.

Someone had been waiting for me.

But how did they know I would be there?

Who would not only have knowledge of when I left the police station in Dayton, but also that Carla was out of town and Daniel would have to bring me with him on this call? How did they even know there would be a call?

About a goat?

"Son of a cookie," I grumbled, whipping open a cabinet and pulling out a box of Nilla Wafers. Tossing one to Winnie, I continued, "they stole the kid!"

"What kid?" Mo went wide-eyed and I shook her off around a mouthful of cookies. It was too dry in my mouth to explain, but I pictured Birdy's hoof between the two rocks. Rocks that were disproportionate in size to the ones around it.

"They trapped the goat with the rocks!" I said, spitting crumbs on the floor. "The bastard stole the goat!"

But how did he know the lady would freak out and call?

How did they know Daniel and I were close enough to be sent?

Unless... Unless it was someone who knew I was at the police station and when I would be leaving. Someone with something to hide who thought I'd expose them.

Someone whose husband was nosing around and could ruin her image.

"Damn," I muttered, picturing the judge and her smiling face. There hadn't been anything Machiavellian in her gaze, but it was the only thing I'd been asked to investigate. She was also the only person I'd met recently with something to hide.

"What are you doing Friday, Mo?" I invited her, crossing back to my bed and unplugging my phone. Careful not to get cookie on it, I scrolled through the device until I found the message from the doctor and his suspected timeline for proving infidelity.

"Chris and I were gonna Netflix and Chill, why?"

I shuddered, knowing full well that Netflix and Chill was code for making the metaphorical beast with two backs .

"I need to stalk a judge who might be trying to kill me," I sighed.

Chapter Ten:
Anxiety Realized

I t was Wednesday and I was fairly certain my gastrointesti-
nal and parasympathetic nervous systems would kill me
long before the shooter ever managed it. Every sound made
me jump, every shadow was a shooter, and my stomach was
burning a hole in itself that had me eating half a container of
antacids every few hours.

My poop could double as blackboard chalk if anyone still
used blackboards.

"I'm not gonna live until Friday," I told Winnie, even
though I could hear her snoring. While she was usually keyed
into my anxiety and stress, just this once she seemed to have
decided I must suffer alone.

"Do you think we could just confront her today?" I begged the dog who twitched her tail in indifference.

"Could you try and offer some real advice? I buy your food!" I was almost shouting but she refused to acknowledge me or the mention of food.

The thought of food sent my stomach rolling over and I ate two more chalky antacids.

"This is stupid! People were trying to kill me in Afghanistan, and I never once had anxiety or GI issues!" Winnie twitched her paw but slept on. "I mean, sure I wasn't the only target. But I was *a* target, and I was fine. Why am I not fine now?"

The empty studio apartment didn't have any answers and Cruz still hadn't returned my voicemail from this morning. My whole body was heavy and I needed sleep, but my heart and respiratory rates refused to go down.

"Forget it!" I climbed out of bed and stumbled into the kitchen to turn the coffee pot on while placing a call to Joseph.

"What?" He answered and I narrowed my eyes on the phone.

"Rude much?" I snapped, trying to grab the combat boot planter that was also a coffee mug.

"After you elbowed me in the gut and threw me to the ground earlier because you thought I was trying to kill you? You're lucky you're not fired."

"Sorry," I mumbled, but it was half-hearted at best. While my fight or flight instinct was definitely tuned to level red, throwing my boss to the ground and seeing him pee himself had been entertaining.

"I need the rest of the week off."

"You what?!" He shouted and I checked my phone. It hadn't been dropped or crushed under the hoof of a bull recently, but I tended to be hard on hardware.

"Joseph?" I asked, trying to see if he could hear me.

"You think I'll give you days off after what you did today?" he roared through the line.

Phone not broken.

Man flabbergasted.

Situational Status: Normal.

"You're... in favor of being near me?" I asked, fingers brushing the boot mug as I pondered why he was both threatening to fire me and indignant that I was offering to give him a break.

Men really were a Katy Perry song, hot and then cold.

I started singing my variation internally.

Yes and then no.

In and then out...

"No! But that isn't the point. The health inspector..." The boot cup tipped and landed on the Formica countertop, splitting in half and sending chips of ceramic skittering to the floor.

"Dammit!" I shouted, jumping back and landing on one of the cracked and jagged pieces. The initial pinch startled me, and I tried to move but slipped on the blood dripping from my foot and landed hard on my ass while my palms brushed against even more shards and a long cut bisected my left palm.

"What's happening, Cynthia?" Joseph shouted from my counter in a small, tinny voice.

"Gravity and sharp objects. Stay out of the kitchen!" I warned Winnie who'd started to come check on me. She looked at the blood dripping on my outstretched palm and offered a soft whimper before laying down at the very edge of the danger area. "Joseph, I'm not coming in. Fire me, don't fire me, I don't care much at the moment. I think I need stitches but I'm bleeding too much to leave my house and I can't leave Winnie here with broken glass."

No additional noises came from my counter and I assumed he hung up in annoyance.

Since I was also annoyed with me, I could hardly fault anyone else for sharing the feeling.

"Alright..." I started, scanning the area around me and finding an untainted section of floor. I used my right hand as leverage to climb my way to a one-legged Flamingo pose on my not bleeding left foot. Gripping the counter, I leaned as far as I could to grip the broom on the far side of the fridge. It slipped through my fingers twice, but I dragged it out and began swiping it along the floor. Glass and blood smeared across the off-white linoleum and the broom handle was quickly slippery with blood.

"What the hell, Universe?" I shouted, just before I heard the fire door at the bottom of my staircase slamming shut and footsteps running up.

"Great! *Now* you send a murderer?"

Winnie had jumped up at the sound of the door and taken a protective stance at the top of the stairs. Four stomps up the stairs and her ears went limp, tail wagging as she looked toward me.

"Friend of yours?" I asked, just as Larry Kirby poked his head out of the entryway. Winnie let out a soft whimper, asking permission to say hi to her former veterinarian. "Yeah, fine, whatever."

Winnie leapt toward the doctor and he offered her floofy ears a good scrunching.

Larry didn't look well. His light brown hair was shaggy, face more lined than I'd last seen it. His eyes had darkened circles under them. His usually muscled frame was wilting. He'd never been body-builder material, reminding me of a nerd who walked into a gym by accident and was too embarrassed to leave so he lifted weights. Now he looked like a regular nerd, and I found myself hoping it was because Amber was slowly poisoning him. I'd obviously help before she killed him off completely, but he deserved to suffer for not only letting his mom dictate his life, but immediately replacing me with Amber.

Yeah, I'd replaced him with Cruz, but he'd replaced me first.

"Hey girl," his rough voice did things to my nether regions that had no business happening while I was standing in my kitchen covered in blood and broken glass. Winnie licked his face, and he inhaled the fur on top of her head. "I missed you too. Smells like your mom spilled coffee on you."

He gave me a sideways glance and I shrugged.

"Who knows anymore. Why are you here?" I demanded with as much warmth as an iceberg. It was our first time alone since the day after seeing Amber ride him. His nose had been broken at the time, a gift from me, and yet he somehow looked worse today.

He studied me from top to bottom carefully. The look was equal parts medically assessing and bodily admiration that sent flutters of pleasure dancing along my skin. Neither felt particularly promising, and I resisted the urge to check what I was wearing.

Whatever clothes I had on were completely meaningless when I was covered in blood.

Specifically *my* blood and more was appearing by the second.

Still... wouldn't hurt to be wearing something that reminds him he can't touch this, I thought and rolled my eyes at myself.

Yeah, because having a man think your corpse is sexy is totally on my bucket list.

"Joseph said you needed medical help and I'm the only doctor he knows," Larry's voice had a gravelly quality that hadn't been present before but I snorted at what he said anyway. It was *sooo not* surprising that the only medical professional Joseph knew was for animals. Larry let out a low chuckle of his own. "Yeah... I told him he was too old to avoid the doctor and he made some sort of comment about hoping you castrate me."

Cautiously, Larry moved into the kitchenette with Winnie glued to his side.

"Stop!" I ordered her and they both froze. "Broken glass. No paws allowed."

Larry looked at Winnie and gave her a little nod of acknowledgement that sent her flopping to the floor with a loud sigh. Turning back to me, he took the broom from me first and propped it on the counter before taking my bleeding hand and wrapping it around his shoulder while he wrapped the other arm around my waist and supported my weight.

"Lean on me. We're going to the couch."

"I don't need... thanks," I said, leaning against him and letting my protest die on my lips.

We hobbled from the kitchen and he put me on the couch. Moving back into my bloody kitchen, he grabbed a dish towel and wet it with warm water before coming back and wiping my hands.

"This doesn't look too bad," he said, squinting through his glasses. Once the blood was clear, I could see the cut was shallow and barely an inch in length. Larry wiped both of my hands and arms, and determined that it was only the one cut.

"Now..." He looked down and I looked down too.

No pants.

Just underwear and a T-shirt.

I shrugged but didn't make eye contact. Lifting my injured foot, he guided it a little higher and started swiping. The cut stung and I winced.

"Sorry. There might be some glass in there."

He set my foot on the coffee table and disappeared into the bathroom. Grabbing a first aid kit and the emergency flashlight I kept on my kitchen counter, he knelt down in front of the coffee table to look at the cut.

"How have you been?"

I blinked at the man, watching him open the kit and pull out green plastic tweezers and an alcohol wipe. Cleaning the tweezers, he flicked on the flashlight and angled it above the arch of my foot.

"Fine. You?" I asked, just as he plucked something off my foot and wiped it on the towel.

"Crappy." He plucked off another piece of glass and then wiped my foot with a clean alcohol pad. The sting was insignificant, now that the glass was gone. After he swiped my foot again, it barely had any blood on it, so I was pretty sure it wouldn't need stitches.

Reaching the same conclusion, he placed a sterile pad on the cut and wrapped a stretch bandage around my foot twice to keep it in place.

"Thanks," I huffed, starting to stand only to be held in place by the doctor.

"Stay here."

Larry got up and went to my kitchen with the dish towel. After wiping down the broom, he swept up the glass, tossing it and then finding one of the wet pads for my plastic mop and cleaning up the blood. Though his movements were certain, he had a listless quality that made me wonder if he might need the coffee more than I did.

Which was confirmed when he saw the now full coffee maker and opened the cabinet above it to grab a mug.

"Where are all your mugs?"

"Dead."

He eyed me over the His and Hers anatomy mugs, the only two on the shelf that had ruined my collection. Above the fridge, aside from the now busted boot, were mugs I'd probably never touch again. I'd thought the universe had let them be as a courtesy, but my luck had run out and I couldn't let any harm befall them.

"There's more downstairs I think?" But I wasn't overly confident. While I had a handful of cups that I'd kept down there for myself, I primarily used paper cups for guests to discourage lingering and encourage to-go coffee thinking.

It also kept me from having to wash stranger germs off my cups.

"Because you're averse to the germs of strangers? Or you just want them to feel obligated to leave?" Larry asked and I gave him a single nod as he filled the innie and outtie coffee mugs and carried them over. He set both down in front of me, righting himself to scratch the back of his head and scan the room.

"Can we talk?" His question was directed at my window and the agonizing hole in my stomach grew bigger. There was not enough intestinal lining left in my biosphere and I was fairly certain the last thing I'd eaten contained battery acid and bleach.

Yeah, the two canceled each other out on the pH scale, but I'm sure it would burn.

"No," slipped from my lips and Winnie punched me in the boob with her paw. "Fine. Not no, but not now. I have a lot going on."

Not a complete lie, but since I wasn't sleeping or planning to move in the next half hour until I was sure my blood clotted, it wasn't a complete truth either. The most action packed thing that may be happening to me in the next few minutes was either throwing up or getting shot.

Possibly both.

"What if I talk?"

His question was more of a statement. He continued avoiding eye contact while drinking from one of the mugs on the coffee table, and I suspected he might have actually been asking. Considering he'd cleaned up all my blood, I mirrored his move and drank my coffee as well. Larry set down his cup, I set mine down as well. We just stared at each other over the coffee table, and he broke first.

"Are you going to listen to me?"

I made a zipper gesture across my lips and twisted it at the end, locking them shut.

"Nothing happened with me and Amber."

I snorted and he shot me a warning look that I returned with a glare.

I hadn't talked.

I hadn't violated the rules.

With my best *Try Me* face, I drank coffee and challenged him to disagree.

"That night of the Fur Pile," he began, referencing the themed fetish party held at his house. It had been hosted and posted by Amber, access to his home achieved with his mother's assistance. While it was clearly a fetish party, the *furry* part was lacking in the guests I'd seen leaving. The fact he was calling it a Fur Pile meant he hadn't seen or learned much during the event. Most of the attendees had opted for the *Mean Girls* lingerie and animal ears philosophy on costumes, including Amber who I'd walked in on grinding herself on a not-quite-asleep Larry.

Since I'd actually been to a *real* fur pile, that part had been on par with the name.

Not that I'd participated... much.

"I really didn't know what was happening. My mom... she has her own agenda, but it was never mine. You're the only woman I want or care about. You have to believe me, I'll do whatever it takes!"

I wasn't sure I *had* to believe him, but unfortunately I did and it made holding on to my anger harder.

My phone made a sound like a yowling cat in the kitchen, and he walked over to grab it while he talked. Setting it on the coffee table beside my empty coffee mug, he replaced the phone in his hand with my mug to go back to the kitchen and fill it.

He really had been the best boyfriend.

"When you ran away at the diner, I didn't know what was happening. She'd invited me to the diner to discuss a business concern, as you know her family was the primary financial backing of my practice and I legally have to talk to her dad... and occasionally her when he makes me."

A reminder that she'd not only given him money but named the super creative Kirby's Critter Care that grated against my skin.

"I didn't let her hold my hand; she just did. Everyone went around saying we were on a date, a rumor she wholeheartedly backed, and then you were suddenly with Cruz. It was like you were just waiting for me to mess up so you could go back to him and you didn't even give me a chance."

My phone yowled again, and I leaned forward, stretching the hamstring of the leg on the table. It popped and stung as much as his accusation, but I managed to grab the little tech box. There were two texts from the judge's husband. Tuning out Larry, I opened the thread, and my heart skipped a beat.

Dr. P: *I had to work late and her phone is on the move.*

Dr. P: *She's headed your way.*

Attached was a Google map tracking her location in real time. Hobbling to my feet, I grabbed sweatpants from the metal rod and looked around for socks. The laundry sack in my corner was slightly over-full as I'd been avoiding my parents' house since the little blue pill incident. Pulling open my plastic drawers, I found an old pair with squirrels that had a small hole in the big toe.

Good enough.

"Cyn! What are you doing?" Larry yelled and I startled, smacking my head on the low hanging ceiling by my bed.

"Ow!" I rubbed the spot and stuffed my feet in sneakers. "If I'm allowed to speak now?

He gave an obvious hand gesture that nearly knocked off his glasses.

"I have to go."

"Why the hell do you have to go?" He asked, anger flashing in his eyes.

"Because someone might be trying to kill me and I have to follow her. Thanks for cleaning me and my kitchen up, stay as long as you want. Lock the door when you leave," I said, grabbing my keys and running down the stairs, the thundering steps of Winnie hot on my heels.

"This can't be right," I said to Winnie.

The judge's pin had dropped in a wide parking lot outside of Yellow Springs and remained there for at least ten minutes. Instead of a terrifying dirt pit or vats of pudding, there was a brightly lit carnival. Bells rang and barkers beckoned people to play their rigged games. Couples and families walked around with cotton candy and plush animals.

It wasn't a shoddy two-bit carnival like I'd seen on this stretch before. Everything gleamed with that "my safety certificates aren't falsified" shine. Food smelled edible and unlikely to kill its consumers or send them fleeing to the porcelain gods for prayer and relief.

A memory that was far too fresh for my fragile GI tract.

"It's what the map says," Larry answered from my passenger seat and I started. He'd gotten in the Jeep with Winnie and I didn't have the energy to argue with him. Instead, I tossed him the phone to be navigator and now I wasn't sure he'd done it properly.

Taking the phone from his hand, I studied the pin and the location.

We were in the right place.

"Dammit."

Wrestling open the door, I hopped out and waited for Winnie to scramble from the back seat and jump out beside me. I clipped her leash onto her pink camo collar and started toward the turnstile entryway. Through the gates, I could see the other carnival attendants had opted for their evening country best, clean jeans and flannel over boots.

My sweatpants and sneakers stood out like a Grizzly in a snowstorm.

Or me when I'd accidentally wandered into a room full of children.

"Ten dollars and no dog," a bored teenager with bottle blonde hair and bright pink lips said without looking up from her nail polish.

"Twenty dollars, I keep the dog, and I don't report you for the vodka cranberry in your 'water bottle'," I countered, and she held out a hand. Placing the twenty in it, she pocketed the whole thing and never made eye contact.

"Welcome to Wonder Carn."

Wow... I thought, feeling invisible for the first time in my life. It was hard to blend at my size, but looking like a blonde Godzilla was not nearly as interesting as a hangnail if you were a teenager under the influence performing a remedial task for minimum wage.

Apparently, my sweatpants wouldn't make me *that* interesting.

"Who are we looking for?" Larry asked, as my eyes swiveled around the brightly lit chaos. It didn't seem likely a shooter would be here. Not only had my attendance been unknown beforehand, but the collateral damage insured immediate capture. No self-respecting pro would do a hit here.

Unless she didn't hire a pro, I thought and then immediately dismissed it. That shot on Monday wasn't an amateur shot.

"We're looking for this woman," I told Larry, showing him the picture on my phone. He joined me in scanning the area. There was a loud cheer from the left and curiosity took us that direction. Spectator density grew exponentially as we pushed our way through a crowd toward a brightly lit elevated platform. Above the cheers, an amplified voice cut through the noise.

"In a surprise last minute entry, the regional champion Judge is here tonight!"

I shoved closer, fighting until my stomach was pressed against a metal barricade and I was square in front of a stage with a long table and five people seated. In the dead center was Judge Anita, wearing a broad shiny belt and a folded paper placard announcing her as "The Judge".

"What is this?" Larry whispered in my ear and I shrugged.

"I know what you know, doc."

"Bring out the wieners!" Microphone man shouted and my eyes went wide in horror as I tried to back away from the stage.

The crowd surged forward and pinned me where I was. From the wings, 5 waitresses in tight fitting tops glided onto the stage with silver trays ladened down with...

"Hot dogs?" I asked, but it was the wrong thing to say. Fur brushed my arm as Winnie leaped onto the metal railing and launched herself toward the stage. She landed dead center between the two rows of waitresses and her tail swung around in full helicopter.

"Winnie! No!" I shouted, but she was gone. She stood on back paws, putting her front on the edge of a tray filled with plain hotdogs and toppling the whole thing to the floor. Another tail wag, and Winnie went to town eating the hot dogs while the crowd started cheering and the judge locked eyes with me and smirked.

"He sent you, didn't he?" Anita mouthed and I vaulted the railing to protect Winnie as she devoured three dozen hotdogs.

Chapter Eleven:
Locked and Loaded

"Come on! Let me out!" I shouted from the back of a police car.

Winnie was in the neighboring car with the rest of the hotdogs she hadn't gotten to finish on stage. The crowd had cheered for her so loudly that the contest had been called off and instead of receiving the cash prize, she'd won the rest of the hot dogs.

My punishment was that I had to take her home after she ate them.

Outside my car, Judge Anita Pestolli was having a loud argument with her phone.

Or her husband on the other end of the phone, assuming he was listening.

He certainly hadn't listened to me.

"I can't believe you would bring that sweet innocent..." I switched from leaning against the window to laying across the back seat. Anyone calling me sweet and innocent was delusional. So far, all I'd learned was that I wasn't the first private investigator the good doctor had tried to hire, but I was the only one to go so far as to tail his wife.

All of my predecessors had wisely chosen not to stalk a judge making me the dumbest PI in the area.

Though the coordinator of the carnival wasn't pressing charges, I didn't have a ticket. The blonde from the turnstile having long since made herself scarce, and Larry not being considered a reliable witness as another non-ticket holder, there was considerable debate as to whether I owed them money, or they owed me a refund.

A decision made more difficult because the carnival was squarely on the border of two jurisdictions, and neither was inclined to take custody of the decision. Dayton because if they made the wrong choice, could end up stuck with me and Yellow Springs because they already were stuck with me, and it was fun to watch me squirm.

If only there were a judge... I glared at the woman who was talking both with her mouth and her hands into the phone. As a court appointed arbitrator, she could legally decide all things. Except not while ripping her husband into pieces for telling a bunch of strangers about her prowess with deep throating... her words.

"Seven-foot frame, rats along his back..." I sang, stomping my feet on the hard plastic backseat. "When he calls your name, it all fades to black."

I stomped out the beat of an American tango, which was probably wrong since the movie was Columbian.

The door by my head popped open and I looked up the nostrils of Daniel Kirby.

"Sup?" I nodded at him, watching a booger wiggle on his nose hairs.

"Why are you always upside down? Did you get bit by a vampire recently?" he returned, pulling on the underside of my arms until I slid to the doorframe and was back upright. Sliding sideways, I sat in the seat properly and looked at him.

"Who called you this time?" I groaned and he smiled.

"Your mom. Dispatch in Yellow Springs, also known as Jenny, gossiped to her husband's mom, the mom lives next door to Mrs. Margot who immediately informed your mother. Your mother called me because she couldn't be disturbed and you, I quote, 'have ruined enough of her date nights'," he concluded and I scowled.

"So... how do I get out?"

It was no secret that when it came to favors, Daniel always demanded payment in advance.

It's how the girls' basketball team all got Mono in high school.

And why half the incoming Kindergartners shared his last name.

"Just say the magic words?" Daniel waggled an eyebrow at me.

"Bite me?"

"The other magic word," he smirked, and I wracked my brain.

"Abra-ca-kiss-my-ass-bra?"

The deputy waggled an index finger in front of my face and I may have lost it. Leaning forward, I shouted.

"Piranha!"

Then bit down as hard as I could.

"Out, Miss Sharp," the judge ordered, and I spit the man's bone-in flesh from my mouth. "Anything you have to say to me?"

Anita looked tense and irritable but that didn't get her off the list.

"Are you trying to kill me to keep your wiener eating secret?" Not my smoothest segue but smooth went out the window a week and a half ago. "Because if you are... could you stop?"

It was the lamest request I'd ever made and she looked between me and Daniel for an explanation.

"Someone shot at her after we left the Police Station Monday. Though I have no idea when she reached the conclusion it might have been you." He spoke while wiping his finger on his pants. Aside from some slobber and tooth indents, the man was unscathed.

Pity I hadn't asked a back-alley doctor to swap a few of Winnie's teeth with mine.

Really need those damn vampire fangs, I thought.

Then I remembered I definitely *did not* want *Daniel* blood in my mouth... or anywhere near me.

"When you told Mo everything and she accused me of being the target. I thought it was an accident since no one would know I was with you, a goat would get stuck, and I'd wander off to try and find it. No one except the judge who decided when I would leave."

"That... wow..." Anita looked at me surprised, but I could see the gears in her head working. "No, I'm not trying to kill you to keep my hot dog eating a secret. My idiot husband would have known where I was if he even once bothered to ask. The man is a damn fool."

"What about your job?" I challenged her, thinking anyone in a public profession might not want word of her extracurriculars getting around.

"I don't participate in contests within Dayton city limits. Though not all criminals keep to a single jurisdiction, it keeps me from being recognized and mocked. A fact that would result in a disproportionately large number of detainees in contempt of court. Again, though, it's not a secret. A lot of people in the court know about it. It's how I got the idea for my stage name."

My eyes drifted closed as I processed not only her words but how she spoke them.

Nothing sounded off or uncertain. No one had been surprised to see her here and the team from within her jurisdiction expressed condolences that she hadn't been able to take home the cash prize. It sounded like she used the money for some sort of kids program, which wasn't really on par with an assassin hirer.

Or a closet deep-throater.

"Sorry," I told her sincerely, letting the muscles in my back relax.

"Don't be sorry, tell me what you know," she said, moving Daniel out of the way and pulling me from the back of the police car. I looked into the neighboring car and saw Winnie snoozing in a bed of breadcrumbs and drool. Anita followed my gaze and popped open the door, whistling once to wake the dog and get her out of the car.

"Impressive."

"Not really. I was a canine handler once too." Her smile as she pat Winnie on her head spoke volumes about her character and I wondered how I ever thought she'd kill me.

Sleep deprivation, loss of coffee mugs and too many True Crime novels, I supplied and there were no flaws in that logic.

"Army?" I pondered, but she shook her head.

"Marines."

"The hot dogs?" I asked, wondering aloud what I'd wanted to know since she walked onto that stage. "Is that a Marine thing?"

"No, it's a stubborn pain in the ass thing, a concept with which I'm sure you're familiar. Some guy said 'no way can a skinny little chick like you ever win a hot dog eating contest unless it was giving BJs'. Never tell a Marine what she can or can't do. Or imply that male gratification is even on her list of skills, much less the top. After I won, I stuffed a whole sausage down his throat... sideways."

"Sure, cuz like bananas, that's how good girls eat them."

Daniel eyed her from around me and I stomped on his foot.

"Leave it," I ordered, and he shrugged before walking off. I followed the judge to a straw bale just beside the carnival entrance and we sat down. Without preamble I told her everything I knew and offered digital copies of the images I'd captured on the hill.

"This isn't really my area," she said, swiping through the photos and stopping on the casing. "I wasn't especially skilled with firearms. It looks like it might be military though. There's no retailer stamp and it has markings showing it was reloaded."

It was a decent observation; one I'd made and dismissed. Looking at it again, I thought her hypothesis had some merit. It had been a long time since I held military issued ammo, but I knew where to find a group of people who probably hadn't held any ammo since leaving the military and could know for sure.

"Thanks, that gives me an idea," I stood and stretched with a few relief inducing pops.

"Veterans Park?" She asked and I smiled, impressed a Marine could make the same connections. She must have done it for the silkies, because she was easily Air Force material.

"Yeah."

"What do you think you're going to learn at a park this time of night?" a uniformed officer asked. He was a bit past his prime, a fact that eluded him if the too tight uniform straining on his gut was any indication.

"Not sure. I'll know when I start asking questions," I shrugged him off only for his hand to clamp down on my shoulder.

"They are homeless people. It's nighttime. You're going to learn they're smelly and asleep," he sneered, and I read his nameplate.

"That's what you think, *Duncan*, but those are soldiers. At least one of them is awake. Night watch on assignment doesn't end when you come home. Unless you have four walls and a locked door, someone is standing guard."

"They aren't soldiers!" he shouted and the judge pressed her hand into his chest, guiding him away before I decked him.

"They are soldiers. You, on the other hand, lack more than just the physicality to be anything useful..." An arm wrapped around my wrist and started pulling me away from the judge and what would probably be The Homicide Victim if I had to look at his face too much longer.

"Let me know what you learn!" she shouted, and I nodded as I was escorted back to my Jeep.

"Where to?" Larry asked and I jumped. Once again, I'd forgotten he was here and had assumed Daniel was the one with a hold on my wrist.

"You can go home with your brother," I gestured toward the idiot in question, having just spotted him trying to teach a group of cadets how to smash an aluminum can against their forehead.

"Pass."

He climbed into the passenger seat of my Jeep and Winnie scrambled across his lap to the back seat. She let out a hot dog scented burp, stretched all her limbs and farted before settling in. Standing outside the open door, the smell hit me, and I gagged.

"Oh my dog, we're going to die," I gasped, but Larry rolled down the rear windows and encouraged me to hop in. "Fine. We're going to a drive through and then we're going to talk with some experts on munitions and survival."

Winnie led us into the encampment. Tail wagging and lolling tongue, she was the least threatening member of the group and our natural leader.

Larry and I held ten Happy Meals in each hand, hoping the juice and apple slices would get a better reaction from the group than it had gotten from me. The veterinarian insisted, as medical professionals do, that a properly balanced diet was a must and apples prevent scurvy. When I told him that French fries make people happy and no one gets apples from McDonalds, he threatened to drop my mochaccino out the window. I conceded, he handed me the coffee and I punched him in the arm.

Overall, it felt like old times and a lot of regret.

"Are you sure anyone is awake?"

He repeated the question a fourth time and I nodded, letting Winnie use her superior hearing to lead us to whoever might be leading the night watch tonight.

"There's my favorite girl," the rough voice of an older woman spoke softly, rustling Winnie's ears and dropping kisses on her head. When she glanced up, I saw the brown eyes and long scar from earlier in the week. "And my favorite disaster."

She squeezed my forearm, and I handed her a handful of Happy Meals.

"Sorry, there are no fries, that one insisted you all needed apples and milk. Claimed he knew best because he's a 'doctor'."

I slung air quotes around the word doctor and received a middle finger from Larry.

Her face mirrored mine before she laughed. It was a scratchy sound, a few of the people sleeping nearby adjusted slightly with the interruption, but snoozed on.

Beside us, Larry was placing little Happy Meal surprises at the entrances to the tarp tents like a cobbler's elf. The high for the next day was in the 40s, so while the nuggets would be cold, the milk and apples wouldn't spoil.

"I suppose cold fries suck anyway," I grumbled and turned to see the woman nodding around a chicken nugget. "I'm sorry, I don't know your name."

"May," she answered after swallowing and I tilted my head.

"First or last name?"

"Just May," she spoke sharply, and I nodded, taken aback by her sudden change in demeanor. Just as quickly, her calm mask returned and I made a mental note to look into her secrets.

Though I doubted "May" would yield much without any additional modifiers.

"Is anyone here an expert in munitions or... distance shooting?"

May brushed nugget crumbs off her hands and popped open the milk.

"Yeah. What do you need to know?"

I pulled out my phone and showed her the images of where the shooter would have crouched, the distance to the road, and then the casing.

"Do you know anyone who can and would make a shot like this?" I asked, ending with the picture taken from the shooter's vantage point. Low to the ground, trees surrounding the spot, only a small opening had a view of the house. I watched as she flipped through the images and scowled harder before she pushed the phone back into my hand.

"Don't come around here, no more." May moved to put distance between us. "Ain't no good following you and I won't end up dead. Not over this. Not again. Leave it alone and survive, but don't drag us down."

She just kept shaking her head while her hands shook.

"But…" I said quietly, not interested in forcing her to help but needing more information before I could walk away. "May?"

The phone in my hand rang and I picked it up without looking.

"Hello?"

"Chica, where are you?" Cruz spoke through the line, his serious tone laced with concern.

"Veterans Park. Why? Where are you?" I repeated his question back and heard a door slam shut behind him.

He let out a long exhale and tension in my own shoulders released.

"I was at your apartment and I saw a lot of blood. Are you OK?" I could hear him climbing into a car and starting the engine.

"Yeah. Why? What happened?"

My heart kicked up a notch as I started heading back toward where the car was parked.

"Meet me at the underground safe house with the tiny coffee cups in twenty minutes."

"What? Why?" I asked, gesturing Larry over and motioning for him to follow me.

"Because, chica, someone tried to shoot me."

Chapter Twelve:
Hidey Hole

"Y ou're lost! Tell me where we're going so I can look it up," Larry repeated on a sigh as we ended up at the same T-shaped intersection facing a Family Dollar. Some of the turns were on purpose to check for possible tails, but largely, I had no idea where I was going. When Cruz had taken me to the safe house, I was incredibly drunk from free shots provided to me by a bar manager to prevent murder in their establishment.

The manager had no vested interest in the man's life, they were just unwilling to lie in a court of law.

Cruz hadn't let me eat, I wore a trash bag as a cape, and woke up mostly naked next to him. Overall the night had been a complete disappearance from my memory that rivaled only the time my mom gave us "magic" brownies and I was accused of arson.

When I woke up beside Cruz, I was hungover and disoriented, gripping any and all body parts in my vicinity.

When I woke up completely, I was happily involved with Larry.

Oh the things you miss out on when you mistakenly think people are better than they are, I thought, checking both ways and turning right. We'd taken the block square to the left and no noticeable headlights were in my rearview. The area wasn't well-lit enough to drive without, but I'd made it a point to stop in a brightly lit box store parking lot and checked if anyone turned with me or kept going slowly.

"I can't give you an address," I told him, again. "Like I said, I was drunk when I arrived and under-caffeinated when I left. Just shut up and let me think."

An understatement as I recalled the shot glasses with handles masquerading as coffee mugs. Three and a half cups and 2000 steps later, I was just awake enough to be annoyed that I didn't have more coffee.

Or my own clothes.

And Winnie had to eat random safe house food that made her gaseous.

Frankly, everything about that safe house had been dangerous to my well-being and Cruz making me go back was just plain mean.

We cruised the Jeep slowly past a row of red brick buildings. On a pitch-black railing was a small red metallic paw print sticker. It was small enough not to be easily noticed, and simple enough to be confused with the work of a child, but I knew what it was.

A little beacon from a past life.

At Lackland, on bite work days, decoys were chosen by drawing little slips of paper out of a coffee mug. Red meant dead... what you wanted to be after all the dogs bit you during training. Not conventional but Cruz led training a little differently in a lot of ways.

We zig-zag circled the block again before parking a few streets over by a metal chicken.

Climbing out, I scanned the street but everything was quiet. Larry loudly slammed his door shut, and I winced.

"Sorry."

Winnie and I gave him our best death glares and scanned the area again. After a shared look conveying the situation, we moved quickly and quietly back to the red paw print sticker. In line with the rail, I pointed to the sticker and Winnie gave it a sniff.

"Seek," I whispered and she followed the railing down, moving toward the stairs and taking two of the steps. She paused, lifting her head and coming back up.

"Is that where we're going?" Larry stage whispered and I shot him a *shut up or die* look.

It was a toss up if the *die* would be provided by me or the killer following us around.

We followed Winnie past three more staircases, watching as she scented each before descending staircase number four and nudging the doorknob. Cautiously, I tested the handle.

It was unlocked.

"Crap," I exhaled, knowing I was unarmed and Winnie wasn't wearing her vest.

You screwed up Sharp, I scolded myself.

Winnie's nose disappeared into the doorway, her tail wagging enthusiastically before she trotted inside. Taking that as a positive sign we wouldn't die, I followed the shepherd mix into the darkened safe house. None of the outdoor lights penetrated the space and the only visible display was the microwave blinking 1200 waiting for someone to set it.

"Were you followed, Chica?" Cruz asked from behind the door. I whipped around, staring into the inky abyss as my eyes adjusted. Winnie's pink collar tags ruffled and I realized he was seated on something, both hands free to love on the gassy canine.

"No. We checked," I answered as Larry closed the door behind us. My shoulders relaxed a little in the dark room. The windows were easily four inches over the top of my head and there was no ambient light coming in. If someone wanted to shoot us in here, they would need to make a hell of a lot of noise or cause a huge disturbance to do it. Cruz stopped petting Winnie and the microwave displayed reflected off his irises.

He was looking at Larry.

"What happened to you, doctor?" Cruz's voice came out concerned and non-threatening.

"Late nights. Trying to buy out the Carters," he spoke softly and I struggled to hear every word. The news that he was trying to buy out Amber's dad to own his own practice was new. It was an admirable goal if it didn't send him to an early grave. Whatever his reason, it was a positive step in his life to not be beholden to a spineless amoeba of microbial slime... and her dad.

"When were you two here?"

"During the Yvette Taylor murder investigation," I answered Larry, moving into the kitchen. Now that my pupils had dilated, I could make out the outline of the coffee maker and the tiny mugs. Using touch, I felt for coffee filters and coffee grounds. The filters were easiest to find, but every metal tin my hand bumped into was empty.

"So... you and he... were..." Larry stammered but I was searching for coffee and didn't really pay attention.

"No. She turned me down for you," Cruz answered. Again, his voice held nothing but honesty and calm. It was comforting that he didn't feel threatened but at the same time... didn't he want to stake his claim on me?

Did I want him to claim me?

Yes, Larry betrayed me.

No, Cruz abandons you all the time.

Maybe you have no idea what you want.

That was a real bummer.

I want coffee.

Since all the thoughts in my head agreed, I left men in the past and searched for what I knew my heart truly wanted.

Coffee.

There was a sense of calm that came with blindly searching the kitchen for the one thing I wanted. My fingers were able to show me the texture of the fridge and the unfinished particle board edge of the counter.

Still no coffee and my eyes were starting to sting with tears.

A warm, soft fur brushed against my leg and put paws on the counter. She sniffed twice, shifted beside me and knocked over a container. Following her lead, I picked it up, opened it and sniffed.

"Good girl," I told Winnie, the most dependable BFF who never needed eyesight.

Slipping the filter in place and adding the newly located grounds, coffee was officially on its way.

Grabbing the carafe, I filled it at the sink. Using the tip of my finger to measure water levels, I added it to the machine and stopped when it reached my hand. Shutting the top, my fingers slid along the bottom ridge and pressed the button that felt like a circle with a vertical line.

The coffee pot gurgled to life and I let out a long sigh of relief that soon there would be coffee.

It was also reassuring that if I ever went blind, I could still make coffee.

"So, fill me in on what happened to you," I told Cruz, leaning against the counter. It had been a few minutes in the safe house and I hadn't fallen over, so I was staying right here until the coffee was done.

Because priorities.

Winnie on the other hand, trotted back toward the men now that she had served her seeing nose canine duties. I could hear her collar jingle and knew one of them was petting her, an image that made my heart smile.

These men were nice to my dog.

"Or you could start by filling me in on what happened to you?" Cruz had a tone that implied I was in trouble. "Since you called me about Arturo and sent that picture, what's happened?"

"I feel like you already know," I grumbled just as the coffee pot beeped. Using my new super alert sense of touch, I reached into the cabinet, touching the crockery until I felt what could only be tiny, handled coffee cups. I looped a finger through three handles and slid them toward me, but one of them resisted.

"Chica, what are you doing?" Cruz broke into my silence and I jerked the coffee cups a little harder. Something moved, sent air rushing past my face and crashed into the ground with a sharp *thunk* and then there was glass everywhere... again.

"Are you OK?"

I could hear them moving.

"Stay. I'm fine! Keep Winnie out of here," I ordered, righting the three cups and putting coffee in them. Chugging one, I admitted defeat and pulled out my phone. Using the ambient light from the phone screen, I found a broom tucked in the corner by the fridge.

Exactly where I kept mine.

Convenient or creepy? I wondered, swiping the bristles across the floor and taking a second coffee shot. No immediate answer came, so I scooped the remnants into the pan and set it on the counter. No point trying to find a trash can.

I'd probably just break something else.

"OK, so someone may have taken a shot that would have exploded my head if I hadn't tripped and fallen, and May doesn't want me anywhere near the park anymore after looking at the picture," I offered the Reader's Digest version while I refilled the two empty coffee shots and carried them to the living room.

Setting one in front of Larry, I put the second two on the far side from the couch and sat on the floor. Winnie came around and flopped beside me, head in my lap while I drank.

"So, what's your story?" I countered his brusque questioning with my own, noticing Larry eyeing my two cups and his one. "If you wanted two cups, you should have asked."

"No, I was wondering why you didn't give *him* one," the question was accompanied with a head jerk toward Cruz. The way he said *him* was a little too childish for my liking, but the man across from me remained passive.

"Because he's fifty percent robot cyborg and doesn't drink coffee. The other fifty percent sold its soul to the devil to be awake and perky when the human side makes an appearance," my first cup ended with my declaration and I moved it to the side to focus on number two. "Now, robo man, speak!"

Winnie let out a soft *woof* and I rubbed her ears without breaking eye contact with the outline of what was either Cruz or a hat stand.

"Your picture yielded results, but not the ones I had expected. Arturo didn't come up, but the woman and another man beside him did. Both are considered missing, lost in a skirmish or an attack of some kind. Everything I had access to was redacted. So I went in."

"Into where?" I requested clarification while trying to drink the second cup much more slowly and avoid standing again.

"Look, I'm Army Criminal Intelligence, but they loan me out. To Homeland Security, alphabet agencies, I have a unique skill set that makes me valuable to the government," he didn't sound especially proud of that. "I have credentials to access any base, field office or safe house owned by the US Government."

"OK, Liam Neeson, but they are trying to kill you. Why would they let you *in* anywhere with that big red X on your back?" Larry took a sharp breath and I realized he was a little behind. He also hadn't touched his coffee shot and both of mine were empty, so I tactically acquired it.

Larry failed to notice until I'd drained his cup and then it was too late.

"They aren't trying to kill me. They just aren't trying to keep me alive," his words were accompanied by a twitch in the shadows that was either a shrug or seizure.

"How is that different?"

"It's different because they'll still give me what I need. Like access to a Homeland Security field office." I started to interject but he cut me off after a non-syllable. "Just stop looking a gift horse in the mouth and listen. Linked into the actual database, I was able to find the names of those soldiers and a report that indicated they were hidden but went missing. I started digging for Arturo, thinking it must have been a server error on my end when it showed him conducting liaison work with a government contractor in the 80s. Before I could dig further, a rifle shot took out the window. The glass was impact proof, so while it didn't shatter, it spider webbed enough to lose its effectiveness. Before I could get up, a second shot cut through the window and pierced the CPU I was working on. The whole facility was locked down, heat seeking drones and spooks scoured the area."

"And they caught someone and waterboarded him until he sang like a canary?"

I wondered why we were meeting in the dark if the spooks handled it. There was no need to be in a safe house if the threat had been contained, but his hesitation filled into the silence that there was more and I was out of coffee. The cut on the bottom of my foot was throbbing, placing my need for coffee at war with my need to stop walking on it.

"No. There was no one there, Cyn. All they found was this," Cruz opened his phone, light concealed by his cupped hand and slid it to me under the coffee table. I leaned back, looking down my body at a gold cylinder with no manufacturer markings.

"OK, so then why not go to another computer away from windows and finish the search?" I asked and he shook his head.

"The servers have been wiped. No one can find squat, in the cyber-verse or in the real world. The files, the shooter, none of them existed moments after that shot was fired," I could hear him scrubbing his hands over his face, the scratching of stubble making me wonder if he looked as run-down and beat up as I felt.

"So..." I looked at each of the men, mentally willing one of them to get me more coffee.

"So... we're out of leads, chica. I have three days left before they send me away and every record that used to exist is gone," Cruz shoved up as he finished, grabbing my three coffee shot glasses and carrying them to the kitchen. "I also think you should stay here until they forget about you. I've got security precautions in place and the government is slightly less angry with me now that I was shot at, so they aren't sending me into the field alone and they admitted I was being sent to look for a burial ground and skeletons, the ones the media dug up from around the same time as Desert Storm."

"Did they give you any more than that? Maybe you can help find what happened to Arturo."

"Or you can let this go and live to drink coffee another day. I can't help you from overseas, and you don't have back-up."

"I have Winnie!" I countered and he choked out a laugh as all three of us turned to the partially concealed dog passed out asleep with her paws over her eyes.

"Yeah, real dependable back-up."

His reasoning was valid and I watched him walk back with the coffee.

"I'm not hiding out in a safe house," I grumbled, giving him an affectionate smile when he set all three cups back down in front of me. "I appreciate that you care, though."

The three of us sat there in silence and Larry asked the question Ian hadn't dared to speak.

"So, you won't hide out, but you'll let this go?"

"Not a chance in hell."

Chapter Thirteen: Range Days

I glanced at my Garmin, the clock on the microwave and empty roadway outside.

"There's time," I told myself, slinging the range bag filled with ammo, gun brushes, solvents and hearing protection over my shoulder. Winnie trotted over, nudging the leash hanging by the entryway with her snoot.

My brain did math again and I set the bag down, clipping on Winnie's leash.

"There isn't time. Joseph was really mad."

We started toward the exit and I grabbed the bag again.

"There's time. No one has tried to kill him."

Setting the bag down again, I sighed.

"He does pay for my coffee and snacks though, I shouldn't risk it."

Staring at the bag, I scooped it up again.

"There's time."

We started down the stairs, Winnie's tail aloft as she paraded her leashed human.

In reality, I had no idea if there was more or less time than what I needed. I had barely been home from the safehouse for five hours, declining both Larry and Cruz's invitation to stay with them in favor of my own, dog-scented space with human sized coffee mugs.

"I don't know if we should go out there Winnie," I sighed.

The shooting range, Shots Fired- owned by Trigger, was an hour away. An hour and fifteen from the dairy. It was 0700, the range opened at 0800, I started work at 1300... Two hours roundtrip... plus at least an hour to shoot and another for questions, factoring in traffic... and the potential demolition that followed me places when Winnie was around...

"Yeep!" Winnie yelped and I stumbled on her outstretched paw that had *nearly* been stepped on. The weight of my bag swung in the direction of travel- aka down- and I tumbled down the last four stairs.

Winnie scrambled out of the way and then appeared above my head.

Tongue hanging out of the side of her mouth, every pant a mockery of my suffering.

"You're evil."

She licked my face thoroughly.

"You're evil and your breath stinks."

Somehow, I got back on my feet. The bag had remained zipped, the dog uncrushed, and my coffee... was still upstairs on the counter.

"Son of witch's tit," I looked up the stairs longingly, then down at the dog prancing to be let outside. "Ugh, priorities."

We shoved through the door, heading down the rear alley with occasional pauses for Winnie to pee on her favorite spots. Despite my interpretation of the hour as cruelly early and only suitable for masochists, parents were being dragged down the street by enthusiastic children lugging around backpacks. Seniors strolled while the Coffee Cabin and Mo's did swift business with the suit and tie commuter crowd. Usually, the Coffee Cabin catered to truckers and tree choppers, offering an assortment of savory breakfast treats in addition to coffee so thick it would hide arsenic.

Must be a plaid and denim holiday.

Winnie and I reached the Jeep, conveniently parked beside a pocket park where Winnie could do her business. Throwing the bag in the car, I waited patiently for the dog to chase a squirrel up a tree, give an older man a proctology exam and pee the Nile River before she signaled she was ready to go.

"Cyn!" Mo ran out of her bakery clutching a stainless steel travel cup emblazoned with her bakery's logo. I took it gratefully and gulped. "Where are you going?"

"Shooting range. Who's running your store?" I asked, noticing that her departure hadn't incited a riot. If she wasn't in there and no one was screaming, it had to have still been staffed.

"I hired some help. Stella's boyfriend, James, specifically," she said and I nodded. He'd worked at the pizza place on Main St and we'd successfully embarrassed Stella into a date. The moderately autistic college student was incredibly smart, but overly clinical in the field of romance.

She has, however, recently informed me that saliva exchange has increased in pleasantness with familiarity. I'd managed to distract her with a question regarding the charge on blood types just in time to not learn what else they had been exchanging.

"I saw Cruz and Larry at your apartment last night," she announced, and I nodded without breaking the seal of my mouth on the cup. "Anything you want to tell me?"

"Thanks for the coffee," I handed her back the empty mug and offered a thumbs up. "See you later."

Before she could protest, I climbed behind the wheel and started the engine. We pulled from the curb, and I glanced in the rearview mirror to see my best friend flipping me off.

"Love you too!" I shouted and stepped on the accelerator.

Shots Fired was modeled after military ranges all over the country.

A long sloped drive led into the side of a hill, wound into an alcove and spat out cars into a dirt lot. The whole perimeter was the rising slope of the hill, elevations keeping properly fired shots in the earth behind it.

Wooden and tin shelters hung lazily over concrete slabs featuring long wooden planks covered in industrial carpet. There were four shelters in a half circle around a dirt space that had a healthy number of large vehicles parked haphazardly in the space. Beside the shelters was a prefabricated structure with a white sign declaring it the "Office".

Leaving the Jeep under a tree at the far edge of the lot, I walked to the office with Winnie trotting happily beside me. For an organization that demanded uniformity and order, the array of cars and their inability to form a straight line called into question the military background of the patrons to a casual observer.

To anyone who served, it was controlled chaos.

A reminder that uniformity and order went against human nature.

The mix of loud fifty-cal booms were interspersed with the sharp crack of a rifle. There were a fair number of pops and ticks, indicating handguns of all calibers were present and accounted for, though the soft ticks far outnumbered the pops. *Twenty twos are the cheapest to shoot*, I thought, inhaling the air tinged with a metallic gunpowder that stuck to the back of my throat.

The taste was like a childhood memory and with it came memories of decimated targets and accolades. Twenty-three wasn't necessarily a child, but I had been young and filled with hope and ambition. Every day I'd go out and show the range master what "shoot like a girl" *really* meant. I'd been tough, always alert even before coffee, and ready for a fight or a frisky encounter with no need to sleep or guzzle water before bed to prevent hangovers.

Now I was filled with coffee and anti-inflammatories with an hourly phone reminder to drink water.

We ambled up the short ramp and pulled open the door. Inside was dark and dusty, stale cigarette smoke mixed with burnt coffee to turn the gunpowder in my throat into a sensory memory from Afghanistan. Underneath it was humidity and body odor covered with a lilac diffuser and coughed twice before deciding short shallow breaths was the way to go.

"Hey," I said to the woman behind the counter. She had toned muscle, weathered skin and blue eyeshadow that may have been tattooed on. The olive drab T-shirt she wore had the sleeves rolled up into tank top length, black pants that may have been cargo sitting just below bony hips on legs that disappeared under the counter. Hanging from the side of her thin, hot pink mouth was an unlit cigarette and I wondered briefly if she knew it was there.

Maybe it was also a tattoo... a realistic 3-D inking of a cancer stick.

"What do you want?" The smoke deepened voice was outshone by the pure indifference and moderate violence laced in her tone. The cigarette moved opposite her mouth, confirming it was real, and with her words came the sweet scent of whiskey. If she wasn't the spitting image of Yzma from that cartoon movie, sans purple feathers, I might have asked her to take me under her wing.

As it was, I was ill-suited to life as a llama and I couldn't make spinach puffs or talk to squirrels.

"To shoot," I said, pulling out my wallet.

"Military only," she wheezed out and I slid my ID card onto the counter. "No dogs."

Winnie wagged her tail, and I rolled my eyes.

"You and I both know you were going to sleep in the car anyway."

Her eyebrows danced across her forehead, and I glared.

"Just because you detect explosives doesn't mean you couldn't benefit from exposure. It's like exposure therapy, getting used to the mundane smells so you can pick out the important ones."

Winnie's tail swished slightly, her paws dancing on the threadbare blue fabric before she paused and let loose a fart louder than the fifty-caliber booming outside.

"Son of a... fine, you win!" I fanned my face while Yzma's older sister eyed us like a drunk man with pictures of Sasquatch. "How much to shoot? I need targets, I got the rest."

One pencil drawn eyebrow hiked to her receding Farrah Fawcett styled hairline.

"We don't usually let the fruitcakes have guns," she inhaled around her unlit cigarette and choked. "What the hell is that smell?"

It couldn't be helped, I snickered.

"Friendly fire. Just give me the targets and take the money?" I slid a twenty across the counter. She replaced the twenty with 4 ten ring sheets and a plastic tag with a lane number.

"When everyone's reloading, you can push the stop to load your targets. Dog stays in the car," she pointed to a sign above her head that read *Range Rules*. "I assume you're shooting hand-guns?"

I nodded because it was too much work to explain I didn't have room for anything bigger in my apartment without finishing the sentence with "that's what she said".

"All guns are always loaded. No harassment will be tolerated. No fighting. Three strikes and you're barred from returning. Clear your own brass. Any questions?"

I shook my head, wondering how dumb the usual customers were that any of that needed stating. Before I could ask, she jerked her thumb toward the door.

We were dismissed.

Emerging from the trailer, Winnie trotted back toward the Jeep and I opened her door. The dog leapt in, spread out and released a long contented breath.

"Working dog my left butt cheek," I grumbled, pulling my range bag from the floor board and grabbing a plain black ball cap from my cache under the seat. "If someone tries to steal the car, wake yourself up enough to get out of it. I can get a new Jeep, but I can't get a new Winnie."

Her soft snore came off a little forced, but I shut the door quietly and directed myself toward the pistol shed.

It was obvious by the giant overhead sign declaring it a "Pistol Shed".

The cracked plywood entrance was coated in peeling green paint that matched the painted green wooden slug in my hand with the number seven. Stepping out from the bright sun into the overhang, my eyes took a moment to adjust before assessing the shooters.

Two men in their mid-twenties were showing small children how to handle twenty two caliber guns while an anxious mother watched. On the far end was an average height woman with a body that belonged on magazine covers, and the half dozen others were men ranging from early thirties to late fifties. Most had one or two handguns on a soft case or a towel, but next to the woman was a blonde man assembling his own personal gun show.

Stepping up to the five-foot stretch with a number seven between two wooden posts, I dropped my bag on the counter. After a quick safety check on my firearms, I pulled out my pink Hello Kitty hearing protection and secured them over my ears, dimming every shot to a minor blip on my auditory radar. Instinct and being shot at had me checking the berms for anyone watching, as well as the line for any potential threats.

You are officially paranoid, I told myself with a mental pat on the back.

Just because you're paranoid doesn't mean someone isn't out to get you.

The red strobe beside my head flashed with a loud buzzer and everyone set down their weapons and took a step back. Every shooter looked left then right, showed their hands, grabbed targets, and headed down range. Joining the throng, I followed a man wearing Bengay as a cologne toward a metal stand with a wooden board.

If I ever went blind, I decided the scent of Bengay would be my new directional sense.

It was far more pleasant than a teenager in Axe body spray.

Or whatever Winnie expelled from her butt.

I was standing in front of board number 7, but something was missing.

"Staples!" Bengay shouted, shoving a wrist into my forearm and offering me a silver staple gun.

"Thanks!" I shouted back, popping my first target onto the sturdiest looking part that remained.

We trooped out and waited for the range to clear. Another hand check, look left and right, the buzzer and red lights stopped. All shooters took a step forward and I brushed my finger on the matte black semi-auto.

Oh man, my hand wrapped around the grip of my Sig Sauer and I got a little tingly. It had been a while since I'd been at a shooting range. While I'd held and fired a gun several times in the past nine months, there had been little excitement in the defensive reflex. Shooting to save a life wasn't the same as emptying a magazine into paper, relishing in the groupings and ring precision. Everything about the shooting range qualified as good, clean fun.

Especially compared to getting blood stains out of blonde hair and dog fur.

Death and dismemberment, even justified, was messy as fluff.

More alarming was how many people had become killed and dismembered in my presence since I was discharged. The number far exceeded the value of that metric in my service record, and

I'd exploded a munitions bunker on my first day in Army MP school.

It's like the universe wanted everyone to know that war zones were safer than being in my company.

Checking down range, I picked up the semi-auto and trained the eyesight on the ten ring about 10 yards down range.

Inhale, time the heartbeat, exhale and squeeze...

The shot exploded from the gun and a hole blossomed just above the solid red circle in the center.

It couldn't be helped, I smiled.

Then repeated the practice, emptying the magazine in my gun and two others before someone pulled the cease fire lever. Ejecting the final magazine and locking the slide back, I set the gun down and took two steps back from the line of fire before sliding my hearing protection down to my neck.

Every shot had been within 2 inches of the first, half in the ten ring.

"Nice work, kitty," a deep male voice said before the crack of his hand hitting my ass broke through the air and I felt his finger curl into my flesh. I whipped around, gripped both of his shoulders and drove the apex of his torso into my knee until he screamed.

Falling to the ground and clutching his junk, I "accidentally" brought my knee up into his nose and enjoyed the satisfying crunch accompanied by droplets of blood splattering my black cargo pants and the ground.

Less clean fun than normal, I mentally scowled. Now I was going to have to change and do laundry to get his nasty DNA filled hemoglobin off my pants.

"You bitch!" He shouted from the ground, his voice muffled by the blood pooling in his nasal cavity. I let out one long whistle. It took a few moments, I assume she spent them yawning, but Winnie appeared behind the man and let out a low growl.

"That is a bitch," my snarl matched her tooth-baring. His genetic material was seeping through the canvas fabric of my pants, sending my stomach into small flips of discontent. "But you are welcome to compare and contrast how hard we bite when I skin you alive, jackass. Your DNA is already on my pants, not like much more will keep me from needing to burn them."

It was the quietest I'd ever heard a shooting range.

A repeating squeak came from the left side as the man on the ground eyed me with malice. The next move was his, but his choice could cost him his life.

"Enough, get out," a soft male voice drifted from the wheelchair that appeared beside me.

"We were leaving," I said, leaving Winnie on guard so I could turn and grab my gun. "I have to put on uncontaminated pants to kneel in cow poop anyway."

"Not you, Sharp. Merit, you're out." I turned to see him gesturing to the man on the ground with a broken nose clutching his penis. Merit seemed an oddly oxymoronic name for the man who would probably sell his mother's heart medicine for stripper singles.

And then grope the strippers against their will.

The man on the ground struggled to all fours, taking a few deep breaths before pushing up. Standing, he rose to an impressive height, bearing down on the man in the wheelchair who didn't so much as flinch.

"What the hell? You subscribe to that 'me too' crap all of a sudden? I thought you were a soldier, you know what and how women are. Then, that bitch attacked me!"

Merit's face had gone red, his blonde hair and blue eyes giving the impression of a large, angry Malfoy. Beside him, I started tapping my fingers one at a time against my pant leg to keep from smashing my fist into new and potentially life threatening parts of his body.

"I was just telling her what a great job she did and she had to be all sensitive..."

The man in the wheelchair slid his hand into its side pocket, pulled a revolver and fired two shots in the dead center of my target's ten ring without breaking eye contact with Merit.

It was both hot and poor range safety.

Bad boys are certainly tempting for a reason, I thought, even as I acknowledged he was twenty years my senior. The age gap wouldn't bother a lot of people, but anyone closer to my parent's age than my age might have dabbled in the same groups as my parents, and I couldn't risk it.

I'd only narrowly avoided second hand incest when the whole Carla, Seth and Larry thing happened and it was unlikely I'd have that kind of luck twice.

"You were warned, you didn't listen. Leave on your own or leave in an ambulance. Your call."

My eyes trailed to the handgun sitting in his lap, his hand steady outside the trigger guard.

"But Trigger..." the seated man leveled his gun at Merit's thigh and I looked at the finger flirting with the trigger.

His middle finger.

"This is crap!" Merit yelled, stomping back toward his shooting station and throwing the pristine arsenal into a metal case. "Just because some oversensitive reservist with a dog shows up and gets all bent out of shape about a friendly tap, you're going to throw me out? Do you even know who I am? I can have you shut down and..."

A snarl came from the back corner and an all-black pit bull with a longer than normal coat, and husky adjacent ears, rose to his feet inches behind Merit. Though not especially tall, the dog had an energy that had every person taking a step back, including Winnie.

As he advanced on the blonde man, I noticed a teddy bear on an orthopedic bed in the corner. This was not a junkyard dog, it was a well loved protection against jerks.

"Call him off, Trigger," the once condescending voice laced with fear. I smirked at the dog and mentally promised him treats if he ate just one of Merit's testicles.

"Leave now and I'll consider it."

Come on, try the dog, pretty please?

Merit nodded, eyes on the dog as he backed out of the pistol shed. He stumbled on the short step, landing on his butt in the dirt before popping up and hauling ass toward a large gray diesel truck. Everything was thrown in the back and he spun out his tires in a cloud of dust before revving down the road to the tune of Trace Adkins.

I let out a mental sigh of annoyance that he'd escaped with a complete set of dangly bits between his legs.

Life's not fair.

I glanced around, expecting people to be holding up camera phones or other manner of techno wizardry I'd have to buy off of them to keep the man in the chair out of jail.

Every soldier stood at attention while the family members held their kids' hands, looking ready to fight and defend. The eerie silence stretched on and Winnie broke through the tension by letting out a booming fart that she wafted for all to sniff.

"Holy hell," Trigger gasped, sliding his gun back into his pocket and fanning his face. No one moved for a minute, coming to life as the smell reached them and they were forced to move or suffer a violent death of asphyxiation. As though being commanded by Winnie's fart, the other shooters immediately hopped to, checking on targets and scooping up brass with an air that nothing out of the ordinary had happened.

"Come with me, Sharp," he said, so softly it was possible no one else had heard it. "Bring your gear and your partner. Shooting time is over."

Chapter Fourteen: An Assassin's Account

"Take a seat," he held open the door at the top of a textured ramp and I walked into a dim office. Immediately inside was a functional desk topped with neat papers and an older computer sitting near a black rotary phone. In front of it was a seating area with a brown faux leather couch and two olive green chairs. The carpet featured the same industrial color and texture gracing the gun tables outside and it was a toss up which had been the original purpose and which the reassigned leftovers.

My money was on the office carpet being an afterthought.

Based on the smell, we were either in the same building as Yzma's older sister or the basement of a casino.

The basement of a casino that doubled as a brothel in an evacuated WWII bomb shelter.

"That is a... smell," I choked out, trying to stand near Winnie's tail so she could fan the air for me. The black dog followed Trigger into the room and stuck his nose between me and Winnie, right against her butt and inhaled like she was air.

"Yeah. Used to be a portable trailer on a junior high school campus. Don't know what it was used for, but I've been to back-alley cock fights in third world countries that smelled better," Trigger rolled to the sitting area, pausing by a mini fridge and pulling out two bottles of water and two cans of iced coffee. He gestured for me to occupy one of the green chairs and put one of each on the low coffee table in front.

"Do you think after you've had it awhile, the smell will get better?"

I perched on the edge of the chair and grabbed the bottle of water. Pulling a collapsible dish out of my cargo pocket, I checked it for misogynist blood before popping it open and putting water in it for Winnie.

My dog was not above eating her own poop, but no way would I let her ingest that man's blood.

It would probably turn her into a demon.

Or worse, a dude-bro.

Holy water did nothing but make them enter a wet T-shirt contest.

"It's been three years. If it hasn't faded by now, it ain't gonna." He took a long drink from his own bottle of water while the large black dog went to a huge bed in the corner and drank from a stainless-steel dish. His tail ended about a foot before I thought it should, paws indicating he could have been bigger and fur suggesting he got brushed four times a day.

Next to him, Winnie looked like a redheaded stepchild from Planet German Shedder.

A world where dog brushes and Furminators were outlawed.

"Ruger," Trigger said and the dog turned his wide head to sniff the air with a stunted snout.

"Winnie," I gestured in her direction. Pointing at myself, I continued, "Cynthia, Cyn, but I have a feeling you already know that."

"Trigger," he gave a curt nod, and I raised a brow to find out if he had another name. "Just Trigger. Anyone I was before is long dead. I've been expecting you for a while now, what finally brought you out?"

His hands wrapped around the can of coffee and my eyes fell onto his trigger finger.

Or where it would have been if someone hadn't removed it.

Based on the scarring, it wasn't done professionally... or neatly.

"Expecting me?" I stammered.

"Heard a lot about you," Trigger began, setting the can down and grabbing a tin from beside his chair. He cracked it open and tossed a treat toward both dogs who immediately gobbled them in a frenzy of slobber and crunches.

"Hard not to," I sighed into my coffee and slouched down in the chair. "In my defense..."

I paused and waited for something to come out, but that seemed to be the end of my thought. My mouth closed again. There was no defense. Some people were just magnets for disaster, and it was far too late to question my polarity.

"Huh," Trigger said, eyeing me carefully over the top of his bottle. Not sure whether he was judging or sizing me up for Ruger to eat, I slid lower in my chair and tried to look... like a guilty child in the principal's office.

In trouble but too cute to murder.

And I'd succeed at exactly the time unicorns farted rainbows that smelled like cotton candy.

Or Winnie met a snack she didn't like.

"If you know who I am, why did you ask what brought me out? Wasn't that in your briefing packet?" I asked from my half-squished position in the chair.

He furrowed his brow and checked the room carefully.

"I know who you are because I keep tabs on all veterans in the area. Someone with your decorated marksman history... I expected you to turn up here needing to shoot the week after you arrived. From what I heard, you found other targets," he rolled closer and dropped his voice. "Who knows you're here?"

"I'm not sure," I replied just as quietly. "I wasn't discreet about pulling out my range bag. Why?

"Who told you I can help you?"

He ignored my question, but I answered his.

"May."

His back went rigid, and a pink tongue slipped out to wet lips that hadn't gone dry. Eyes shifting back and forth, I could see his throat work but the gentle pulse visible beneath his skin remained steady.

"You were a sniper." It wasn't a question, but he nodded anyway. "The casing and the shot I'm interested in, they couldn't have been taken by just anyone. I'm assuming you were deadly accurate to get the nickname Trigger?"

His face cracked into the first almost smile I'd seen today.

"Started calling me that after my capture and questioning," he held up both hands and wiggled the index nubs. "Military humor."

"Is that why you left?"

"Nah, losing my fingers was fine. So was getting half of my intestines removed when a gunshot wound perforated that. Same with my kidneys and the half plus dozen concussions. Nope, they didn't kick me out until I couldn't walk," he smacked the top of his leg. "I'd like to say the last injury had the best story, but this was the only one I did to myself."

My stomach rolled over and I fought the urge to ask why.

I knew why.

It was the same 'why' I'd seen etched in every face at Veterans Park.

You could offer your body, your life and your mind for the country, but they were hard pressed to do anything in return.

Not after someone marked your file as "Unfit to Return". Trained not to ask for help and no longer provided it by force, you just faded out of the system. An estimated 6000 veteran soldiers committed suicide in a year according to a VA study, and still no one gave them the tools to save themselves.

They all became just another casualty.

A name on a rock.

Surplus.

"I'm sorry. I understand if you don't want to help."

It came out as a whisper and Winnie pressed her head into my lap.

"Not as sorry as they were," his bitter laugh made the hair on my neck stand on end. It was a little too Heath Ledger in Batman and I wondered if beneath the surface was a man two steps from the ledge. "So, what did May say I could do for you? What is this mysterious shot?"

Hand shaking, I pulled my phone from my pocket and took a dozen deep breaths before opening the image.

"Someone is trying to kill me," I showed him the picture of the shell casing. Then scrolled through the tracking route to the vehicle and back to the firing point with a shot to where I'd been standing. He studied each image for barely a second before his eyes went back to mine.

"Professional," he commented and I just nodded. "Not a lot of people can make that shot. Not surprised he missed, that kind of range needs near perfect conditions."

"He might have if I hadn't fallen over..."

"A true marksman would have known to anticipate that. Your gravitational anomalies are well-documented. It was sloppy reconnaissance and even sloppier shooting considering anyone could track the location of discharge and the idiot left the casing. What were you looking into?"

"Missing goat. My friend thinks maybe the shooter stole the goat but the plausibility of that has too many variables." I tried to remember who would have known Daniel and I were together and Carla had ordered me to help the man on a recorded message that anyone could have heard, It was most likely recorded when she went out of town last week, well enough in advance to line up the shot.

Still, the judge would have been the only one to know *exactly* when I left.

Her and the officer's at the station.

"Before the goats," his eyes were watching mine for a tell. It felt like he could read my mind and was waiting to see what I came up with.

If it would be the truth or a lie.

Joke was on him though; my whole face was an over-expressive tell and I had no idea which emotion was plastered on it at any given minute. Like one of those clown paintings that changed with different angles, my face gave everything and nothing away. "What brought you to May?"

Oh, that.

"Arturo Denicourt."

My eyes zeroed in on his before I spoke, but they didn't shift in the slightest.

Either he'd already known or he was that good at hiding his thoughts. Neither was improbable, but only one answer leant itself to finding out the one answer I needed: why wouldn't Arturo go home?

"What's that got to do with me?"

He rolled back to his coffee can and chugged it. I mirrored the move, only to find my can of cold coffee was empty.

Why is the rum always gone? I sighed internally and tried to poker up my face.

"Like we discussed, you're a sniper," I shrugged but he didn't buy it.

"May wouldn't have sent you here after seeing those pictures. She'd have told you to run."

I blinked at the man.

"How do you know she would say that?"

"Because that's what a smart person would do. May's seen enough, she's one of the smartest people I've met. You don't survive what she has if you're dumb."

"Are you saying I'm not smart?"

I scowled, weighing my outrage over the potential truth in his implication to decide if I was willing to punch him over the jab. Much as it hurt to admit, my decisions these past few days made a solid case in his favor.

And my hand hurt from having just punched a man in the face.

"No. I'm saying that she gave you this information before she knew it would kill all of us. Only a stubborn pain in the ass would keep going," he switched to taking a swig of water. "And everything I know about you puts you squarely in the stubborn pain in the ass category. So why me?"

I blew out a breath.

Stubborn Pain in the Ass was probably going on my tombstone.

Right beside *Told you you can overdose on coffee.*

"You were reassigned to a military prison during one of your recovery periods. She mentioned you saw a file, one that current service members can't find or find records of ever existing. Incarcerated for years and now it's like he doesn't exist," my hand grasped the water bottle, sloshing some out as I squeezed too tight. "His son wants him home. And I want to know why someone is shooting at me and my friends. But mostly, I want to protect the people in that park. Whatever it takes, nothing happens to them because of me."

Trigger nodded but sat there silently.

"There's also a photograph of him that someone had when they were released... him and his newborn son with a weird cryptic message..."

The man moved, almost imperceptibly, but I knew the picture meant something to him.

Ruger lumbered to his feet and dropped his large head in the man's lap. Absently rubbing a thick ear, Trigger seemed to search his mind for a decision. Ruger's tongue fell out of the side of his mouth and every pant made his dopey smile grow wider. Winnie let out a soft rumble and I looked at her, expecting jealousy or condemnation of the dopey beast.

Instead, her eyes focused on something in the far corner. If the wall lined up, it would have been the corner with a shared wall to where the registration counter sat. In the poorly lit trailer, it was hard to make out, but I climbed to my feet and Winnie led me over, pawing at each of her ears as though they had filled with fleas.

It reminded me of the time we went to a nanobot farm and Winnie destroyed a transmitter for hurting her... ears.

We approached the corner, noting that from this angle, a small quarter sized hole was letting in the too-bright sunlight. On the discolored carpet, immediately beside the hole, was an oblong capsule that reminded me of a dog poop bag dispenser. As we got closer, a small buzzing tickled the bottom corner of my jawbone.

Every step I moved closer, the sound picked up speed and I froze in place.

I motioned for Winnie to search it.

She sniffed twice and sat without getting any closer, but the fever-pitch whirring remained steady.

There was only one choice.

Pushing her out of the way, I grabbed the device and ran for the back door.

"What the hell are you doing, Sharp?" Trigger shouted as I flung the black capsule as far as I could toward the firing berm sitting beyond the large caliber rifle range. Halfway there, the tingling got worse in my ears and I counted down to impact as the crescendo held. Above the range, a cloud of fire ballooned up in a sizzling pop that rained ash on the ground and stuck. Everything was bathed in the orange and red glow, some sort of adhesive accelerant keeping the flames alive on the otherwise non-combustible ground.

"Son of a bitch!" He scrubbed his hand against his face and I turned to see both Winnie and Ruger leaning against him. I was prepared to comfort, reassure, and offer snacks if necessary.

But instead of fear, his face displayed a resolute rage that promised retribution. "Those mother-"

His exclamation was cut off by the wail of fire trucks.

"Did you call fire?" I asked, watching the red truck climb the drive, followed by two squad cars. Trigger shook his head. "Where do you keep your ammo? If that was a self-destructing listening device, they might have company. Stay sharp and stay armed."

"If they've tagged me, I need you to take this. The reason for the picture should become apparent."

He leaned forward in his chair, using a thumb to feel around before sliding an index sized envelope out from between his seat and his chair. The paper was still warm, but I flipped it over in my hand.

"Open it alone and don't go anywhere by yourself. If anything happens," he nodded toward Ruger. "Take care of him. This ain't a war I'm equipped to win, Sharp."

Chapter Fifteen: Record of Lies

Using every ounce of stealth I possessed, I ran to the rear of the building and tried to time my breaths with my heartbeats. Crouching low and pressing my back against the wall, I listened for any and all signs of life on the other side. I motioned to my partner to circle the building and draw eyes, a job she was born for.

Winnie was the distraction, and I timed my movement based on the fading jingle of the tags on her collar. I just needed...

"Cynthia!" I winced at Joseph's voice and turned around.

"Hey, boss," I said casually and then walked into the barn like I hadn't been trying to sneak into work three hours late.

Winnie needed to work on her Scooby and Shaggy skills if we were going to keep our jobs.

As it was, now I had to try and lie.

Not a skill I possessed.

"Did you just get here? I haven't seen you yet."

The ear piercing shriek at the end was a bigger giveaway than the untouched work in the barn.

"Cynthia," he warned and I puffed out a breath while I washed my hands and grabbed latex gloves to begin my rounds.

"OK, I know I'm late. But I have a good reason!" Armed with a clipboard and thermometer, I headed toward the cow's milk collection container first.

"Enlighten me, Cynthia. What incredibly important thing couldn't possibly be skipped to keep your ass employed?" He was standing behind me, but I could hear the eye roll in the skeptical voice dripping with annoyance.

"I had to go to the shooting range."

Popping open the first container, I took measurements, noted them, and then sanitized the thermometer.

"Explain!" Joseph demanded without making it a question and I sighed. There was no way to explain. Sure, the shooting portion and the talking with Trigger portion were easy enough, but how do I explain the assault investigation and questioning? Or explain the napalm related substance still ablaze when they arrived?

Note to self: don't punch pompous politicians.

"Uh..." I looked over the cow's glands and ears, checking the pressure on the milking equipment attached to her udders. I inspected her gums, teeth and nostrils but found everything about her healthy and adjusted.

What I failed to find was an answer and I could feel Joseph's eyes burning a hole into the side of my head.

"Remember how someone might be trying to kill me?"

I chanced a glance at him and he didn't look nearly as angry as I thought he would.

Maybe he finally decided to get his blood pressure and cholesterol checked.

Or met up with Mr. Meden for some herbal medicine that he puff, puff, passed.

"You mean someone besides me wants to kill you?" I shrugged at his implied threat.

"Not to minimize your feelings, because your feelings are valid and you deserve credit and support in your willingness to express them."

I'd moved on to the next cow. Despite the reasonable nature of going to therapy, I wasn't above mocking the things I learned there.

Or sharing them with people who would probably never go themselves.

A good two for one sale was hard to pass up.

"In the four-quadrant graph of people who want me dead, where ability is the X axis and desire is the Y-axis, your point is practically an outlier. If we graphed it, you'd ruin the linear regression slope and be removed for more accurate data display. So don't let your blood pressure *rise* over the *run* of your mouth."

I mentally patted myself on the back for remembering math terms and hopefully bamboozling Joseph into leaving me alone. If slope calculations didn't do it, who knew what would. My memories of anti-derivatives were limited to making the swooping shape that reminded me of music notes.

"What if I scatterplot your guts all over this farm?" He challenged back and I snorted, quietly impressed he knew what one would do with a four quadrant graph. "I can do it, Cynthia! I have a tractor!"

Looking over the top of the next cow, I studied his face and decided that it was stubbornness and ego motivating his threat. Though I didn't doubt he'd poison me in a heartbeat, dismembering me would drastically cut into his drinking and dressing up with Winnie time.

No, there was something else there.

"What's going on Joseph?" I spoke calmly, even as my stomach burned with apprehension. I studied his clothes, the area around the barn, and glanced through to the slower than normal ice cream shop. It reminded me of the scene in Old Westerns where the gunslingers face off on the deserted road while the townsfolk peered through windows and a tumbleweed rolled by.

Scrubbing his hands on his face, Joseph plucked his hat off his head to fan himself.

"Some men came by last night."

"Came by where?" I decided continuing to check the cows was a better use of my time than agonizing over what the ranch manager had to say.

"Here. My wife and I had a bit of a disagreement, so I came here to give her some space," he shifted from foot to foot. "I was out in the back area..."

"Screaming at produce," I supplied, startling myself at sharing my knowledge. It was the only blackmail I had on him, and I just gave it up. Though I'd known for over nine months, I'd never actually learned why he hated the eggplants so much.

Jealousy seemed the obvious reason, what with the emoji meaning, but I hadn't wanted to ask.

"Yeah..." He didn't seem the least bit phased. Maybe he'd seen me on my nightly excursions. "These guys showed up in black cars. They were wearing all black, talking too much for trespassers, but they didn't belong here. Somehow, they went into the barn and then broke into the back of the ice cream parlor. Nothing was in their arms, they didn't seem to be stealing, but as I got close enough to yell at them to leave, I heard them talking about you."

I stiffened. That wasn't where I thought this conversation was going.

Worse, I hadn't expected the man to listen to intruders, much less use them to garner information.

I'd put him squarely in the Han Solo, "shoot first, ask questions later" category and I might owe him an apology.

"They were saying there was a lot of blood in your apartment, and someone had cleaned it up. They didn't know why they had to come to bumble fudge nowhere when you were clearly dead. Well, they didn't say fudge..." I nodded for him to keep going.

He spent too much time with children at the ice cream shop to swear freely.

"After they left, I searched the barn and the shop. Found these little devices, like big plastic pills. Couldn't find any lenses, but I... they looked like they had microphones. Before I could think it through, I drove them out to the back forty and buried them. Today... there was a smoldering hole in the ground and I thought when you didn't come in..."

My eyes stung with sentiment, and I deflected quickly.

"Aww!!! You like me! You don't want me dead!"

"I don't like you!" He swiped at his face. "It's just really hard to hire people. And you didn't call."

"You like me! You like me!"

"Cynthia!" His pink tinged ears were at odds with his concerned expression.

"Sorry."

I stared at my boots and then stuck a hand in my pocket to grab a small packet of chocolate chip cookies. I handed him the pouch and looked as remorseful as possible. When all else failed, food was my best strategy for apology.

"When I left the house today, I didn't know some jerkwad would touch my butt and I'd break his nose."

Joseph accepted the cookies and snorted.

"Don't know why. You're always punching people in the face." He opened the cookies and ate one. It was too true to argue with, so I shrugged it off and got back to work.

"People should stop underestimating women if they don't want their testicles reascended and their facial cranial muscles dislodged. I'm not a medical professional, but those men are practically begging for facial reconstruction and gender reassignment procedures, services I'm offering for free. I should get a medal... or a plaque even."

He snorted again but didn't comment.

"We good?"

He shrugged and then toed the dirt beneath his feet.

"Do you know what those people wanted?" He asked, then held up a hand. "Don't tell me what it is, but if you know... handle it. Maybe hide out from your apartment for a while..."

"You sound like Larry and Cruz," I mumbled and he crumbled the now empty blue pouch of cookies. "All of you should know better. I'm capable of taking care of myself and no one scares me out of my home."

"No one said you can't. We just asked you not to make it easy on them, kid," he reached up to pat my shoulder as he walked passed and left the barn. Staring down at the brown cow in front of me, my mind flitted back to the envelope Trigger had given me just before emergency services arrived. I'd opened it in the car, below the dashboard, in the tunnel of a car wash.

Because it's not paranoia if people really are out to get you.

Inside was the address to a storage facility in an industrial park and a four-digit gate code. There wasn't a unit number, or any reason I could think of for Trigger to store something there. A second piece of paper had longitude and latitude coordinates that pointed to a spot between Dayton and Yellow Springs that I couldn't visit in the daylight hours without drawing attention.

Tonight, however, it was game on.

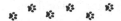

"I'm still not sure why you insisted on coming," I hissed at Winnie as she let out a grunt of annoyance. The Jeep had been built for off-road terrain, but it hadn't been built to take that terrain comfortably. Every rainstorm for the past decade had eroded the dirt road into a maze of ditches and potholes that sent Winnie bouncing toward the roof of the car. My neck cracked and popped as the seatbelt held me down, but couldn't stop the intense side-to-side jostling, and part of me considered that letting the assassins get me would hurt less.

The other, stubborn, part said "Hell no, we won't go".

As usual, Stubborn Cyn won out and we were bouncing down an unmarked road in an unfamiliar place at sunset. Every section of the sky was streaked with a different color, oranges and pinks mixing with the fading blue in a beautiful rainbow that I'd normally enjoy. Instead, every second spent looking at the sky sent me into a panic that I wasn't checking my surroundings.

Considering my surroundings were flat, undisturbed farmland as far as the eye could see, it was unfounded. My rear view mirror showed nothing besides the dust cloud my tires kicked up and a steadily more likely to throw up Winnie bouncing in and out of frame. Wherever Trigger was sending me, it was the perfect place to maintain a visual defense in all directions.

It was also a great place to murder someone without witnesses.

My stomach clenched again. It was impossible to know if Trigger was a friend or foe. Trigger, the residents of Veterans Park, Judge Hot Dog Eater... all of them were hiding something.

We hit another deep rut and the whole Jeep was briefly airborne at which point Winnie gave in. On her way back down, she threw up dirt, grass, possibly goat poop and half the dinner I'd given her before we headed out. The smell sent me careening toward the shoulder and bringing the Jeep to a stop.

Before the door was all the way open, my partner barreled out and flung herself onto the ground, rolling over onto her back and wriggling in the dirt making Winnie sand angels. It reminded me of the time we made a harrowing landing on an unmarked airstrip overseas and a few of the lesser soldiers tumbled out of the C-130 and started making out with the tarmac .

"But did you die?" I asked the dog and then caught another whiff of her vomit. "Sweet cheese and crackers. Maybe you did."

Grabbing a stack of napkins from the door, I scooped the vomit out of the car and dumped it on the side of the road. Not wanting to litter, I pulled a poop bag from the center console and tucked the napkins inside. I tied it closed and stuck the bundle on the rear tire outside of the car, scanning in all directions.

Aside from a cow or two, nothing stuck up from the ground. Checking my GPS, we were only about twenty feet from the coordinates given. Leaving all the car doors open to get rid of the smell, Winnie and I walked forward until the little dot representing me was nestled in the circle of the dot representing my destination.

We were still absolutely nowhere.

Instead of being on the road, we'd veered three feet into the shoulder. This was one of the few sections that wasn't fenced, a small ten-foot wide block strip that ran between two wooden posts marked with barbed wire to indicate boundaries. Each side formed an L shape about twenty yards back with the meeting point dead center in the strip.

"Who buys a box of land?" I asked Winnie, startled to see her nose working the ground. She didn't so much as glance at me before heading into the box of dirt, weaving back and forth. As she approached the rear boundary, her nose slowed. Fewer sniffs, but much longer and deeper.

Before she sat and looked over her shoulder.

Oh good, explosives.

A bomber bought a block of land in the middle of nowhere, buried the bombs and then gave the coordinates to an ex-assassin who owns and operates gun ranges... Or maybe decided on his own to send any people who might interfere to an early, and very scattered, grave.

"He's trying to kill me."

But that didn't really add up. Trigger wasn't really an assassin, more like a fixer.

One who worked with explosives.

That probably could have easily killed me without sending me on a treasure hunt.

"Crap."

I moved slowly toward Winnie, checking the eroded dirt for tracks. Both the land strip and the neighboring lands had been hit hard by the rain a few weeks back. Large valleys cut through the dirt, the farms on either side sporting green shoots of grass interspersed with small stacked rocks and signs of livestock pounding the earth.

The box in the center was baked dry and hard as rock.

Winnie whimpered and I looked back at her.

"What's wrong?" I asked, watching her nose. It was in the air, whirring in a full three hundred sixty degree circle as she tried to isolate whatever smell was causing her distress. Her paw went to her nose, then her ear, while the rest of her shifted uncomfortably.

"Winnie, come!" I ordered her but she laid flat on the ground over her find. "Come on..."

I ran toward the dog, telling myself I was light as a feather and my feet barely touched the ground as my boots slammed into dirt. I got to Winnie, offered her a treat and tried to attach her leash to get out of here.

Nothing that caused her discomfort was something I wanted to be near.

In a first for her, Winnie ignored the treat, tilted her head and started digging.

The ground was tough, her too-long claws scratching deep gouges in an already uneven surface. Surrounding the spot where she'd started digging were small popsicle stick crosses. They must have fallen over in the rain, each cocked at an odd angle. Instead of names, it looked like a graveyard for ideals.

Courage.

Action.

Trust.

Fidelity.

Unity.

Winnie's nails scraped metal and I turned away from the crosses. CATFU covered a few too many military operations, but it was the only indicator I had that we were in the right spot.

It also meant we probably shouldn't be here.

"Winnie, out," I ordered. Moosing her to the side so I could look into the hole she'd dug. A bright red metal latch stuck out from a rectangle with a collapsible metal handle.

"Ammo can?"

Sliding my fingers into the handle, I jerked the can, but it was stuck. Winnie circled, pawing at her ears and nose. Leaning my weight back I put all two hundred plus pounds into dislodging the ammo can, but it only gave an inch.

Winnie circled faster and let out a soft whimper.

This was bad.

This was definitely bad.

With a final yank, I got the top piece free and pulled the metal latch. The ammo can creaked but wouldn't open.

I tugged again, Winnie's whimpers turning into howls.

The latch popped off and I flipped the lid back to see a four-inch-thick file folder with papers spilling out in all directions. Pulling the whole thing out, my eye caught on a small red blinking light peeking from beneath the can. When I shifted the box to get a closer look, the light blinked faster and Winnie howled.

"Oh crap," I said, stuffing the file into the waistband of my pants and grabbing Winnie's leash.

"Run!" I shouted and we took off back toward the Jeep. The toe of my boots caught on the divots, but I didn't dare slow down. "Run faster!"

We cleared the shoulder and were halfway back to the car when Winnie let out one long ear-piercing howl and a burst of light cut through the twilight.

Behind us, where there had once been a random strip of land, was a smoking hole in the ground.

Chapter Sixteen:
Holed Up

"What was that?" I whispered, even as I slammed my head against the desk I was hiding under. "Did you hear that?"

A long loud snore rattled the small wooden shack that served as Joseph's office on the farm. Peeking out of my sleeping bag, I watched Winnie sprawled out asleep on the air mattress I'd set up between the desk and the door. The office wasn't really sized for holding a desk, an air mattress, a full-sized human and a full-sized canine, but it was the first place that came to mind when I walked into my completely trashed apartment.

Despite being very small, the area around Joseph's office was flat and clear. With small windows on each wall and a strategically placed camera, I had an uninterrupted 360 view of... farm animals. The file was stuffed into the bottom of my backpack with freeze dried coffee, two pounds of cheese crackers, a collapsible teapot , and a single burner camp stove.

Barring my discovery by murderers, I could survive with nothing besides this backpack and a freshwater source for days. Winnie, on the other hand, was already complaining that I didn't get the "good" treats when I started throwing things into my bag in a panic.

Winnie truly was not suited to a life on the run.

Not that surprising considering how often she refused to run... or wake up.

"Winnie! We're supposed to be stealthy! Keep it down!" Her next snore shook the shack and I let out an exasperated sigh as I tried to calm the rapidly beating heart in my chest. "They touched my underwear and broke my last two coffee mugs!"

A warm smear streaked down my cheek, and I swiped at it angrily.

"Don't you start making water works, face. We need to find out who these people are," I stared at my backpack like it held a severed head. "But to do that I need to look into the file."

I'd thrown the folder onto the Jeep's floorboard when we'd escaped what would likely be considered ground zero or the sight of an alien abduction if anyone ever discovered it. A picture had slid out of a man in half-military clothing with severe burns, bloody gashes through pouring out entrails and what looked like toes stuffed up his nose.

The picture had discouraged me from opening the folder and seeing what else was inside.

"It can't all be that bad... right?" I tried to give myself a pep talk even as I pictured the horror scene that was my apartment. Whoever had been there had been searching for something, that much was clear. A lot of people had keys, so the intention could have been something as simple as needing to borrow a cup of coffee.

A lie I told myself until I saw the message written in blood on my bathroom mirror: Die, Bitch.

Sure, not that creative, but the crude drawing of an X-eyed stick figure and her dog had me out of there in seconds.

Nobody threatened Winnie.

No one.

"If you want to know who did, you have to open the folder."

My arm grabbed the bag and pulled it closer, even as my brain screamed at it to stop.

The hand on that arm then opened the backpack and grabbed the folder while my heartrate spiked.

Together, the arm and the hand pulled out the folder as my two most vital organs warred against the urge to lose consciousness and have a stroke.

The folder fell onto the floor and I stared at the blank cover. Unlike in movies, there was no catchy title or mission name. Not even a big red "Top Secret" stamp.

It looked like my medical record, thick and filled with records of catastrophes.

"Disturbing," I whispered as I flashed back to the photo in my car. "Definitely don't want that in my medical record."

Picking up a pen from under Joseph's desk, I used it to flip back the cover and braced myself for pain and suffering.

Perhaps another explosion.

Instead, there was a table of contents for the enclosed reports and findings. Arturo's name was the most often appearing series of characters followed by mission, intel and massacre.

Massacre?

My stomach flipped and I pulled the whole thing closer. After reading the summary, I flipped to the reports and the statements from the Officer in Charge as well as the civilian contractors who witnessed the "un-necessary jeopardization of a complete military unit".

There were rumors of independent outfitters playing both sides just before Operation Desert Storm. Despite the growing tensions, this group capitalized on adding fuel to the fire. A covert team went in, tracked rumors and stories for weeks only to come up against a group of mercenaries armed with American weapons and specialized training.

There was a firefight, one that had numerous casualties on both sides. The squadron leader, Arturo Denicourt, was accused of leading his men into a known ambush that resulted in their capture and execution. After his "cowardly" retreat, the soldiers left behind were killed on a secure broadcast. There was an image of their bodies lined up and laid out, hands tied behind prone backs and sacks over their faces.

A fact that sat at odds with the statements indicating no living service members had been left behind and the deceased ones recovered several hours later.

There also wasn't a list naming the victims or record of family notification.

A man hunt for the group leader ended with his death and dismemberment at the hands of a contractor. Initially listed as identity unknown. No known connections to active watchlists.

No groups took ownership.

Then an anonymous tip led to his capture and...

The dismembered body I'd seen was the supposed leader. I studied it again, fighting back vomit. My own countrymen did this, despite the rules of engagement and legal standing of trial. Contractors were still held to the same standards as soldiers and whoever had done this hadn't abided by any known peace accords.

I flipped the picture over.

Taped to the back of the image was... "Andrew Marks?"

Winnie was still snoring and didn't comment.

It was a staged High School senior year photo of a pimple faced male. His chin was fairly narrow, eyes somewhat beady and the smile wasn't friendly. Flipping from the back image to the front, I tried to figure out if there were any tell-tale characteristics that this was the same person.

Since the man on the front was severely disfigured, there wasn't enough to compare. The report identified the decedent as Mahammad Rajeem, which stood at odds with the whiter than Wonder Bread kid taped to the back.

There was no flesh left on the dead guy for me to classify a nationality.

On impulse, I shot off a text to Cruz with the picture of Andrew Marks with a question mark and a skull and cross-bones emoji.

I'd have encrypted it, but the cracked lens on my camera was almost as effective at making the image blurred enough to be anyone.

Setting both pictures aside, I grabbed the stack of screen grabs pulled from the supposedly secure video sent to... I double checked the report. No one knew the intended destination of the video but Eagle Enforcers had intercepted it.

Eagle Enforcers... my brain connected it to something earlier in the report, but I focused instead on the images. The close up of approximately seven soldiers sporting a bullet hole in the back, with perfectly even lengths of rope and dirt crusted fingernails but...

"Where's the blood?" I asked aloud and flipped through all the pictures again. Aerial view of all of them, close up of each of their hands and gunshot wounds. No faces, no identifying markings...

And none of the wounds had blood at the entry point.

The ground around the bodies didn't have any blood either. It also lacked any sort of displacement in the dirt, like the victims had been placed there already dead.

Dead bodies were the only ones that couldn't move and make dents in the sand, but if they were already dead, why were they tied up?

Half of the bound hands were done at awkward angles. It reminded me of biology class when the frog's legs had already succumbed to rigor mortis, and we had to snap the bones to dissect it.

Did someone tie up dead bodies?

I checked for autopsy reports, curious if any of the arms were broken, but came up empty. There was no detail on the victims, no names, ranks or familial notifications.

It was like a massive plot hole in a CSI show.

"No record of execution, no blood, signs of rigor mortis when being tied up... did someone execute cadavers?"

A distorted recording of "There She Goes" erupted from my pocket and I screamed.

"Oh dog, hello?" I answered my phone, receiving face licks from Winnie who'd been startled awake and thought I was dying. My heart rate agreed with her, and I wondered how long my cardiovascular system could survive going this pace because it wasn't going back down.

I might have to take up smoking Mr. Meden's Skunk Stash.

"Cynthia! Where are you?"

The deep voice cracked on the vowels, and I pictured a woman in her 80s with blue-grey hair. Stooped shoulders, floral themed shapeless apparel... No name came with the image.

"I'm at the farm. Why?" I rubbed Winnie's head against my cheek. It was a big place and finding me with that information alone wouldn't be easy.

"I need your help! I'm at your office and it's all dark!" Her words were interrupted by a thick wet coughing. "Someone stole my car and I need you to find it!"

"Why don't you call the police?" I asked, wondering how my phone number was easier than 9-1-1.

"I did! That good for nothing dum dum said he was busy and it was your turn to earn your keep in this town." She tutted at the end and it turned into a hiccup that ended on a burp. "I'll just go in and wait for you to get home. Looks like there's another person waiting on the same thing. You should post your business hours so people don't..."

"What other person? Don't go inside. Go home, text me the last known address of the car and don't open the door for anyone but me," I scrambled up and started stuffing pictures and papers back into the folder. I heard a few more hiccups and then what was potentially both a burp and a fart.

Drunk old lady near would be murderers, so not good.

When it was mostly put back together, I tossed it in the backpack and grabbed Winnie's leash.

"What is wrong with you? It's just a black car. Couple of men inside."

"Listen to me, Mrs..." I had no idea which one of the senior citizens was on my phone. If her breath matched her voice, she'd had enough that her name may have escaped her as well.

"It's Mrs. Elliot, Cynthia. You kids these days have the memories of..." My brain pulled up her face, hair and the unfortunate memory that she'd kept the church Bingo money in her unmentionables drawer and hadn't been wrong since I was dirtying diapers.

Her words.

"Mrs. Elliot, go home. Don't look at or talk to those men. Text me the car's license plate and the last known address of your car."

I was only offering to look for her car to get her away from my office. There was no way I was going to look for her missing car, but as long as she believed I would, the woman would return home to safety and I could finally get some answers.

Winnie and I hustled toward the Jeep, Mrs. Elliot sounding prickly on the other end as I fought for air.

"I can't send you an address, Cynthia!" she shouted over my panting.

"Why not?" I asked, starting the engine and backing out of the parking lot.

"Because it's been stolen for twenty years! You need to find it so I can smash it to pieces for the insurance money!"

I hit the brakes and listened to the engine tick.

"Your car has been missing... for twenty years?"

"Yes! My good-for-nothing husband bought it and when I said no, he hid it somewhere. Never even saw it except when I noticed a few thousand missing from the account. He tried to swear it was never there but you know my numbers are never wrong. Did I tell you about-"

"The car Mrs. Elliott. Tell me about the car!"

"So impatient, always 'skip to the good part'. What happened to enjoying the journey?"

I let out an exasperated breath and glanced around the farm for something sharp to impale myself on but came up blank. My plan to get her to go home so I could confront the men in the car was waylaid by my desire to break into Joseph's liquor stash and let whoever was in the car take on Mrs. Elliot.

As usual, my money was on the old lady.

"Anyway, he's dead, I need you to find it and set it on fire!" She cackled and I smacked my head on the steering wheel. To my left, a shadow darted across the field, and I moved the Jeep to shine the low beam parking headlights toward the figure moving toward the back forty.

Two figures and they were holding something with a dim green glow.

"OK, go home and I'll come by to help with the car."

I hung up before she could criticize my generation for yet another thing and turned the Jeep off. Winnie and I got out and tried to move with stealth.

We failed almost immediately when the side view mirror cracked after colliding with the center of my chest.

"Ow..." I hissed, rubbing my sternum and grabbing for Winnie's leash.

The dog was gone.

"Winnie!" I whisper shouted.

Nothing.

"Winnie!" I stalked toward the moving figures, trying to keep to the shadows and listen for the sound of her paws hitting the ground. "Winnie!"

The two shadowy figures picked up pace, and I heard the gentle metallic clink of Winnie's tags.

"Shoot the dog!" A male voice shouted and I picked up my pace, reaching for the handgun in my cargo pocket.

"I can't see a damn dog. Find the devices, you idiot!" The second voice was also male, but a lower baritone to the original guy's alto. I raised my gun and sighted toward the sound, but there was nothing to see.

"Get the damn-" Alto voice started, but was cut off by a shout, a thump and then silence.

"Gilroy!" Baritone started and I gave up on stealth. Flicking on my flashlight, I angled it up at a man in all black with a square jaw hidden by a ski mask, and a beer gut that strained against the rib-knit shirt he was sweating through.

"Stop!" I shouted, and he turned around too fast. Winnie was moving too fast to stop and she plowed into him. The man screamed and fell backward, disappearing completely into the darkness.

I ran over to Winnie, gun at the ready with my flashlight hand crossed under.

"Winnie, clear!" I ordered. She turned abruptly and I stumbled, dropping my flashlight while sliding forward like a batter stealing home. My arms scraped the sand and I slid to a halt, my head hanging over the edge into a giant crater.

"What-" my flashlight caught up and rolled down the side bouncing end over end to land with a metallic clunk on a disturbed concrete rock bed.

The light rolled a little more, revealing two bodies dressed all in back with small red splats beside them and heads at unnatural angles.

Chapter Seventeen: Joint Ops

I woke up sore, tired and wishing I was in bed.

Not necessarily my bed, but not under a desk in a sleeping bag with my backpack for a pillow. Winnie had retained custody of the air mattress as my intruder warning alarm and my hand had stayed wrapped around my gun all night after the dead bodies were carted away. After questioning, identification and large amounts of paperwork, both deaths were classified as an inexplicable accident.

At least on paper.

Gilroy the Alto was fresh off the turnip truck.

A literal turnip truck, as he delivered produce for one of the major grocers in the area. While detained in the back of a police car, I'd read on the mobile data unit that he'd been arrested previously for voyeurism, electronic manipulation, explosives possession and petty theft.

It was likely his devices that had created the crater that killed him.

Baritone, however, was the reason I was locked up.

Captain Dick Preznall, presently suspended and under psychiatric review for fitness of service, was the second dead body. When my initial response was to ask Judge Pestolli if I still had to show up for the Skid Marks hearing, they thought it was a planned attack on an eyewitness and respected law enforcement professional.

A claim I was both too tired and too annoyed to refute, so I remained in custody.

If not for the fact I could nap in a locked police car surrounded by law enforcement professionals, I'd have found the situation inconvenient. Since one of their own was part of the group trying to kill me, it wasn't a restful sleep but still safer than my ransacked apartment.

My backpack had remained in the Jeep and rather than risk anyone looking through or for the file, I instructed Winnie to sit inside on alert.

At least four less-than-seasoned officers had peed themselves by getting too close.

The memory brought a smile to my face while I popped my shoulder, back and hips. Each pop and snap reminded me that I was way too old to sleep on the floor.

It also reminded me that if they'd managed to kill me, it probably would have hurt less.

But noooo, you're too stubborn to just die, my brain snickered.

Really, it was true and a little insulting that the master controller of my body didn't have a greater sense of self preservation. My phone buzzed with an unknown number and I stared at it while considering if it was safe to talk to strangers before coffee.

The answer was no, but I answered anyway.

"What?"

"You sound like shit, chica," Cruz chuckled through the line and I angrily pressed the end call button lamenting the loss of the handheld phone receiver and cradle. No one calls me before coffee and then insults me.

At least not a body that had once been very intimately connected with mine.

Phone buzzing in my pocket, I took Winnie with me down to the barn. At the far end was a quasi-break room with a kitchenette and an industrial coffee maker that spewed sludge for the half-alive.

Blissfully, the sludge was already brewed and I poured a cup that smelled like burnt mud. Since it had a similar consistency to pudding, I grabbed a handful of sugar packets, ripped off the tops and dumped the crystals in.

When the stir stick remained upright in the cup after I stirred it, I grabbed a spoon and dug in.

As promised, it was disgusting.

But now that I'd had it, I decided to answer the phone in my pocket.

"Yeah?" I spoke around a steaming mouthful of sludge.

"Did you drink coffee?" Cruz asked, sounding like a more subdued version of the man I'd hung up on.

That'll teach him.

"More or less," I spooned another lump into my mouth and swallowed through the bitter burn. "What have you got for me?"

I heard his response in my head before he could speak and I growled into the line to stop his joke.

"You used to be more fun until someone tried to kill you. Where did you get that picture?" The question came out light and easygoing but the unknown number hinted at his own hesitations and fears.

"Found it. Who is he?"

"Andrew Marks is a runaway from Greenbill, Alabama. Last seen at the age of 15 in 1985 when he left school and never came back. Reports say there was a history of abuse in the home, but nothing ever stuck. A body was found in the childhood home, the pictures a gnarly. There wasn't enough for an ID, but they think it was his Dad. The remains showed signs of being strangled, then dismembered, and covered in burn marks. He was discovered a week after Andrew was seen leaving school and the estimated date of death matches that departure, but the body was too large to be Andrew Marks."

His voice was carefully neutral, but I felt sick at the implications.

Was Andrew the mutilated man in the photo? Or was he the person who'd mutilated him?

"What about the license plate of the car Mrs. Elliot saw in front of my building?" I compartmentalized the first part into Future Nightmares and kept spooning caffeinated sludge into my mouth.

When the older woman had sobered up, she apologized for her drunken outburst and sent me a photo of the car in front of my building. It had an out of state plate with government tags that kept Anita from getting through the red tape to the owner.

"Expired government contractor plate..." Cruz flipped through paper on the other end and I scraped my spoon around the mostly empty coffee mug. "Eagle Enforcers, last operated overseas in the early nineties... Plate not fully... That's weird, this name..."

Cruz trailed off but my synapses started firing simultaneously.

"Get me everything you know about them," I ordered, hanging up the phone and grabbing my backpack from under the table.

"Winnie!" I whistled and she trotted out of a cow pen, straw sticking out of her fur. "Come on. I need a computer."

Breaking and entering wasn't really in my skill set.

If it were, I'd have used Amber's computer to frame her and lead the killers there. As it was, there were very few places I could think of with multiple computer terminals, secure internet access, and people who wouldn't question my day-old clothing, rumpled hair and dog. The list of people who owed me badly enough to risk their computer and life was an even smaller circle and only one spot sat at the intersection within a reasonable driving distance.

Dr. Pestolli's office computer in the Veterans Affairs hospital.

"So... I'm really sorry," he muttered again, propping open the fire door off of the parking structure. Winnie and I walked in and made straight for his underground office. Like the Haunted Mansion, it had no windows and only one door and offered the chilling challenge of not running out of it screaming.

"Do you need... anything?"

He stood in the doorway watching me boot up the computer and I shook my head.

"Best if you go on your rounds and lock the door behind you. Stay away for a couple hours and you never saw me," I said, not looking directly at him while plugging my phone into his CPU. This next bit was going to be tricky and if there were any cameras in the hall, he wasn't going to get away with squat.

"Right," he responded, letting the door close behind him. It clicked locked and I got to work pulling up the encryption sequence program Mrs. Margot's niece had provided me for petty revenge and general tom foolery.

Her niece was a hacker, some sort of gray hat if my ten minutes of internet searching into the subject was to be believed. The woman had been instrumental on multiple occasions in identifying leaks, lies and losing information. This particular sequence was meant to get me into the Sweet Pea Police Department Personnel records to modify Daniel's resume and qualifications after he tried to call me a two-bit investigator from the sticks.

Sadly, Carla had caught me changing his previous job title to Butt Licker and threatened to give Winnie cheese if I didn't put it right.

Chief Sharp was either really mature or really good at her job. Maybe both.

Since the system I wanted into was also a government personnel file, I could only hope it would function the same. Using the employee log in screen and the name of the now deceased captain, I initiated the encryption to enter the user portal as a dead man.

If the system was set up properly, I'd be flagged and descended upon by the Men in Black immediately. My hope was that they were as inefficient as every other government agency and it would take a few days to mark the account inactive.

As the green loading bar worked its magic, I looked around the doctor's office and saw photos of his wife, diploma and board certification as a specialist of... something typed in an illegible font. Proctology, maybe? Winnie could give him a run for his money in that area if someone taught her what abnormalities in the area smelled like... assuming cancer had a smell.

It also could have said Podiatry which Winnie had zero skills in the field of.

The entire medical field appeared to have taken a Hippocratic Oath with a secret subsection dedicated to ensuring anything they wrote would be completely illegible.

A soft double beep came from the desktop and I was looking at the former Captain's employee dashboard. Despite my curiosity regarding his pay and beneficiaries, there were only two pieces of information I needed and neither of them related to the fate of his income.

I clicked on his applications submitted tab and scrolled through work history until I reached his 1980s and 1990s entries. Unlike most men of his age in law enforcement, his work history didn't reflect military service. He'd been born in the 1950s and I scribbled his social security number onto a piece of paper to check whether or not his "number" had come up. A lot of men had been drafted to Vietnam... What were the chances he wouldn't go?

And what are the chances they wouldn't let him?

For a fifteen year period, he held increasingly responsible positions as Field Analyst, Operations Support and finally Acquisitions Manager, the managing agency listed as Contract Specialists, LLC. The address was listed as international and worldwide, so I copied the name, opened a secure browser to search for the holding company that owned the LLC.

"Crap," I said, even as the computer showed what I'd already suspected. "He worked for Eagle Enforcers, Winnie. What are the chances it was just a coincidence?"

Her dancing eyebrows indicated that she didn't believe in such things.

That or she was cooking a really juicy fart and wanted me to let down my defenses.

The company didn't have a website, but Preznall's resume had a contact phone number. A quick reverse-address search and they had a registered location in Dayton, about two blocks from the police station.

Something metal clattered to the floor in the hallway and Winnie whipped her head around at the sound of someone shouting.

"What are you doing down here? This isn't a public area," Nurse Pluto's voice carried and I fervently wished that Dr. Pestolli's office had a window.

"We were looking for uhh... The..." a deep voice responded and I ran it through my memory banks for familiarity. "The ice machine?"

His voice went up at the end and I could sense Nurse Pluto's rising hackles with a frosty reply.

"Then why are you standing beside a vending machine in an employees only hallway?"

An image of the machine came to mind and I knew they were just around the corner. If I left now, it was a clear shot to the parking structure exit. Popping the door lock quietly, Winnie and I stepped into the hallway and moved slowly toward the fire door, listening as a man tried arguing with the God Of War in nurse form.

"Our friend is down here; we just need to visit her!" a woman supplied and her voice gave me pause.

I knew her. How did I know her?

We stalled a second too long.

"There! It's her!"

I chanced a glance over my shoulder and saw two dark suits with semi autos pointed in my direction.

"Run!" I shouted to Winnie and she led the charge toward the green Exit sign. A shot ricocheted off the cement walls and I fought the urge to duck and just kept running. My fingers crashed into the metal release bar and another shot destroyed the green sign, showering the floor behind me in sparks while we ran to the Jeep.

Winnie hopped in the backseat the second the door was open and I turned over the engine, flooring the gas pedal just in time to see the two suits occupying the doorway in my rearview mirror. While the man had his gun aimed at the back of my car, the woman had a cell phone pressed to her face, sparks from the ruined sign catching the small rhinestones in her inch long manicured fingers.

The Kardashian Wannabe from the donkey photo incident was a trained killer working for the bad guys.

"Essie should have *so* let Esther trample that lady," I huffed, watching marked police cars with lights and sirens descend on the hospital. "Now what?"

Chapter Eighteen:
Lost and Found

"**N**ow what?" turned out to be an invalid question.

After circling the area for ten minutes, we went on a quest to find the puppeteer holding all the strings.

Winnie and I drove to the address listed for Eagle Enforcers and found a vacant lot. It wasn't fenced off, under construction, nor tainted with the black soil of a recently exploded land mine.

It had crab grass covering a sandy surface between two residential units in a suburban tract outside of Dayton. The houses surrounding it teemed with life forms- children playing with balls in driveways, adults hosing off their walks, small dogs yapping at the windows, and various homeowners conducting landscape maintenance... Everything was perfectly ordinary and absolutely terrifying.

"When the robots invade, it will look exactly like this. A 1950s sitcom came to life," I whispered to Winnie, even though we were in the Jeep and strategically parked well out of earshot with the engine running. A kid shouting about missing Paw Patrol on television calmed my nerves. "Definitely not robots... yet."

Hand on my keys, I prepared to kill the engine and start asking questions, hoping in vain that I would walk into a TV screen instead of down a residential street. Like someone decided the world's biggest television set belonged in Ohio masquerading as a suburb. The phone rang, startling me so badly, I accidentally activated the call.

"Cyn?" The voice came from my car's speakers, and I checked the caller ID.

Unknown number.

Stuck in the suburbs with an unknown caller? *Hello hell*.

"Yeah?" I asked cautiously, trying to Google the digits.

"It's Pluto. I need you to get back here," the nurse from the hospital said, voice humorless for the first time since we met. "As soon as you can."

The Jeep was already in drive, and I turned out of the suburban bliss that would haunt my nightmares. It felt like driving out of a movie theater showing the world's worst movie.

"On my way, what happened?"

"Someone shot Arturo... it doesn't look good."

Arturo Denicourt looked out of place in the too-bright hospital room.

His once looming frame was laid out with a sheet draped over his lower body. Instead of a cigarette, his lips held a breathing tube in place while a clear sack provided liquids into a weathered arm of leathery skin. An expression filled face gone slack with medication and sedation offered a glimpse into his life before the military.

Before someone ruined his life.

Ruined a lot of lives.

The idea that somewhere out there was a person or a group of persons that had killed a bunch of soldiers made my skin crawl. Thinking that the man clinging to life in front of me was somehow made to feel responsible... made my blood boil.

He didn't deserve to be in surgery.

And he didn't deserve to be punishing himself.

Not based on what I'd seen.

"Where did this happen?" I asked from the other side of the observation glass. A team of medical professionals were dancing around him in a choreography involving sharp objects and extreme lighting. None of them, including the pea green scrubs and hospital gown could make this look elegant or anything other than terrifying while happening to someone other than me. "When did it happen?"

Beside me, Dr. Denicourt was rubbing at a tear-stained face trying to keep himself together. It was an admirable effort, but his father was shot in the shoulder. The trauma to his human form was proving non-life-threatening, a minor reassurance to an average person.

To a child watching his father bleed?

He'd earned the right to fall apart, despite the Hippocratic Oath. As an audiologist, he wasn't able to help in this area, but he looked compelled to lay his doctorate on the line for any medical promise of success. Without any ability to make that happen, the man should have at least allowed himself to cry openly and loudly.

Like a soap opera actress discovering her lover is her father-kind of bawling.

Instead, he just stood there. Looking less alive than the man on the table.

Reaching out, I gripped his shoulder, jolting him back with a start.

"Sorry... I... did you ask something?"

His composure broke and the tears started falling. Cautiously, I repeated my question.

"Just before the shooting downstairs. It's why the cops were so quick to get here, he was shot on his usual collection rounds," everything was half incoherent with snot, but I got the general idea. He was picking up recyclables and someone had fired on him.

221

"Was it a drive by or close-range?"

I was unable to get a sense of the wound through the glass and standing here felt wrong. If I wasn't helping find answers, then I wasn't helping at all. Dr. Denicourt shrugged and I scrunched up my face trying to weigh the possibility of getting info from the man.

Not great. At least not about this, I decided, and switched gears.

"Did they arrest whoever was doing the shooting downstairs?" I tried not to sound too concerned. We'd been standing in the open for ten minutes and I hadn't bothered to check my surroundings. A gunshot wound to the shoulder wasn't life threatening if kept clean and dry.

Not thinking to check for additional gunmen was.

I checked the area and found the ward secured with limited entry and exit points.

"Yeah. They're in holding over at Dayton P.D."

"OK," I nodded and offered the man a gentle shoulder pat of reassurance. "Hang in there."

Stepping away, I walked down the hall, checking doors and rooms for hiding places and signs of entry. At the very end was a mop closet and, after checking the hall one last time, I ducked in to use my phone.

"Judge Pestolli?" I asked when a grunt came over the line after four rings.

"What? Do you know what day of the week it is?" She grumble-shouted and I looked down at my Garmin... dead. I pulled the phone away from my ear to check the screen, cracked. I tugged at the waistband of my pants but all I saw was pink.

Right, don't own Day of the Week undies...

"Not really, no. But I need your help," I said into the phone and movement on her end told me that she was working toward comprehensive human status, so I waited. Circling the closet, it held cleaning supplies and bathroom supply refills.

"With what?"

Water came over the line and I assumed she was filling a coffee maker of some sort.

"Two humans were arrested for shooting at me in the hospital," I started and all movement on her end stopped. "No one got hurt, but someone also shot one of the homeless men from the park. I think I know why, but in order to find out who, I need to know the social security numbers and names of the people in custody."

"What do you need that for?" Her distrust came through the line.

"Because the address linked to Captain Skidmark's former employer is a vacant lot. His resume doesn't even have an address, just a name and a number. The number linked to the lot, but the business itself doesn't have a digital presence. If I can find the W-2s filed by the employees, I can get the EIN of the company and maybe find a better address. One that is actually a place?"

She seemed to consider my words carefully before resuming her coffee prep. I crossed my fingers that whatever was coming out of my mouth made as much sense as it had in my head. My knowledge of taxes, tax IDs, and employer/employee record keeping was limited to the minute amount of research I'd done to get Sharp Investigations into compliance and a ten-minute Schoolhouse Rock video about how bills become laws to a really catchy tune. It left out a whole bunch of important factors, lobbyists and questionable funding, but it gave the illusion we knew what we were doing.

It also gave me the impression the government was gaslighting children, so score one for the Communists.

"Why would the address be more accurate on a W-2 than a resume for an employee tasked with keeping their secrets? Also, how did you see his resume?"

"Because no one messes with the IRS. The fastest way to get caught running a scheme is to not pay taxes on it. They are also a government contractor and while they aren't well-known for good judgment, the department of defense can work Google maps. They'd see a vacant lot and look into it... as would the IRS when the business didn't show any sort of operational base payments..."

The verbal vomit worked at avoiding her question regarding my digital B and E.

"Whoa, slow down Skippy. One conspiracy theory at a time," she took a long drink, and I made a mental note to get the brand of her amazingly quick coffee maker. "I can get you all of the EINs and tax filings you want, they're public records and I know where to look. But what happens after you have the address?"

"I go and talk to the landlord or tenant of said address and say 'hey! I see that you're paying some people who want to kill me, what's up with that?' and then maybe someone will arrest them?" It was not one of my better plans, but it was the best I could come up with on no sleep and inadequate coffee. If the good judge were here, I'd totally steal hers.

"Also, I don't just want the address. I want a complete payroll list of everyone who has filed as an employee of that business for the past... twenty years? Or that they filed an employee payment to or for... how the hell do taxes work?"

"No one knows how taxes work. All I know is you pay them and you don't go to prison or have to live in a sailboat off the coast of an uncharted island. If I can find the information you need, will you come up with a better plan than the one you just told me?"

"Like creeping around outside the private residence of who-ever has the highest income listed until I catch him twirling his mustache and laughing evilly over the piles of money and corpses with a big cup of whiskey?" I asked, inspecting the shelves in the storage closet. I'd absent mindedly begun shifting the toilet paper, surprised they kept bleach behind something that went directly on human skin. Behind the bleach was surface disinfec-tant, which was as odd as the bleach, considering you'd need easy access to both. Facing it on the opposite wall was glass cleaner, paper towel refills and... more bleach?

"Damn," I moved the small line of bleach bottles, noticing they matched all the ones on the other side. Positioned in the space behind them was a large bundle that didn't quite fit on the shelf. The lump wrapped in a hospital gown didn't move, a positive sign it might just be hidden laundry someone didn't want to do.

I tugged it slightly until an arm flopped over the side and smacked me in the face.

"Eee!" I screamed, dropping the cell phone from my hand and sending it clattering across the floor.

I stepped back, hoping it still worked and tripped on the mop bucket. Before I could stop myself, I grabbed the nearest item to keep me from falling.

Unfortunately, it was the hand of the dead person.

More unfortunate, the body was not secured to the shelf and the corpse tumbled off the shelf and pinned me to the ground.

With my head in a dirty mop bucket.

"Help!" I shouted as two security guards burst into the room clutching handheld radios.

"Oh, thank god," the first man said, gripping the corpse under its arms and pulling it off. The second guard looked around, noticing the open gown and his coworker touching the skin of a dead person, went pale and vomited into the mop bucket that was still holding my hair.

Chapter Nineteen: Displacement

"I can't believe you found Mr. Petrosian!" A lab coat said from the other side of my shower box. "He's been missing for days, and we were starting to think the worst."

While I personally considered being dead and stuffed into a closet shelf an example of "the worst", the hospital staff had other ideas. Hypotheses that he'd been abducted, walked into traffic, fell asleep in the morgue and was confused for dead, or buried himself alive in the center court garden were all vastly worse than having your dead body neatly placed on a shelf by bleach.

I shampooed my hair a fourth time and still felt unclean. Getting crushed by a corpse and vomit on my hair had earned me exactly two minutes and twenty-six seconds of quiet in my shower before rubbernecking medical professionals and over-en-thusiastic security staff insisted on hearing the story and filling each other in on the man I'd found.

"Can you believe she found Pete?"

A new voice joined the first and I waited for the story to be repeated once again while I stood naked in water.

After getting me out of the mop bucket, I was swiftly relocated into a patient room with a private bath for "hygiene reasons". I had no concept of how long I had been showering, hot water not being a concern in the hospital, but my pruney flesh indicated it had been awhile.

And in that while, at least ten people had walked into my "private bath" to talk about Pete and ask questions.

None of them considered my nudity or showering any reason to shut the door and leave.

Apparently naked in a hospital was not a barrier to conversation and privacy was a relative term.

"Actually... we don't know who the dead guy is..." A third voice joined the first two and I held my breath. Whoever this new person was sounded both terrified and excited at having the juiciest gossip in the room.

"What do you mean 'we don't know'? It's Pete, I've been giving him his drugs for years. I know Pete," the lab coat turned away from my shower stall and I waited for an explanation out of the latest arrival. The character described in the anecdote portrayed Pete Petrosian as a squirrely patient residing in the psychiatric ward. The man was prone to "wandering off" and getting handsy with himself while other people were watching. He had a fear of needles and blood that made him ill-suited to patient life, and a bad-habit of "cheeking" his meds and complaining of auditory nuisances no one else could hear.

He was the human version of Winnie and apparently couldn't be bribed with peanut butter or porn.

Nothing in the depiction painted him as a criminal, an imposter, or especially good at hide and seek before he either crawled on a shelf and died or was killed and put there.

No one had yet seen fit to gossip about the manner of death as it was apparently the least interesting part about the dead man in the closet.

"That's the guy who said he was Mr. Petrosian, but now that they're autopsying him... the blood types and fingerprints don't match, his missing Naval record populated our system an hour ago and his dental records and physicality don't match either... The real Mr. Petrosian had a family, one who's been mourning his death overseas for a few decades," I expected one of the others to gasp at his declaration, but it would seem the drama in my head was not on par with the drama outside the shower stall.

People pretending to be other people for medical care might be more common than street walkers.

"Ms. Sharp?" I jumped out of my skin at the sight of a nurse knocking on my shower door. Her head barely reached the midline of the shower and even without the raised floor, I knew she wasn't more than five feet tall.

"Yeah?" I asked, shutting off the water and looking at her through the tempered glass.

Five feet tall and 100 lbs. Winnie was bigger than her.

"We have some scrubs for you to wear," the door opened slightly, and a threadbare hand towel was passed to me. It looked like something that might get the job done in pediatrics, but I'd need six more to become anything even remotely comparable to dry.

"Do you have... grown-up sized towels?"

It was challenging, but I managed to wrap the small square around my hair.

"Yes, but..." my eyes sharpened at the frame, and I popped open the door to face a nurse with eyes the size of dog-dishes. "There's a bunch of armed people here and they're asking to see you. I thought you might want to... run?"

I blinked at the small woman, guessing her age at 18 or 19.

"Nah. But if I can have those scrubs, I'll make them really uncomfortable by not wearing a bra and undies."

She passed them over and I choked.

"Are these... yours?" I asked and she nodded, face bright red.

"I thought you... would be shorter..." It was too much, I doubled over laughing. Shorter was about to be the least of my problems when I had a thigh the same size as her head. "I can try to find..."

"Don't worry about it," I smiled at her and pulled the scrub top over my head. The boxy fabric had zero stretch and once my arms were inside, it was obvious the size medium would have to be cut off me. Arms pinned nearly to my side, I squatted to the pants and pulled them up, wrestling the fabric over the round spheres of my butt and having to shimmy them past hips that challenged the tensile strength of the thread holding them together.

I glanced in the mirror at my look.

The shirt was a crop top, my boobs were pushed to my ears and beneath my belly, the pants were cutting off circulation to my lower extremities and had already made an angry red line in my gut. If they had been green and purple, I'd have looked like The Incredible Hulk in Bruce Banner's clothing.

"Well... that's a look..." I stammered, turning toward the now scarlet nurse. "Take me to the gunmen!"

I raised a fake sword in a Monty Python manner.

"Are you..." her voice dropped to a whisper. "What if they kill you? You don't want to die dressed like that!"

The laugh that slipped out was hysterical.

"At this point, seeing me in this is their punishment for trying to kill me."

I gestured for her to lead the way and marveled at her tiny frame and voluminous curly black hair. A lesser woman would have been wearing a neck brace just to support the raven bunches beside her ears.

All speaking stopped when I walked into the room.

"What are you-"

"Holly, we have other-"

A wolf-whistle silenced everyone, and I turned to the red-headed bombshell in the door.

"Hot, right?"

I motioned with my hand the length of my body, knowing that my sister-in-law would support my unfashionable choices.

Just like she supported my psychotic niece, autistic nephew, and brother, Carla was dependable and just weird enough to not arrest my parents for... There were so many things she could arrest them for. It was best not to fall down that rabbit hole.

I turned back to the young woman I thought might be Holly.

"Are these the 'bunch of people with guns'?" I asked and she nodded.

"Don't tell them about the..." she made a running gesture with her fingers.

"Your secret is safe. That's my sister-in-law, Carla Sharp, Sweet Pea Chief of Police. The goofy looking idiot next to her is Daniel, he married the high school diva and transmits diseases. Two people though, is hardly a bunch unless..."

A third person stuck his head around the doorframe.

"Larry? Do you have a gun?"

"Just the one in my pants," he cracked a grin and I heard a few women behind me swoon.

I blushed hard at the third person giving me a heated once over. He still looked exhausted and scraggly, but his eyes had some of their normal humor and light back. The overly graphic humor was new, but it was possible he'd been forced to spend extra time with his brother and some of the douche-ness had worn off.

If my arms worked, I might have hugged him.

"What's a Sweet Pea?" Holly asked and every other nurse in the room shrugged. She turned back to Carla and the woman performed a herculean miracle by not laughing. "Is it a place or a fictional place? Are you in a TV show? What channel is it on?"

"It's a town, not too far from here. It has been on TV, but mostly it features in YouTube videos starring Cyn and Winnie. I need Cynthia, does anyone in this room have additional questions for Ms. Sharp?" Everyone shook their heads and I smiled before performing an exaggerated bow and exiting.

"Where's Winnie?" Larry asked immediately after I exited the room. Before I could process the movement, he tugged off his sweatshirt and pulled it over my head. Grabbing something from Daniel, a cold piece of metal preceded the loud *rip* of fabric. A breeze on my back came with a delight release of pressure and I took my first deep breath since being crushed by a dead body.

"She's guarding the car... and thanks."

Now that my arms functioned, I pulled off the open backed scrub top and stuck them through the sweatshirt holes. Larry moved the blade to a side seam of the scrub pants and started sawing at the drawstring.

"Never thought my hottest fantasy, cutting you out of your clothes, would happen in front of my brother."

His breath tickled my neck, and I could feel his fingers trying to wander. The tight fabric against my skin didn't yield to his hands or the knife, a fact that was both reassuring to my sanity and disappointing to my raging hormones that could use the shot of dopamine. "It's been so *hard* since we broke up..."

"Enough, Larry," Carla scolded, and we followed her down a staircase to the Employees Only hallway. The shell casings were gone, but the exit sign still featured bullet holes and exposed wiring. "Walk me through what happened here."

Deciding it couldn't hurt, I told her about borrowing Dr. Pestolli's computer to look for Preznall's past employers. That Nurse Pluto had given me advance warning, but I got tripped up when one of the women from the Princess Farm Incident turned out to be a shooter.

"Eagle Enforcers? I know that... why do you know that?" Her face was now carefully blank and I poker-faced back at her.

"How do you know them?"

"Answer me first?" She raised an eyebrow threateningly and I crossed my arms under my chest.

"No. You first."

I had flashes of images from her past life. Working as a honey trap agent for alphabet agencies nationwide, if she knew them, she could be both a threat or in danger.

There was so much about my new sister-in-law that was a complete mystery and I couldn't risk Trigger or the folder. Not when so many people were shooting at me recently.

"Target or client?"

"Both," she answered and blew out a breath. "When are you going to start trusting me?"

"Back at you, Carla," I countered, and she seemed to reach some sort of decision.

"Eagle Enforcers was a military contractor. For several decades, they operated almost independently under the blanket of US operations, but they overstepped. A few agents, myself included, found ourselves receiving orders from someone new. They'd hacked the system and were using us, but by the time we figured it out, they'd ghosted. No records, no databases, just a blank slate that used to be a multi-million dollar corporation," she paused, considering her next words carefully.

"They've been linked to past incidents, ones that never quite came to light, and no one was held accountable."

"Like a massacre in Kuwait for which a man was imprisoned for 20 years?" I asked and she nodded once. "Why hasn't anyone done anything? Arturo's been on the streets-"

"You found Arturo?" Her gaze sharpened and I tilted my head, confused.

"Yeah, his son works here. He's been living in the park but someone shot him. He's in surgery upstairs."

Carla pulled out her phone and started running back into the hospital.

"This is Carla, lock the building down. They're cleaning house and they've infiltrated the staff," she shouted into the phone, and I took off after her. My legs impeded by the too small pants, I had to take three times the normal amount of steps I'd normally have and she still had a significant lead.

"What the hell? Are you saying Dr. Denicourt is a fraud?" I fought to get air in my lungs as we went after her.

"I'm saying Arturo's son still lives in Phoenix and has been searching for his dad for two decades."

Chapter Twenty:
Locked Down

D r. Denicourt was gone.

With him, he'd taken his patient files, records and wiped his digital identity from the hospital computer. Time stamps coincided with the discovery of the corpse in the closet and his suddenly reappearing digital identity.

"I don't understand," Dr. Clyde said for the fourth time and I still had no response for him. I'd gathered everyone I'd interacted with in the hospital, everyone who'd known or told me about Dr. Denicourt in a conference room. In the room was a live feed to the recovering Arturo Denicourt, conveniently located across the hall with Winnie guarding the door.

It was impossible to trust anyone else with the man's life.

And since Winnie couldn't use a radio, we left Daniel with her.

Then we also had to leave Larry because Winnie immediately peed on Daniel's shoe in dismissal of his authority.

Since someone had washed and returned my clothes to me, I felt secure in not offering him any sort of apology for his urine soaked shoes.

Cargo pants and a stolen sweatshirt really made a woman brave.

"Cards on the table. When did you meet the man and when did he start showing an interest in the homeless population nearby?" Carla asked, but Nurse Pluto was fiddling with a cell phone and Dr. Clyde was too pale to manage more than breathing. Her anger flamed brighter and she tried again.

"Who remembers when he got here?"

Neither hospital worker changed their behavior.

"Someone answer me!" she shouted, hands flung in the air and I snickered. If it weren't for her stacked appearance, the short woman could easily have passed for my niece having a tantrum.

"You need to calm down, chief," I mocked before freezing in terror when she whirled on me.

"Shut it, Sharp!" she barked and I raised my hands in surrender.

"Here."

Pluto shoved the phone at Carla, and I glanced at the screen. It was a time stamped diary of daily interactions and encounters around the hospital.

"I have a hard time interacting with people. Often, they are so quick to demand I fit in boxes Male or Female and I want to be in a box labeled 'Mind Your Own Damn Business. These Are My Pants and You Aren't Getting in Them'. So, I started a digital diary documenting my interactions. It made me feel like an explorer of an alien planet keeping a log of the new and unusual world around me. Also useful in preventing some of the more hostile remarks when you look like you're always documenting everything."

I marveled at the detail of the nurse's blog, reading it over Carla's shoulder. It reminded me of a scene in Star Trek where the voiceover narrates a captain's log, but one that had a few too many curse words for public television. Every interaction was detailed with physical characteristics and oddly specific notes on vocal inflections that would have been useful for any alien to understand non-verbal communication.

Also helpful for people who can't read social cues and I made a mental note to suggest this to Stella.

"What date am I looking for?" I reached over Carla's shoulder, stealing the phone to read the dates at the top. "This was only four months ago. He's only been here two months?"

Pluto nodded, eyes moving like a flashback was playing.

"It feels longer. Which is surprising... It's like he showed up one day and it felt like forever had passed with him always here. He just sort of creeped into every aspect of life here, and at some point he started asking questions about patients and the homeless people in the area... Were we... did we get... *Single White Female*-d?"

We all shrugged, but it sounded right.

"What now?" I asked, looking up from an incredibly detailed description of the man's chin cleft and light scar above his lip. Little nuances I'd never noticed... but the face that came to mind wasn't that of a distraught doctor... it was...

"Wait..." I gave Pluto the phone back and went to my backpack in the corner. Pulling open the zipper, I tossed freeze dried coffee, packets of cookies and crackers. At the bottom was the spilled contents of the file folder. Before I could fish around for the picture of Andrew Marks to compare, I instead found a different photo I hadn't seen stapled to a one page document with a post-it note stuck to the top.

"That's Pete," Pluto said from behind me, and I nodded as I scanned the single page of text.

"Says his name was Leon Tsolakyan. Served a short four years in the late 1980s, was recruited into Eagle Enforcers and incarcerated in 2019..." I flipped the page over to see a scanned image. It was a woman in a hospital bed with a man standing beside her, holding a small bundle with a face. Below was a copy of the note Cruz had read to me: *The missing have nothing to lose. Find the answers.*

"What year did Arturo get out of Military Prison?" I asked the room and all of them gave half shrugs except Carla who started working keys on her phone.

"May of 2017," she said, but held up a finger to prevent us from speaking. Her eyes darted back and forth across the screen. "He was released early, though not by much, and they said he left with nothing more than a few clothes. Refused for his family to be called, refused to accept a ride... he just walked out and walked away."

"What are you reading?" I walked over to check her phone. "That's his prison record... and military file. Cruz said it was gone, how are you viewing it?"

My phone buzzed and I pulled it out to see a text from an unknown number.

Unknown: *Cleared a blocked pipe. Enjoy the wave.*
Unknown: *You should have asked me sooner.*

"Is that a cracker emoji?" Pluto asked and I nodded with a stupid smile. When Cruz couldn't find it, I'd assumed the data was purged or corrupted. I never thought to ask Mrs. Margot's niece if it could be recovered. "Who refers to themselves as a cracker?"

Carla and I shared a look before we both burst into awkward laughter.

"Her great aunt," I answered, tears streaming down my face that were equal parts hysteria and humor. "Calls her a cracker because she thought 'hacker' was a typo and she mistakenly mentioned 'breadcrumbs' in reference to cyber tracking..."

Pluto remained sober faced and Carla joined me in shrugging.

"You might have to know Mrs. Margot for this to be funny."

Again, crickets, so I tried to put my responsible adult face back on.

Me: *Did you trace the blockage?*

I didn't expect an immediate response, tucking the phone back in my pocket. Usually "The Cracker" only used a phone number once. She claimed it was safer.

I'm pretty sure she just wanted to confuse the Auto Warranty robots.

Or she was the leader of the Auto Warranty robots.

"Cracker Jackie set all the missing files free..."

"Cracker Jackie?" Carla asked and I shrugged.

"No one ever says her name... and honestly, I prefer not knowing. So... Leon arrived at the prison two years after Arturo left," I crossed the room to a whiteboard and picked up a dry erase pen. Drawing a single line across the board, I put a hashmark toward one end labeled 2017 along with the phrase "Arturo Released". A few inches later I added a second that showed 2019 "Leon Goes to Jail". I slid down the board a few more inches and marked "March- Fake Dr. Denicourt arrives in Ohio".

"What else can we put on here?" I asked the room and Carla spoke up.

"Leon was released two months after he went in." I marked it down.

"When did Petrosian get here?" I directed my question to Dr. Clyde since he was the psychiatrist.

"About a year ago..." He reflected on the memory before shaking his head. "That's not right."

Walking out of the room, he returned quickly holding a laptop that folded over into a tablet. He was balancing the base on his left forearm, typing with the right and scrunching his face in concentration.

"Back when he first came in... there was a Pete Petrosian record. The man had been treated pre-deployment here, but it was a paper file. It took a few days to try and consolidate the files, and when I found the hard copy, he was listed as MIA presumed KIA from a classified mission. I scanned it into the record, thinking I should get it updated, but three weeks later, the scans and hard copy were missing. Only... I still had the scans in my email and I saved them to a flash drive..."

He passed over the computer and I read the man's physical descriptors. Though his heritage was likely Armenian by name... the photo could easily have had him playing Middle Eastern in a Hollywood film. It showed his last field mission as a joint operation with a SEAL team and a Ranger contingent that required inoculations performed on site at the medical center. The inoculations were consistent with deployment to the Persian Gulf region and...

"I know that man," Carla breathed, and I looked down at her beside my left elbow. "He... he was ours?"

Pulling out her phone, she worked the buttons again and pulled up a grainy video recorded off a television set. The quality was inconsistent with her device and I suspected it wasn't her recording. My eyes widened at a man coming into frame and condemning the American scum, stating that they were getting retribution for their people. One by one, propped up soldiers were shot and dropped in the background. In the foreground,

Pete Petrosian remained stoic, watching the deaths of his own people.

"Pause it," I said, and Carla complied even though the footage was no clearer paused than it had been in motion. "Slide it backwards... there."

A work light was visible just off frame, but beside it was the barrel of a rifle aimed directly at Pete.

"He's the scapegoat. They... they framed him for the murder of soldiers."

"So then... where is he?" Dr. Clyde looked at me and Carla. My stomach rolled in waves of acidic nausea. "And why would they need...?"

But I couldn't listen as I went back to my backpack and pulled out two photos- the man I'd pictured and the one who haunted my nightmares.

"I don't know what they were hiding... but I know who did it," I said while separating the top picture from the back and setting them side by side. Nurse Pluto sucked in a breath at the sight of the fleshless and dismembered form lying on a dirt floor. Doctor Clyde dry heaved into the trash can, re-affirming that he'd never been in a war zone.

Flipping over the second picture, I revealed the face of Andrew Marks. The chin cleft and scar on his upper lip were more pronounced in the drawn face than it had been on the grown man parading around as a medical doctor. Cruz's words clicked into place, the man may have killed and mutilated his father... and kept going.

"Andrew Marks? That's not his name..." We all turned to Nurse Pluto whose face was scrunched in either concentration or an effort not to vomit on the table.

"You know him?" I asked at the same time Carla spoke.

"What did he tell you his name was?"

"I knew him as Agent Dremmer. He was reviewing medical records as part of a missing person's investigation... said he only needed descriptors to see if any of our patients matched."

The nurse looked angry.

"How did I not realize Denicourt was Dremmer?"

"Probably the same reason I didn't realize he was Lincoln Lutheran- founder and leader of Eagle Enforcers," Carla muttered, and we all stared at the slimy faced image on the table. The dark, haunted eyes burned into my mind, sending me into a trance that broke when my phone rang and I pulled it out.

"Judge?" I asked, starting to recognize the number.

"Are you still at the hospital?" She asked, in the background there were sirens and the hum of two-way radios.

"Yeah, what's wrong?" I was already moving to the door, motioning for Carla to follow and listen in.

"Two officers were just found murdered and mutilated in their homes... both of them have Eagle Enforcers on their resume."

Chapter Twenty-One: Cockroaches in the Cracks

"You... they found them like this?" I asked, but it was a stupid question based on the average height of the crime scene workers. The bodies themselves were perfectly normal, reclined in chairs and facing the television set in sweats. No blood stains, or evidence of physical assault, just two dudes drinking and watching a TV set that was possibly older than I was.

Their hands, however, were dangling from the ceiling fan on alternating blades from their...

"What is that?" I studied the fleshy wrinkled blobs slowly oscillating in the room...

"Oh my dog, no!"

I clapped my hands over my eyes and wished there was pepper spray on them.

Capsaicin burning out my retinas would have been less painful than looking at dangling scrotums.

"Yeah... the weirder part is the absence of blood," Carla said from beside me and I chanced a peak between my fingers.

"Yeah, I noticed the clothes were clean, but they could have changed the bodies?"

Screwing my courage to the sticking place, whatever that meant, I examined the room again. Not as an unfortunate bystander, but as a trained observer who was definitely not avoiding the ceiling.

Sweatpants, fully covering the lower body of two paunchy white males. Arm nubs, carpal or maybe radial bones were exposed, without any staining or discoloration at the removal site. Same with the light brown leather recliners, carpet and hallway to the kitchen.

As though they had been killed, drained of blood, dismembered and placed here with no effort whatsoever.

"It's almost like the pictures in the file..." I mused, and Carla turned to me sharply.

"What picture?"

"Of the execution. The bodies looked staged, no blood, an awkward job tying the hands like rigor mortis had set in, no indents in the dirt like they had struggled... no photos with face shots..."

I stared at the two men, studying the serene look on their faces. They were definitely not alive when someone cut off their junk.

Pretty sure no one smiled that big during castration besides Lorena Bobbitt and any other female beaten and raped repeatedly.

Nip that problem in the bud, so to speak.

Moving on from the expression, I looked closer at the faces. I wasn't expecting to know either man, but a shadow cast across the face on the left brought up a memory of carnival lights and police cars.

"That's Duncan..." I commented, just as Anita walked in.

"I was wondering if you'd remember him. The second was at the park when the incident with Skid Marks went down. I'd heard rumors he was hand chosen by Captain Preznall and placed in a location well away from where the take down was happening. Just..."

Her face showed conflicting emotions about the man's death. It was clear neither of them was a great human, but still... they were people.

"Do they have families?" Carla asked and Anita looked to a uniformed officer wearing Sergeant bars. "Sergeant Baton?"

"Duncan does... or did. His wife is separated from him, and he hasn't seen his kids in years. Rumor is he didn't want to. Having adult kids around made it harder to get women the same age as his daughter. Oliver has been divorced for two decades, no kids... I know we're not supposed to speak ill of the dead, but I can't say this isn't a result of their own life choices."

Sgt. Baton did a double take looking at Anita, as if recognizing the un-robed judge for the first time.

"Judge... should you be here?" She shifted uncomfortably and Anita tilted her head in a Winnie-style response.

"It's just... you're a judge. At a crime scene? Pretty sure that's not how this works, ma'am."

Carla and I snickered, but not because Sgt. Baton had stated clearly what everyone was thinking. We laughed because we knew Anita, a former marine, hated being in an office and not out doing. The same way Carla and I could never hang back and wait to be filled in, Anita had a need to see for herself...

"Shh..." I whispered as Sgt. Baton and Judge Pestolli began sharing their thoughts on current cases. Behind the chairs, at the eye level of a much shorter person, was a framed picture in a bright red frame. Taking the long way around the chairs, I arrived at the wooden folding table without any dangling bits touching my head.

At first glance, it was a picture I'd seen a million times.

A group of soldiers in various parts of their BDUs, lounging against a wall. Some were smoking, some holding guns, all of them a strange mix of worn out and excited. There were a few wearing the standard military aviator shaped wire rim glasses popular in the nineties, the ridiculously emphasized bridge as much a statement as the bushy eyebrows peeking out over the top of them. The soft sand coating each soldier's boots was a fine grain that clung and lingered in every crevice, a sand I knew too well from my time in Iraq.

To this day, I'm still convinced my boots shed a little every time I move them.

It was on closer inspection that something was off. The uniforms were close, but not quite right. Where the name tape usually sat was an embroidered logo. Patches weren't consistent with military dress and appearance standards for those wearing the button up top, the T-shirt color an inconsistent shade for any combat branch I'd encountered.

My nose was practically pressed against the picture when the embroidered logo clicked into place with my memory.

"Everyone needs to walk out of the room, calmly and slowly," I spoke over my shoulder, obscuring the picture from view by the rest of the room. "Do not pick up or collect anything, just walk out."

Sgt. Baton gave me a questioning look, one that was reflected in the staff all around her.

"Trust me," I mouthed, and she nodded once, signaling all the forensic workers to take a break. No one spoke as a few dozen feet shuffled toward the door and only Carla, Anita and I remained.

"You too," I said to both of them but neither woman moved. "Seriously, please? And call an EOD tech... or whatever the police equivalent is?"

I was hoping it still included the phrase Explosives and Disposal, as I still didn't know how Ordinance came into play. The first two phrases, however, were going to be key to their work.

Carla caved first and took the judge by the arm, leading her away from the living room. I heard the front door open and close before I breathed out the breath I was holding.

Counting slowly back from five, I spun on my heel and sprinted the ten feet to the front door. Six steps in, an ear-piercing whir sliced through the air.

Stumbling through the front door, I fell onto the sidewalk just as the bodies erupted in an expulsion of shrapnel and body parts. I could hear alloy nails pierce the drywall of the room and shattering glass of the old television set, or maybe I'd imagined it based on the brief glimpse I'd managed when it all went sideways.

"What the hell, Cyn?" Carla shouted, but the ringing in my ears refused to hear more than a whisper of what was spoken. "Sharp!"

I blinked up at her, wondering for the first time if I was the only adult to ever have to physically look up at her. Her mouth kept moving and a wash of red and blue lights flooded the sidewalk, but I couldn't hear much more than a tea kettle whistle attached to a hammer.

"Trap. It was a picture of the Eagle Enforcers... probably from Kuwait in the 80s or 90s... There's eight people in the picture. Duncan, Oliver, Preznall, Tsolakyan, Merit, Marks and the woman who looks like Yzma's older sister from the shooting range. All part of the Enforcers. In the background though, there was one more. Need to go to Shots Fired. He's in danger."

"Who?" I saw Carla's lips form the words, but there still wasn't any sound. Climbing off the sidewalk, I examined the scrapes on my hands and arms, swiping at my chin that came away red with blood. Noting the rip-stop cargo pants hadn't stopped one of the knees from ripping, my shoes held up and my shirt was blood and body part free.

I would live.

"Gotta get to Shots Fired..." I whispered, hoping it would come out at a reasonable volume. The whistle had downgraded, the hammering more sporadic and I was certain the hearing damage wasn't permanent.

For the best, really, the VA would not cover treatment for hearing aids if I got blown up and went deaf after retirement.

Or if they did, the amount of paperwork might be worse than just being deaf.

Stumbling forward, my balance failed. My face was heading rapidly back toward asphalt when a strong arm looped through mine and pulled me back to standing.

"Thanks," I mouthed to Larry. He nodded and pointed me toward his waiting truck, Winnie's head sticking out through the back window. "Arturo?"

Larry pointed to Carla and mimed a locking gesture with the word "Daniel" mouthed and I nodded, pulling up the directions to Shots Fired on my phone and showing him.

"Why are we going to a shooting range?" His voice made the first normal sound I'd heard.

"Because Trigger and Yzma might be in danger," I thought of the hanging testicles of her teammates and flinched at the potential equivalent used on her weathered and wilted frame.

"For two very different reasons."

Chapter Twenty-Two: Abandoned Range

"This isn't good," I whispered to Larry as he turned off the main road and encountered a chain across the driveway. Though the flimsy plastic barrier wasn't

"Maybe they're at lunch?" Larry suggested and I gave him the dirtiest look I could muster. It was three in the afternoon, well past lunch and too early for dinner.

"Closed early?"

The shoe marks on the ground suggested Trigger hadn't been the one to lock it. My knowledge of his dedication to being a safe haven for soldiers made his willing closure more unlikely than his being the owner of the shoe prints.

Up the long, sloped drive I could make out the rough outlines for each of the sheds serving as a firing line. Beyond the hum of Larry's engine, it was silent.

No pops of 22s or fifty cal booms.

Gone was the soft chatter of soldiers and the occasional engine as a shooter departed or arrived. It was like entering a ghost town the day after Armageddon.

"Let's go girl," I said to Winnie, climbing out of the truck and waiting for Winnie. "Don't drive up for at least five minutes."

Larry opened his mouth to argue, but I raised a finger in warning.

He nodded and set a timer on his phone.

Winnie and I shared a look before heading up to the chained entrance.

My handgun was tucked into my cargo pocket, and I pulled it out. Muzzle low with a two-handed grip, Winnie and I walked around the chain post and moved quickly up the hill. The slope was more than I'd prepared for, the scabs and bruises shouting through the exertion, but I worked hard to keep my breathing even and silent for our approach.

Behind us, I could hear Larry getting out and the links of the chain shimmying against the metal pole, but we needed to get there before him. Before the sound of his engine gave us away.

Before he could make himself a target.

At the top, we paused to the rear of a dumpster and listened.

Aside from a semi-truck rumbling by on the road below, the range was silent.

"Ready girl?" I whispered and Winnie let out a soft whimper. "Search."

Her nose dropped to the ground and I watched her head. She went left, then right, before making a hard right toward the pistol shed. Her paws ate up the dirt and I huffed along behind her, noting that there were no cars in the parking lot.

Though she wanted to go a different way, I circled a storage shed. Having her scent the doorway and peering through the small window. Inside was an old motorcycle and a reload station, both pristine and clearly used by... someone.

Winnie pulled toward the pistol shed, but I shook my head.

"I know, gun powder is your specialty, but we're looking for Trigger..." *Or a killer.*

I dragged us up the ramp to Yzma's domain of hassling would-be shooters. The door was slightly ajar and Winnie sniffed the opening. She looked back at me and pawed the crack until the door opened. Pulling her back, I dropped down and waited.

The air and the range remained still. No suddenly appearing gunmen.

We moved inside slowly, gun at the ready and hand on Winnie's collar.

No one was inside.

The counter was neat, a lipstick-stained coffee mug sitting next to the old-fashioned register. An empty pack of cigarettes in the trash can, no blood on the floor or walls, and no dismember human parts displayed for all to see.

No signs of a struggle.

No evidence of disaster.

I released my breath and tried to calm the heartbeat pounding in my ears. Checking the small space, everything had remained neat and undisturbed. If they'd taken Yzma, they'd done so without resistance. On the back wall, I found two Honda keys on a single ring with a Master lock key, the same brand as the storage shed. Pocketing both, I let Winnie lead us back out of the room.

The second we were outside, her whole body lurched toward the pistol shed, shaking loose my grip. She didn't run, but I had to power walk to keep up. At the pistol shed, Winnie lifted her head and scented the air.

She sneezed twice and sniffed again.

"Yeah, still gunpowder," I whispered and she tilted her head at me. "What? It's a shooting range."

The dog sneezed again, her tags shaking in an eerie echo off the metal pistol shed. Cautiously, she took two steps in, and I followed with my hand back on her collar, ready to pull her back and protect her furry body with my own. Just around the corner was a sun-drenched firing line, the bench free of shells and shooters with the red lights flashing ominously.

However the range came to be closed, it was made to look purposeful.

We walked the line, checking over and under each shooting position, Winnie sniffing. At the far end, her ears flattened and a soft growl slipped from her lips. I raised my gun slightly, but we were at the ramp leading to Trigger's office and there wasn't anything there.

"What is it?" She growled again, louder, and stalked up the short ramp. Hand gripped tightly on her collar, I let her pull me along until we reached the door and I saw the first sign something was wrong.

Blood smeared the metal handle of the trailer.

"Damn," I pulled the sleeve of Larry's hoodie down and gripped the handle. When the door opened, I dragged Winnie behind it, gun at the ready.

The inside was silent, Winnie scrabbling her claws against the metal to get inside the trailer. I took a long slow breath and the smell was as horrible as it had been before, but a metallic taste stuck at the back of my throat and I double checked my sweatshirt sleeve.

No blood.

The blood on the handle was dried.

What was inside... probably wouldn't be.

"No," I warned her and peered around the door, eyes adjusting to the darkness. Dirt crunched behind me and I whipped around to see Larry on the firing line, hands in the air. "Stay!"

Larry took another step closer and Winnie pulled me toward the door.

"You both suck," I muttered and took a step inside, dropping to the ground at the sight of a figure seated at Trigger's desk.

"Don't move!" I ordered the hunched human form, noting that the chest remained still. I crept closer, releasing Winnie as I got closer. A haunting pair of blue eyes bulged wide, permanently fixed on a spot on the wall, never to blink again.

My grip on Winnie's collar slipped and she ran straight to the back corner of the office. Amid her whimpering, I took a longer look at the man in the chair.

His lifeless head was resting on the left shoulder, rigor mortis having made him look permanently perplexed. The exposed torso sported a long, deep slice. Just above belted pants, someone had arranged his intestines to be spilling from his abdomen.

It was Merit.

"Well, at least you're not..."

Winnie's whimpers turned to sharp barks.

"What..."

A trail of blood led to the dog bed in the corner. Panting heavily beside Winnie was Ruger, deep cuts in his side.

"Larry!" I shouted. "Larry!"

I moved quickly to Ruger, sliding the water bowl closer to see if he'd drink. Winnie lowered her head to lick one of his injuries and I grabbed her.

"No," I ordered, watching the husky pit bull mix loll his tongue in the water. A stampede sounded on the metal ramp and Larry filled the door holding a random piece of plywood trim like it would bludgeon someone.

I was too scared to mock, tears stinging my eyes. I rubbed the spot between his eyes trying to offer affection without causing him more pain.

Larry was frozen in the doorway.

"Help him!"

The veterinarian came to life, dropping the wood and running over to us. His sharp focus was all business, quickly checking over the injuries and shaking his head. Gentle as he could, the man probed each patch sporting blood, but he didn't discuss what was obvious.

Ruger was seriously injured and he'd lost a lot of blood.

"We need to get him to the clinic," Larry gently slid his arms under the dog, eliciting a whimper that nearly crushed my heart.

"It's OK, buddy. It's OK," Larry whispered and lifted the dog in his arms. Gun at the ready, I led us out and back to the truck. Popping open the back door of the extended cab, Larry placed Ruger gently on the rear seat. A few towels littered the back floor and he placed one over a cut to seatbelt the dog onto the seat.

"Winnie, shotgun," I ordered and she took her post in the passenger seat.

"Where are you sitting?" He asked and I shook my head.

"I need to call someone about this... and I need to find Trigger and Yzma."

"Cyn..."

"Larry..."

My phone alerted me with a message from an unknown number and an address popped up from Mrs. Margot's niece with a name: Andy Marks.

I quickly plugged it into my phone and studied the tiny map that popped up.

The address was within ten miles of the range. The last name matched the fake doctor, as did the shortened version of his first name and I had a bad feeling.

But I couldn't share it with the man in front of me.

I needed him to save Ruger.

"Go, Larry! There isn't time!" I slammed his truck door closed and despite the head shake and muttering, he backed out while I called Carla.

"One dead at the shooting range. I'm headed to the address I just texted you... I don't know who has jurisdiction but send them," I hung up and forwarded the address.

Racing to the old shed, I pulled out the keys and released the padlock. Walking up to the bike, I grabbed a helmet and stuck the key in the ignition. Looking at my phone one last time to memorize the directions, I silenced Carla's return call and stuffed the phone in my pocket.

"Please don't let him have hurt Trigger," I whispered to no one and roared down the drive toward the road. "Please let Larry save Ruger."

Chapter Twenty-Three: Domino Effect

If I wanted to murder and mutilate people, this is where I'd do it.

Killing the bike engine, I stared at the address GPS sent me to.

A line of trailers, camper, pop up and tent, went from the beginning of the parcel to the far end with just enough space in front of each for a single lawn chair. Each lawn chair was accompanied by the withered remnants of suburbia, a rusted tricycle sat beside a deflated sports ball, its color faded in the unrelenting sun.

Despite being just outside Dayton, it was like being transported back to the Middle East. Around the land plot was cracked and dry earth, baked into oblivion where nothing grew. Instead of soft sand, swallowing every sound and scene, the hard packed dirt gave a clear view for miles and amplified every sound.

Without the bike's engine, it was deathly quiet.

The property was a few miles off the main road, but no cars came this way. Those still on the highway flew past without noticing this road, the trailers, or anyone over here.

Assuming there even was anyone over here.

A shiver of fear ran up my spine.

Taking cautious steps forward, I crossed the road to face the first trailer.

It had 1970s brown stripes, still hooked to an ancient pick-up on blocks. On the ground below was a hodgepodge of footprints, all sizes and shoe types, permanently imprinted in what must have once been mud. Crouching low, I peered under the trailer and saw an inch of the tire was partially sunken into the mud.

These were definitely not *mobile* homes.

Standing on tiptoes, I peeked through the frosted window on the flimsy door. Despite the sun, no light permeated the interior. Moving left, I tried looking through another window, but the interior remained blank and empty.

Potentially not even a *home*.

"You really are stupid," a woman said from behind me, accompanied by the long pull of a hammer. "You just made my job easier, though. Walk."

A hard piece of metal poked me in the ribs, directing me toward the trailer farthest from the road. Taking two steps, I listened for how many footprints followed.

At least two sets.

Easier to go with them then risk alerting whoever took Trigger and Yzma.

"Go check for the dog," the woman ordered, and the taloned claws of the vicious Viv popped into my head.

"She came on a motorcycle! How the hell would the dog have gotten here?" a grouchy man responded. He was clearly the brains of the two, but I didn't recognize the voice. Either we hadn't met, or he'd been completely forgettable.

"Don't question me! I will shoot you!" Her shrill squawk would have made Winnie howl if she was here. As it was, I wished my hearing wouldn't have recovered from the explosion so I couldn't hear her.

"Give it a rest," an aged voice cracked through a speaker attached to a Tioga trailer with neon orange faded stripes. "You are both disposable."

A snicker slipped through my lips and the butt of a gun slammed into the side of my face. My cheek cut against my teeth, and I tasted blood.

Turning quickly, I spit the blood onto her carefully made-up face and perfectly slicked hair.

"You bitch! You ruined my hair! Do you know how long I spend to look this good while your half-baked fat ass walks around-"

A shot rang out through the trailer yard and where Viv's head had been screaming was an empty neck with the splash zone covering the mountain of a man beside her. The torso remained upright for a few more seconds before the headless corpse crumbled to the ground.

My mouth worked like a hooked trout for a few seconds before I looked at the flesh mountain beside her who gestured for me to keep walking.

"Seriously? You're covered in..."

He cocked back his fist and slammed it into my gut, doubling my body over. He took advantage of my lack of air to fling me over his shoulder like a sack of potatoes.

We moved quickly between trailers and as I caught my breath, I started fighting.

My knee folded into his torso, fingers clawing at his T-shirt clad back, feet aiming for the soft flesh between his legs.

Mountain Man's stride never broke, and he shoved open a trailer door with his foot. I was struck instantly by the cool, dusty air. I paused for a second in my fight and he retaliated by turning suddenly and smashing my head into the door frame.

Squeezing my eyes shut against the bursts of light and the pounding blood in my ears, I nearly missed the metal clank of a secure door opening. A wave of stale air tickled my nose before I found myself falling, back slamming into the ground and stealing the air from my chest again.

Struggling to breathe, the man above me positioned himself on a short metal ladder. Jerking my arm, I flopped over and bit back bile as pain sent waves of nausea coursing through my gut.

Before I could push up to all fours, I was once again airborne on the back of a man the size of a mountain.

The jostling was too much with the pressure on my ribs, I threw up down his back.

"What the…"

His hand reached around, feeling the damp, chunky remnant on his shirt.

"Bitch!" he shouted, throwing me to the ground. His foot flew out to kick me, but I rolled away like a steamroller until I ran into something metal that jerked slightly.

"Nice job, calvary," a harsh grumble came from somewhere above me, and I opened a single eyelid.

"What can I say? I live to make an entrance."

My eye slid closed so I could process what I'd seen.

Trigger was in a folding metal chair, tied around the center with a thick length of paracord. His face had bruises and a few cuts. Blood stained his khaki cargo shorts, but I could still tell they were khaki. Either it wasn't his blood, or it wasn't that much.

"How much of that blood is yours?" I asked, hearing my own chest whistle like a tea kettle around what might have been a punctured lung.

"'Bout half. Took some of that asshole Merit with me before she killed him," he sounded darkly pleased with himself. "He hurt my dog."

"He did that to Ruger?" I gasped for air around the words. "Now I wish Andrew had cut off his testicles like he did the other two."

"Andrew?" Trigger's single word sounded like a question, and I opened my eyes to try and look at him.

"Yeah, Andrew Marks. Head of Eagle Enforcers? Everything is in his name. The business, this address, the..." I ran out of air and tried to suck in as much as possible before I continued. "I mean, you were following him in the desert."

"That little punk? He couldn't manage a hemorrhoid outbreak, much less an operation. Andy is behind all of this," Trigger's dry laugh caught me off guard. "Can't believe I bought that load of bull about making amends."

"Andy is Andrew, isn't it?" I wheezed.

A pair of boots showed up in my periphery and I turned to them, glancing up thin green pants covering chicken legs.

"Yzma?" I asked, wincing at Trigger's dry laugh. "Are you OK? You were in the picture. Someone is killing everyone in the picture."

"Kid, that's Andy. The most brutal old hag to ever crawl from the crypt and torture men..."

Her boot went up and I grabbed it, sending her to the ground.

Using the seat of Trigger's chair, I went to my knees and looked down at the woman who I thought needed my help. She didn't look brutal or dangerous.

"Seriously? You?" I looked at her flailing noodle arms as fake Dr. Denicourt arrived and pulled her from the ground.

"Are you OK, mommy?" he cooed, giving her a look that made my neck hair crawl.

"Yes, baby," she replied, caressing his cheek and I gagged again. "But I think we'll need to teach this little bimbo a lesson. After all, we can't leave any witnesses."

She turned suddenly and put two rounds into the mountain of a man's chest.

"I love spring cleaning."

Chapter Twenty-Four: Eagle Enforcers

"This is creepy, right?" I whispered up to Trigger and he nodded. "Like... Bates Motel creepy?"

"At least in the Bates Motel, that was his real mom. Andy is just some creepy neighbor from Andrew's childhood," Trigger muttered. "She killed his guardian... made him watch. She made him watch a lot of things."

"Seriously? You mutilated those people? And became obsessed with a child? What is wrong with you? Were you dropped at birth?"

Motion from the corner of my eye had me turn just in time to receive a backhand across my cheek.

Since the hand belonged to Yzma, it was like getting hit with a declawed cat paw. Startling, but not especially painful. In deference to her ego, I fell over onto Trigger and glanced up at him from his lap, head swimming in the pain radiating from my ribs.

Can you shoot? I mouthed at him.

His eyes move down and up in a nod.

"Get up, you moronic, worthless..."

Her words were lost in the sting of my hair being jerked backward, popping muscles in my neck that might have belonged in their previous location. Eyes forced upward; I could see into Andrew Marks' nostrils and the eyes floating above them. Eyes that had seemed genuine and loving toward a long-lost father were now dead to the world. Blank and deranged, it was hard to imagine what he'd seen.

Even harder to imagine what he'd done.

What he might have been forced to do.

Maybe he really did miss his father.

"Get her up, baby," his mother cooed, and I considered vomiting again, but my stomach was empty. Tension increased on my ponytail and my whole body was dragged backward and then shoved forward into standing. The world swam, but I appeared to have avoided any head trauma if the sharply focused fall out shelter was any indicator.

"So... is this where you tell me why I have to die?" I asked, sliding my hands into the cargo pockets on my leg and confirming my gun was right where I left it.

The irony that Viv had suggested Mountain Man "look for the dog" and hadn't thought to check me for weapons was further proof that she must have managed to live this long out of sheer spite.

No way was she smart enough to have made it based on her life choices.

Problem was, Trigger was on my left.

The gun was in my right-side pocket.

And both of my sides felt like the ribs were ready to be served in barbeque sauce.

I have to let one of them hit me again, I winced at the thought. Being hit was a part of my life, but letting these two touch me meant I was going to need to bathe in Purell.

Twice.

"It's just business. That first group was doing good work for years, selling info to the US and guns to the insurgents. The first time they almost got caught, the frame job on Arturo was brilliant. But as time went on and the conflict ended, they went on and I replaced them until we lost the contract. Then Eagle Enforcers went underground, mercenaries and murderers, but we kept some of the perks. We weren't the only ones who knew what was happening in Kuwait and there were still people in high places willing to pay to keep it quiet."

Though the villain's speech was boring, it kept Andy distracted as I moved closer to Trigger's chair and tried to think through a plan that wouldn't get everyone killed.

We do not shine with planning.

"I had no idea that first crew was leveraging information and fear for their own benefit and cutting me out. It brought me great joy to cut them out the same way I cut out Andrew's father," she snickered but my eyes snapped to the son who recoiled in horror before going blank again.

"You... burned and skinned and mutilated that man?" I asked, forgetting for a moment that I had a different goal in mind.

"He was trying to get between me and my son. The man was a liability and my son needed to learn the price of insolence," she caressed his shoulder and my face spoke before my mouth could lie.

Upper lip curling, I felt the disgust between my eyebrows just as Andy looked at me again.

"Don't make that face, wench. You have no idea! No idea what I went through for him!" She stomped forward, pulled my hair, spinning my body to face the man tied to his chair. I used the movement to disguise my own turn and leaned a shoulder on Trigger's leg.

"Andrew! Are you going to let her talk to mommy like that?" Her shriek was joined by heavy footfalls bearing down on me.

I was running out of time.

The insane woman released my hair and I fell forward.

Shoving my ribs into the metal chair, I let out a scream and stuffed my hand under Trigger's upper thigh, leaving the gun concealed where he could reach it.

Sucking in another breath, I prepared for impact in whatever form it would take.

A half heartbeat later, my head was hauled backward, and my body dragged across the floor until forced upright flush against the fake doctor. Every part of him rigid, his heartbeat racing with a slight tremble in the fingers he was fighting to get free of my hair.

Andrew wrapped a forearm of coiled muscle around my neck, applying just enough pressure for the heartbeat in my chest to sound like a jackhammer in my ears.

"Hold her still, baby," the creepy old woman pulled out a serrated fishing knife as she bore down. My eyes lingered on the slightly red tinged hook at the end. "We won't be killing this one quickly or slowly. She deserves the full experience of my ire. This little witch is going to spill her guts just like that freeloader Merit and then I'm going to send them to everyone who needs a reminder that I'm in charge."

"Ew! You better clean that..."

Andrew's arm pressed harder, cutting off my words on a wet hack.

My eyes crossed to multiply Andy into a half dozen silhouettes.

All versions of her holding a dirty knife threatening to contaminate me with Merit's remains.

"Who knows about us?" She asked, playing with the serrated edge against the pad of her bony finger. "Who knows about Arturo?"

The jackhammer had been joined by a cicada, buzzing behind my ear and dimming the sharp focus of my eyesight.

"Who knows!?!" The knife swiped out across my cheek and a small drop of warm blood slid to my lips. "I'd forgotten all about Arturo until Dick Preznall started causing a racket, trying to get information and using my connections to get someone inside that prison only to botch the whole thing. Then I have to get my son to clean up his mess."

Her knife swiped out again, nicking my other cheek but I couldn't think about the pain. Stars were bursting behind my eyes, Andrew's arm applying more pressure with every word slipping out of his psychotic "mother's" mouth.

"Answer me!" Her arm flew out again, but my vision was getting dark. When I expected to feel the sting of a blade, a shot erupted into the concrete cavern and the arm around my neck went slack.

Blinking twice, I tried to clear my vision when another shot removed the hand from the woman in front of me.

A third, and she was a lump on the ground.

Trigger, gun at his side, was slowly fading from view when another voice filled the room.

"Cyn!"

But I couldn't keep my eyes open anymore and it all went dark with a wave of head spinning oxygen.

Chapter Twenty-Five: Full Pardon

Three weeks had passed since the glue incident, but I was once again at the scene of a medical catastrophe.

"Can you just sit still for two seconds!" Pluto shouted, but Arturo wasn't having it. Instead of Winnie ripping off medical leads, the man was doing it himself, shouting about being imprisoned and forced to wet himself like a baby.

Apparently, Marines were not babies.

Who knew?

"You need to stop," Trigger said from the neighboring bed, trying to sit up with only one functioning arm. "Some of us are trying to get our beauty rest over here. Now piss yourself like a man and shut up."

"Speaking of, I brought you a visitor!"

My smile faltered when he looked at the door nervously. The man had been carried from the underground bunker by Daniel and they found one of his arms had been sliced up the center. There was significant muscle and nerve damage, the repair of which had kept him here longer than he intended.

Not a huge leap considering he hadn't planned on staying here at all.

"I don't..." Trigger's voice cut out and Arturo stopped fighting when Ruger hobbled into the room. One of the cuts had nicked a tendon on his leg, an injury that would never fully heal. Larry had cleaned and stitched all the wounds, the dog missing a half-dozen patches of fur.

Like his human, he was having a hard time resting and recovering.

"Hey boy," he whispered, eyes misting over.

Larry followed Ruger with Winnie who was oddly subdued.

"What's wrong girl?" I asked her, and she came over to butt her head against my hand. I crouched down, nuzzling her neck. We had only been hospitalized two days, but Winnie had visited.

"I wouldn't let her eat the contents of a biohazard bag," Larry sighed and Arturo snorted a laugh. Hearing his voice, Winnie perked up and took a flying leap onto his chest. She nailed him with two paws to the solar plexus that stole his breath just long enough for her to give his face a tongue bath without reprimand.

"Damn dog!" He muttered, even as he wrapped his arms around her back and rubbed her scruff.

Opposite him, Larry had lifted Ruger onto the man's bed. As soon as the great black beast had settled, both dog and human were the most at peace I'd seen since becoming injured. Looking at the pair was too much for my fragile physical state and I swiped at my eyes before sitting gently in a chair beside the wall.

"Shouldn't you be back in your own room, Sharp Attack?" Pluto asked.

"Not sure. They told me I might be eligible for discharge today, so I assumed that meant I could leave and give my room to someone else?"

Pluto gave me a dark look but was interrupted from responding when a new person entered the room after a gentle knock on the open-door frame.

"Excuse me... I'm looking for..." His eyes landed on the man in the corner, currently weighed down by 90 pounds of dog. "Hi?"

He scratched the back of his head, shifting uncomfortably, but the eyes matched more than Andrew's ever could have. On the bed, Arturo's fist clenched and opened, Winnie giving him small head butts of encouragement.

"S-son?" he choked out and a small girl with green eyes in a wide face peaked out from behind Roberto. "Hello?"

The little girl clutched her dad's leg, looking up at him for direction.

"Kace, this is your grandfather," the voice mangled with emotion had the same gruff quality as his fathers. "Art-Da-... this is your granddaughter."

Arturo's eyes moved between the man and the small girl.

"We've been looking for you... but... well... if you'd like us to..." Winnie jumped off the bed, walking up the small child and stuffing her nose under the girl's dress.

"Winnie, out!" I shouted, startled when Arturo burst into laughter and the little girl followed suit.

"Sharp, that dog is a menace."

I couldn't tell who'd said those words, but it was true either way.

"Roberto, I... I'm sorry," Arturo began, but seemed to run out of words there. "I let you down."

A new guest walked in without knocking.

"Sgt. Arturo Denicourt?" He spoke, looking up from a document to see everyone in the room staring at his rank.

A full bird colonel.

Pluto was the first to recover enough to speak.

"Here, sir."

They gestured toward the once homeless man's bed and the colonel approached with the paper extended.

"The United States Department of Defense would like to present you with a full pardon. Crimes for which you were accused and sentenced have been discovered to be staged. You were framed for atrocities you did not commit and served a sentence you did not earn. Please accept our apology, financial restitution and..." The colonel looked around the room, everyone silently observing Arturo for his reaction.

"Those men," he whispered and the colonel shook his head.

"Staged. All of it. That recorded execution wasn't your team. They robbed a mass grave to frame Private Petrosian for a crime when you were getting too close to finding out they were the ones giving weapons and training to the enemy."

"They?" He asked and I realized no one had filled him in on the whole "Eagle Enforcers Were Committing Treason and Financing Political Candidates with Blackmail and Secrets" thing.

Another story for another day.

"The contractors... I apologize, I'm not authorized to share the complete details of an ongoing investigation," he shifted awkwardly as across the hall a news story announced a former president in custody for accessory to murder, conspiracy to commit fraud and tax evasion.

"See? Taxes... they'll always come after you for taxes," I said to no one in particular, but yet another person walked in and I was starting to question whether or not this hospital believed in security or patient privacy.

"I'm here to take that one home," Carla said, pointing at me.

"You," her finger moved to Trigger. "Have to stay two more days. But I talked to the hospital administration and Ruger can stay with you."

"This is your son, this time?" she asked Arturo, pointing at Roberto and Kace.

"Yeah... not sure why anyone believed the other guy, but I was hoping by playing along I could learn something."

"Did you?" She looked skeptically at his head as though he may have received head trauma.

"Don't get shot," he muttered, and Carla let out a strangled laugh.

"Fair enough. There's a lot to sort out," she looked pointedly at Trigger, then Larry and finally me. "Are you ready to go home?"

"Yeah, I guess," I shrugged, stretching the kinks in my back as I stood to an angry symphony of pops. "Can we stop somewhere on the way home, though? Someone broke all my coffee mugs and none of my bowls have handles."

"About that," Larry's ears turned pink and he shrugged his arms out of a backpack I'd missed. Unzipping it, he pulled out a mug with a German shepherd wearing a party hat and emitting a fart cloud.

"Cruz called me, said... well... A lot of things. But Winnie's birthday is coming up, so I thought we might start rebuilding with her."

"My coffee cup collection or..." I looked at it again, turning it in my hands to see the back had a note.

Like a Winnie fart, my love for you lingers. ‑LK

"I... Thank you."

"You're welcome, Cyn. You're the only one who will ever be welcome," he gave me a meaningful look that stole my good sense.

Our eyes met and I leaned forward, giving him a quick kiss that left a look of longing on both our faces. A yawn escaped my lips and I fought the urge to lay down in a hospital bed for a nap.

I'm told napping in a hospital is how living people end up in the morgue.

"I need coffee."

"I need you. Let's see if I can make both of us happy," he answered, slinging an arm around my shoulder and whistling for Winnie. Moving through the door, his hand slid down my arm, lacing our fingers together.

We left the room, hand in hand, with matching smiles.

Afterword

If you are on social media and follow military groups, you've probably seen the #22ADay referencing veterans who commit suicide. In true science student fashion, I had to research this (social media has burned me before) and found a single page summary of VA research stating the number is 6000 a year, an average of 17 a day.

This is still too many.

If you are or know a veteran, remember that struggling and asking for help does not make you weak. No human is meant to carry this alone, and no one would shame you for seeking out and asking for help.

If they did, I'll totally let Winnie bite them. She isn't real, but Perry is and trust me when I tell you- she has teeth and they are sharp.

Sgt. Rex, *Until Tuesday*, and the movie *Dog* (only the last one is fiction) are excellent examples of the phrase "if you're not ready to reach for a hand, you can always reach for a paw".

I hope you see a dog today.

'Til Valhalla.

-Noelle, Perry and Padfoot

Sneak Peek of Book 8: Itching Against Ignorance

Chapter One: Overwhelming Generosity

"If I move this one here... and that one there..."

My hands looped the blood red yarn around pushpins surrounded by the images of every resident of Sweet Pea, Ohio. It was like a mural of murder victims, taken while they were dripping blood-yarn in the final howls of death. None of the images were flattering, none of them taken with consent or the intent of establishing reasonable allegation. Reasonable was beyond me at this point.

We were in blind blame territory and this entire mural was just for my own sick amusement.

A cackle slipped out as I looped another piece of yarn and circled a single picture repeatedly. It was her... it had to be. No one else would have the power to orchestrate such a targeted attack of generosity.

And no one else would risk incurring my wrath... Assuming I had any.

The jury was still out.

"I'll get you my pretty..."

"Please don't tell me you've lost it."

My skin jumped away from its muscles while I whirled around, brandishing the sharpest object available to me at the source of the voice.

A thumbtack.

Against Mrs. Margot.

She was 100 when I was a child, which meant she was probably a thousand now... or a supernatural being. Vampire, werewolf, mummy... something that looked dead but wasn't.

"Will you put that damn thumbtack down and stop trying to figure out what immortal being I am? We've been over this. I'm only 85! And I can't be taken out with a thumbtack. Remember? You tried when you were six, Cynthia."

My lavender eyes flutter down at her shrunken frame.

"I don't remember... I was six. And only a vampire would know that I was trying to figure out if she was a vampire. I'm getting garlic!"

Spinning on my foot, I turned toward the rear of my office and the door to my apartment above. The entire space was about 900 sq ft, divided into two levels so I could easily get up there and back before Mrs. Margot could hobble out on her walker. Usually, I didn't have garlic cloves, but there was always garlic salt in my cabinet.

It would be perfect for taking her out if she was a vampire *or* a snail.

My first step collided with the hefty fur log half pressed against my leg.

Gravity brought me down, my body falling the almost six feet between my head and my feet. Consciously, I angled myself away from the German Shepherd Malinois mix on the floor to prevent undo trauma. With the number of times I tripped on her, you'd think she'd learn to give me some room.

She might argue that since she was always *right next to me*, I should take care to go around her.

I landed shoulder first, head tucked against my shoulder. My outstretched arm flopped down onto Winnie's tail, and she screamed. The impact sent a sharp stabbing pain down my arm with a loud *pop,* and I joined her in an agonizing howl. I was used to falling, and being injured, so it wasn't as much about pain as just a primal need to scream.

For hours, into the sky while cursing the world.

Maybe not the entire world, but cursing Florida, bigots and men sounded right... though Florida was already cursed, so maybe that was a waste of a curse.

If curses were like wishes and you only got three, someone definitely already took care of Florida.

I could use my third one to curse chickens, goats or whoever designed coffee bags with that inadequate glue on the foldy-tab so it fell off when you tried to open the bag and you were forced to rely on that clear sticker.

Where was I going with this? My brain acknowledged its own rambling even as my mouth continued screaming like an overly dramatic poltergeist. Instead of mental relief, my throat became dry and scratchy, my brain continued to hum with thoughts and curses, every part of me a contorted mass of ruminations and pain I could never piece together.

"Will the pair of you shut up? At least one of you is fine and the other screaming about it will do absolutely nothing to fix you. Honestly, Cynthia, you and the whole Sharp family are the most dramatic lot of fornicators..."

"La la la.... I am not listening," I shouted over her, refusing to hear any more allusions to my parents' sex life that was both public knowledge and public spectacle.

Absolutely nothing was private about their private lives and I, for one, knew more than enough.

They say no one wants to know how the sausage gets made, but an up-close look at how you got made is far more traumatizing.

It also, strangely, involves sausage.

Taking a few deep breaths and closing my mouth, I declared myself screamed out. My brain wasn't as easily quieted, pondering the meaning of life, the universe, and everything... I know it was supposed to be 42, but aside from that movie about baseball and my brother's age, it didn't offer any real insight.

Maybe I needed to be 42 to get it... a question for Seth if his daughter hasn't killed him.

Mrs. Margot cleared her throat with an unnecessary amount of indignation, and I put on my sweetest fake smile.

"How can I help you?"

Directing my question at the fiberglass tiles and metal supports that comprised my ceiling, I gave up the smile. Actually, it was Mrs. Margot's ceiling. She owned the building, including my office and the studio apartment above it where I lived and slept... when I wasn't slowly losing my mind and refusing to sleep. Aside from my one-woman crusade to stop the unwanted generosity of townsfolk, I was dealing with an existential crisis that followed the celebration of my twenty-ninth birthday and separation from my long-term on again off again Larry.

In one year, I would be thirty and all of my "quirks" would solidify into permanent personality traits... I wasn't ready to be permanently anything.

"Are you going to get off the floor?"

It was phrased as a question, and yet it didn't feel optional. Once, in a fit of insomnia and irrational fear, I'd tried to count the black dots in each of my ceiling tiles. After 1,989 spots, I was cross-eyed and no closer to sleep or legal insanity. That had led to trying to count Winnie furs before ending with counting coffee beans and dividing them one bean at a time into the six dozen coffee cups that had appeared in a twenty-minute period.

Which was only... I glanced at the white clock on my wall with black arms and black numbers on a white face. It looked like the clock in every schoolroom, ever. The sight brought back memories of bullying, friendship and Larry... it haunted me so stunningly.

I should stop looking at the clock.

Why was I looking at the clock?

"I repeat, Cynthia, get off the floor!"

Right, I was trying to figure out how long it had been since I tried to count the ceiling tile dots...

The answer was six hours.

Or 12 hours... without the AM/PM designation, I couldn't be sure what was day or night anymore since I'd given up going outside, exposure to sunlight, and human interaction as well as sleep.

Only some of those choices were mine, but all of them felt right.

Like making a cup of Keurig while waiting for the drip machine to make a full pot. Without sleep, human interaction was impossible, and sunlight was never necessary to begin with.

Except as it applied to photosynthesis for coffee plants.

"Cynthia, I will give you to the count of three. One."

"Ah, ah, ah," I mimicked The Count, and the feet of her walker crept closer, aiming for my head.

I refocused on Mrs. Margot's face. She did not appreciate my Sesame Street reference.

In fact, she looked genuinely perturbed.

"Two."

"Yes, ma'am," I sighed. Hauling my size 18 frame off the floor and stumbling back toward my desk, the canine I'd served with, Sgt. Winnifred Pupperson, ambled along beside me. My shoulder had come unseated from the ball socket, but my best furry friend looked completely fine.

Minor miracles, since her former vet was on a three-year lesbian cruise and the fill-in commercial vet was my ex-Dr. Larry Kirby.

My doctor was a revolving set of ER workers, and I was this close to filling my frequent flyer punch card.

"If you want me to take care of anything that requires a computer or paper, I can't help you."

With a sweeping gesture, I drew her attention to the completely obscured surface that used to house my business operations equipment. The second-hand monitor and CPU from a reformed porn publisher, a blotter calendar with recurring charge dates highlighted, wired keyboard, mouse and mouse pad completely obscured by coffee cups.

Several dozen coffee cups of various colors, shapes, and volumes. Each one emblazoned with dogs, a farm, or some manner of witty or snarky saying.

All of them mysteriously materializing in or around my office, apartment, car and one on a cow at the dairy while I was checking her over.

It was creepy and impressive since I hadn't seen a soul.

Maybe it came from the cow herself?

Mrs. Margot, however, did not seem dissuaded by the new collection.

"Why don't you put them away, Cynthia? As I understand it, your previous collection was destroyed. Just place them where those once lived... honestly..."

She tutted at me, and I narrowed my eyes at her, glancing between her and my string art conspiracy theory board.

Could it be...

I watched her hobble on the walker and dismissed it. While she could get around reasonably well, I couldn't conceive of her having the motivation to hunt down townsfolk and collect coffee mugs. No... Carla had all the leverage to do this to me.

Her glaring image judged me from the wall where it sat framed by red yarn.

"Will your partner be joining you or has Sgt. Winnifred forgotten her manners?"

The dog in question, retired from the Army alongside me, had flopped onto the floor again and was now doing a sideways wiggle on her back. Rear paws kicking out, front tucked against her chest, the dog could have been scratching her back or jazzercising. Whichever it was, she managed it in perfect time to the music coming in from the public library next door.

"Baby, I'm just gonna shake, shake, shake, shake it off," her tail thumped in time to the beat with each foot kicking out to punctuate the claps before the bridge.

"Considering she wrecked your BINGO hall and tried to blow up Florida, I don't know where you got the idea she had manners." Scoffing, I tried not to roll my eyes even though I had resting sarcasm face.

It was like RBF for people who used dark humor to process their trauma.

Jiggling my dislocated shoulder, I stifled a scream and decided it was well and truly out of place, but I would need coffee to get it back in. Picking up one of the coffee cups and putting it next to the coffeemaker, I tried to choose what to put inside the cup with my magic bean water. "It's like you've never met us and think we somehow developed social skills and competence."

A sharp side eye from Mrs. Margot attempted to maim me, but I elected to take TayTay's advice and... well, ignore it.

Only Winnie could work a tail shake like that in our dynamic duo.

I'd probably un-seat another ball joint if I tried.

"And I can't put the damn coffee cups away because when the old ones went down, the shelf broke and I don't own any tools! I tried to buy some tools, but I ended up in the grocery store buying cheese and coffee creamer... and then I went to... somewhere. Probably work? Definitely not bed because it smells like Larry, and he's gone..."

I blinked at her, wondering when she'd lost focus.

"When did you last sleep, Cynthia?"

"Do you want some coffee?" I replaced her question with one of my own, gesturing the cup in my hand out to her. Beside the coffee maker was another full cup, one I'd apparently poured and forgotten about at some point. I poked the side and discovered it was still lukewarm.

Like the inside of a Tauntaun.

Snickering at my own joke, I waited for Mrs. Margot to answer while I chugged the tepid liquid.

"I do not want coffee. I want to know why you aren't sleeping," she scowled at me. Ambling slowly over to the front window, she ripped back the heavy drapes and let in the morning light.

A sharp hiss at the brightness passed through my lips as I looked through the front window. It was adorned with our names in vinyl letters:

SHARP INVESTIGATIONS, CYNTHIA SHARP AND SGT. WINNIFRED PUPPERSON, K9.

Only Winnie had earned rank and title.

My name looked like what my mother would call me when I was in trouble, and she couldn't remember my middle name was Natasha.

Outside the glass, people ambled up and down Main St in the not-so-sleepy town of Sweet Pea, OH. I'd been born and raised here, but it had never felt like home. In a search of a sense of belonging, I'd gone to school in Colorado, joined the Army and started my career in Texas with no luck. After seeing a few parts of the world and some other parts of the country, I wasn't sure anywhere would ever feel like home.

Winnie's tail bumped my leg, and I amended myself, the only place that felt like home was beside her.

Through my window, I watched the average citizens of my average town continue on with their mediocre lives and wondered at the key to their happiness. Nothing about their movements was hurried or motivated... It was unclear if they had places to be or were simply enjoying the cooling temperatures of early fall. Either way, I was mildly envious of them as they enjoyed the trees' early-stage death drop of foliage. September had barely arrived, but pumpkin spice everything had already made its way into Mo's bakery, the Coffee Cabin, the lube section of the adult stores, including Phil's Curious Courtship, and my coffee maker.

Mankind's greatest invention and the only love in my life, besides Winnie, I could trust not to let me down. The little orange light on the maker was off... the coffee maker should never be off... though the carafe was getting darker.

Except it was getting darker from the top and not the bottom... strange.

"Cynthia!"

My head jerked up, and I shook off the cobwebs.

"Hmm?"

"Why don't you ask one of your male... friends... to fix your shelf? Would you be able to sleep then?"

I shook my head slowly, looking into the empty coffee cup still in my hand.

"I don't have any man friends. Cruz went away and Larry.... Is dumb. His whole family is dumb... and my bed smells like him.

I want to wash the smell away, but I can't because then it's gone, and I can't have it back because he's a little mama's boy and I have some pride! Somewhere..." I stared down at my desk. There was just enough space to use as leverage to push my shoulder back into place. Bracing my forearm, I chomped down on my lip and pushed.

The wet *pop* was unnerving, but I'd managed it without crying... more than I already was. I looked out the window again, waiting for the mist in my eyes to clear before addressing the vampire in the room. I'd read once that I wasn't supposed to show weakness to vampires, or maybe it was predatory men.

Potentially, it was both.

"What about your intern, Stella?" She tried again, and I pointed to a pile of confetti in the corner.

"She quit and brought me a pile of resumes for potential new people. Winnie ate them."

The mist in my eyes was clearing and I could once again see the blissful town with its cheerful people and its happy coffee that they could make because everyone they cared about hadn't jumped ship and abandoned them to their own inner thoughts.

"No one has abandoned you, Cynthia!"

Almost inner thoughts... I clarified, wondering if that too would escape my lips. A shadow momentarily blocked out the sun, and I darted out the door like a drunken troll.

"You!" I shouted, an accusatory finger leveled at the rather expansive chest of my brother's wife and the town's sheriff... or chief.

"You did this..." I tripped over a collection of coffee mugs on the sidewalk. They fell over, and I toppled after barely angling myself away from the shattered ceramic. I landed on the shoulder I'd just popped back in and felt it threaten to slide out again. Frustrated, I blinked up at the sun and the outline of my curvy in all the right places, sister-in-law. The shorter version of Jessica Rabbit, with an equally sexy voice and lethal hands. My squinting eyes marred my attempt to glare as I fought to keep them trained on her for signs of guilt.

She just stared down at me.

"This sidewalk is unclean. You should get up," she advised, and I waited for the horror to fill me. I'd seen things on this sidewalk. Horrible things and yet...

Horizontal on the sidewalk was actually kind of comfortable, a weird discovery since my bed had felt possessed by fire ants recently. I closed my eyes against the sun and the second I did, everything else faded and I fell asleep.

About the Author

E. N. Crane is a fiction author writing humorous mysteries with plus-sized female leads and their furry friends. She is one of two authors under the Perry Dog Publishing Imprint, a one woman, two dog operation in Idaho... for now. My dogs are Perry and Padfoot, the furry beasts shown above. They are well-loved character inspiration in all things written and business.

If you are interested in joining my newsletter, please subscribe here: https://e-n-crane_perrydogpublishing.ck.page/578ed9ab 37or on my website, PerryDogPublishing.com

You will receive A Bite in Afghanistan, the prequel to the Sharp Investigations Series, as a thank-you for joining. I only have one newsletter for mental health reasons, so both romance and mystery are on there! If you only want one in your inbox, follow Perry Dog Publishing on all socials to stay on top of the latest news... and pet pics.

Made in the USA
Las Vegas, NV
11 December 2024